Arise, O Phoenix

*For Fith —
with all my
best wishes!
Lisa*

Arise, O Phoenix

a novel

Lisa K. Drucker

July 2012

iUniverse, Inc.
Bloomington

Arise, O Phoenix

[NOTE: This book was written in the immediate aftermath of the September 11 attacks.]

iUniverse books may be ordered through booksellers or by contacting:

iUniverse
1663 Liberty Drive
Bloomington, IN 47403
www.iuniverse.com
1-800-Authors (1-800-288-4677)

ISBN: 978-1-4759-1037-7 (sc)
ISBN: 978-1-4759-1039-1 (e)
ISBN: 978-1-4759-1038-4 (dj)

Library of Congress Control Number: 2012906101

Printed in the United States of America

iUniverse rev. date: 5/1/2012

To all the heroes and victims of September 11, 2001.

To the brave men and women—police, firefighters, emergency medical technicians, and civilians—who risked, or even gave, their lives to save others on that terrible day.

And to the brave men and women who defend and serve our country each and every day.

May this book ever honor all America's heroes—not just those of September 11, but of every fight for freedom—and ever be a tribute to their courage, selflessness, and devotion to the liberty and justice for which our country stands.

God bless them all. God bless us all. God bless America.

[**NOTE:** *The author is a proud supporter of the Robin Hood Relief Fund* (www.911relief.robinhood.org) *and the Wounded Warrior Project* (www.woundedwarriorproject.org).]

Fear not;
for I am with thee.

—Isaiah, 43:5

A Note from the Author

I wrote this book during the weeks directly following September 11, 2001, because I wanted to capture the way I felt about the events as they unfolded.

Although the characters are fictional, their emotions and reactions are very real, and are intended to pay tribute to the experiences of the actual survivors and heroes of that day. I chose fiction as the genre for this book in order to symbolize that day's significance in a way that would show our collective sharing of the tragedy and its effects on our lives.

Whatever our own experiences of that day were, may we never forget all that was lost.

Acknowledgments

Many thanks to everyone who helped make this book possible.

To the amazing team of talented professionals at iUniverse, my thanks for all your efforts, dedication, and hard work. You all are a pleasure to work with. Elizabeth Parker, the book's original evaluator, thank you for your thorough professional review and glowing praise. Ben Hudson, Kathi Wittkamper, and Dayne Newquist, thank you for your guidance and care throughout the process. Shawn Waggener, thank you for all your help at every step of the production process. My thanks also to the design team for the incredible cover and elegant interior of the book. I also deeply appreciate the Author Solutions team. Alan Bower, thank you for all your support and efforts. Joel Pierson, thank you for your advice and encouragement. Laurel Brettell, thank you for all your assistance and amazing enthusiasm from the very beginning—and for your consistent kindness and generous spirit—I am especially grateful to you.

To my brother, Irwin, and to all my friends and family, thank you for your support, encouragement, and love.

Russell Mendola, online marketing and tech guru, an extra-special thank-you for your brilliant website development and design, for all your savvy advice, and most of all, for your friendship.

Finally, to my parents, who have always unconditionally loved and believed in me. This book would not have become what it is without you, and neither would I.

BOOK I
ON OUR OWN SOIL

$\mathcal{B}$y 5:15 a.m., Cameron Burke was running along the Potomac. He ran every morning, no matter the weather. "Just like the mail," Patricia, his wife, always said. *Ex-wife*, he hastily corrected himself, wondering when it would become automatic. He could still hear her saying the words, her voice tinged with what he now realized was bitterness, though for years he had thought it was acceptance.

His feet hammered the pavement. He exhaled rhythmically. Maybe bitterness was too harsh. Maybe it was only resignation.

His pedometer cycled another round.

No, it was bitterness. Better to just accept it and move on. She'd known what he was when she married him: driven, tough, honest, decent. Her description, not his. Within the past year or so, he had suddenly become an inflexible, monomaniacal workaholic. Again, her description. His daughter, Margaret, called him "the casualty of Mom's self-improvement juggernaut."

Burke couldn't help but chuckle at the thought, even though it made his breathing uneven and running more difficult. Margaret was the light of his life, her wry sense of humor a source of constant delight, despite their constant battling over politics and much of what that entailed, which Margaret referred to as "life issues." Nonetheless, she was "her father's daughter," as Patricia always referred to her, and Burke loved it—always had, always would.

His pedometer finished cycling his last round, and he slowed to a walk. Patricia had a lot to say about everything. He'd never realized it until they divorced a little less than a year before, and he shook his head at his own ignorance. He'd missed all the signs, after all, hadn't he? Despite the fact that Margaret assured him Patricia was the loser, not he. "She's my mother, so I can say that," she had punctuated her pronouncement, with the innocent confidence only a twenty-

3

two-year-old can possess. As long as his daughter didn't blame him for the breakup, it didn't matter who else did.

He walked back to his apartment for coffee and a quick shower. He had to be at Langley for a meeting at eight. He was ready for it, though. As always, the run had given him what he needed: clarity, focus, determination. He hoped the meeting at Langley wouldn't run on forever. He had to be back at the Pentagon for another meeting at ten, and didn't relish either one—he hated meetings.

Burke shrugged again, the door to his apartment in sight. September 11 was starting off like any other day. Which could mean anything at all in his line of work, but that was the deal, and he had agreed to it a long time ago.

Cameron Burke held his head in his hands. *How could this have happened?* he wondered for the umpteenth time that day. It struck him suddenly that, in the wee hours of December 7, 1941, the day had seemed as innocuous to Americans as had September 11, 2001—until just past 8:46 a.m. eastern daylight time.

Just a few hours before, he'd been finishing his daily run and thinking it was an ordinary day, even though he knew that there was no such thing for anyone who spent his life doing what he did for a living.

Burke lifted his head and swigged now-cold black coffee from an ancient mug, grimacing. No more time to grieve, though. Not for him. He had already received his orders from the president, albeit by means of a few layers of brass—find out who did this, and show no mercy to the perpetrators or to those who harbor them. All Americans would soon be advised of how the president intended to respond to the attacks: protecting our nation in self-defense, finding the perpetrators in order to obtain justice, preserving the ideals and freedoms on which—

4

and for which—our country had been founded. The president's response was in line with Burke's personal reaction, so the orders had come as a blessing. He could focus on the task at hand now, and he felt grateful that it supported his own moral convictions. He hadn't been that fortunate with every mission he'd been assigned to over the years.

Burke refused to let himself think about the friends lost at the Pentagon. Not to mention that if his meeting had been scheduled for nine o'clock instead of ten, he might have been lost too. He knew all too well that survivor guilt could be lethal, so he willed such thoughts out of his consciousness. For his colleagues as well as for Burke, jobs at the Pentagon signified at least a reduction in the danger they had accepted in connection with their chosen work. You might think about dying every day when you were in a war zone or a country hostile toward America and democracy, but you never thought about it in between assignments when stationed on our own soil.

To add to his concern, Margaret was now living by herself in a loft in SoHo (a gift from him and Patricia when Margaret had graduated from Pratt on a full scholarship), where she was able to "refine her art and live by her principles," as she put it. Unable to get through to her by phone, all he could do was pray she was safe. Given Margaret's antiestablishment nature, the Financial District was probably the last place on earth she'd ever be. Burke smiled wryly at the irony of his gratitude for Margaret's dedication to the liberal views that had caused so much contention between them ever since her late adolescence.

As a native New Yorker and former firefighter—and with his cousin, Dylan, and old friends still among New York's Finest and Bravest—Burke feared that all too soon he would be learning of losses close to him, even if Margaret was safe. He prayed that she *had* to be safe, especially once he'd seen the Twin Towers collapse. *There, but for the grace of God, go I,* he thought. Had he been near the towers or the Pentagon, unless he'd been rendered unconscious, Burke would have stood with the rescuers, shoulder to shoulder, trying to help as many of the victims as he could. Even with the specter of death and destruction descending and palpable, he would have been among those running into the smoke and flames without hesitating, fighting to save lives while as many as were able to were struggling to escape.

Serving and saving were in his bones. Always had been. He'd been one of New York's Bravest until he went off to Vietnam, where his service led him into the military-intelligence special operations that became his life's work and true calling. Feeling powerless in the wake of the tragedy was the worst part of it for Burke. Not being able to know for sure that Margaret was all right. Not being able to be there saving and serving. Not being able to help during the nation's greatest tragedy, especially when he had been spared by the grace of God, not just that day but in so many other life-threatening situations over the years. He knew he had to get beyond those feelings—guilt, rage, helplessness; sometimes alternating, other times commingling—but right now he didn't know how he would.

Burke had no regrets. Given the chance, he wouldn't change anything he'd done. Except for one thing: Josselyn. If only he had *that* to do over again. ... But he would never get the chance, so it didn't matter.

Shaking his head as if to cast off the recollection, Burke grabbed his bag and swept out of the room without looking back. The best he could do right now was to focus on the enormous task that lay before him and keep putting one foot deliberately in front of the other, every day, until walking—and living—became second nature again. He'd had to learn how to do that once before; he could do it again. He had no choice, then or now.

Josselyn Jeffrey was downtown, not as a reporter but as a "civilian." That was the way she thought of herself when she wasn't working on a story. A workaholic, such times were few and far between for her. When she wasn't working on a book, she was writing for the *New York Times* or the *New Yorker*, or doing something for one of the charities she supported. In fact, on the morning of September 11, she took the subway from Brooklyn Heights to Lower Manhattan to meet with some venture capitalists about a foundation she wanted to set up to promote literacy. Arriving at eight thirty for a nine o'clock meeting at the World Trade Center, she decided to walk around a bit before going inside. At first she thought about going up to Windows on the World, but then she opted to enjoy the fresh air instead.

When the first plane hit, Josselyn Jeffrey was all of two blocks away. Etched forever in her memory—her heart and soul—was the conflagration, followed by the eerie sucking in of air as the plane disappeared into the steel-and-concrete-and-glass bastion of Lower Manhattan; and then, worst of all, the screams and falling bodies, many of them—God save them—in flames. Hellish images far too horrible for the mind to really even process.

On impulse, Josselyn rushed toward the towers, buildings she saw from her brownstone's windows every day and had come to love. Her only thought was not to break the story but to help in whatever way she could. As a reporter, though, she would certainly tell the story, could never resist the compulsion to document what she saw, heard, felt; she related to the world and understood it through her words. She was no stranger to disaster zones, having covered far too many.

She rushed to the towers, moving quickly despite her high heels, as though magnetized toward what she was witnessing, her mind racing between thoughts of how beyond horrible the images flashing before her were, and yet how surreal it all felt. She reached into her bag to find the press badge she always carried with her. Groping, she found it, never breaking her stride as she pulled it out by the chain it hung on. She looped the chain over her head and let it fall around her neck.

Choking on smoke but still pressing on, she suddenly realized what made the whole thing feel so simultaneously horrible and surreal: It was a beautiful day, crystal-clear and sunny. How could a plane hit one of the Twin Towers on a day like this?

She had arisen with the dawn, as usual. From the top floor of her Brooklyn Heights brownstone, she could see the lofty towers and, seemingly suspended between them, a strip of sky limned pink and violet by the rising sun. Josselyn was glad suddenly that she had never taken that daily sight for granted— no matter how many times a day she looked out her window to see the downtown skyline, she was awed by the ingenuity and sheer moxie that American architecture symbolized. It would never be the same again.

The same persistent thought seized her mind: On a clear day, what pilot could crash into one of the Twin Towers? It would be like missing a mountain. True, she hadn't seen the plane actually hit; perhaps the pilot had lost control, and the plane had spun into the tower. No, she had heard a plane; she had looked up, surprised to see it flying so low, but then had not thought about it in the intervening moments—that is, not until she saw flames shooting out of the gaping hole in the North Tower, debris flying from the building, and the airplane disappearing into the inferno. She realized in a fresh burst of horror that part of that debris had been people, immolated in this awful catastrophe. Descriptive words that she had used throughout her career flooded her brain: gruesome, macabre, hellacious, nightmarish, catastrophic, apocalyptic—not a one of them could adequately reflect what was transpiring, or how those witnessing it were feeling and responding. Words failed.

Now, in the midst of the despair and the surreal, hope came at last: people streaming into the street, from the lower floors of the North Tower or from surrounding buildings, she wasn't sure which, and firefighters going in. In that precious moment, hope was a lifeline, actually palpable around her. New York's Bravest had come to save the day, as always. It was no coincidence that the fire department was the only official service bureau in the city that its occupants never cast aspersions on: New York unabashedly adored its firefighters.

Josselyn reached the Twin Towers, and what she saw on the ground sickened her almost beyond what she could endure. It was so horrible, she couldn't even process in her own mind how she felt about what she saw. Images of stories her mother had told her about the Holocaust—the "Shoah," she'd called it—swamped Josselyn suddenly, her memories and the smoke now choking her simultaneously. *Don't go there now,* she told herself, the deafening din making it impossible for her to know if she'd only thought it or had actually said it aloud. *This was some sort of horrible, horrible accident—or something—not the twisted, calculated plot of evil, hate-filled men.*

Someone's cries caught Josselyn's attention, and she turned in the direction of the sound. On the curb behind her sat a young woman no more than twenty-five, bloodied and sobbing, the oxygen mask an emergency technician had given her dangling, unused, in her hand.

Josselyn knelt beside the young woman, gently attempting to put the mask on her face.

The young woman, obviously weak from shock, pushed Josselyn's hand away with surprising firmness. Lifting her eyes to meet Josselyn's, she said, "My fiancé works on the 105th floor of the North Tower. I came to meet him for breakfast so we could go over some last-minute additions to the invitation list for our wedding. We were going to have breakfast at Windows on the World. I was supposed to mail all the invitations today." Her sobs overtook her again.

Josselyn wrapped her arms around the young woman, letting her weep.

"He's going to be very upset with you when he finds you aren't using this mask," Josselyn said, feigning a brightness that was the last thing she felt.

"He's never getting out of there. I just know he isn't." Her sobs ceased, giving way to a leaden tone even more heartbreaking. "Whatever hit and cut me might have been part of his office."

"You can't give up hope. There might be a roof rescue like there was in '93." Her coverage of that story rushed back into her mind.

The young woman's expression was inscrutable. Too numb to even know what she felt, Josselyn supposed. "I don't think so. I can only hope that he'll be able to jump. Maybe he already has. Please don't let him have been one of the ones who were on fire, though," she added hastily, clapping her hand over her mouth as she digested the horror of what she'd just said. "Oh God! Please don't let him suffer. Don't let anyone suffer. Let the smoke get to everyone who can't get out." She said this in a calm and steady voice, as if praying, and she seemed to draw strength and serenity from the words.

"Amen," Josselyn said, her voice calm and steady also. She let her heart and soul invoke God, and she drew strength from that, just as the young woman had. Josselyn knew all too well the horror in this young woman's eyes, the horror of imagining someone you loved dying in flames. That same horror had haunted Josselyn's mother for her entire life, spreading to Josselyn in an osmosis of empathy as uncanny as it was undeniable.

"Did you come here to help?" the young woman asked suddenly.

Josselyn nodded.

"You can't help me. Maybe there's someone you *can* help. Keep praying."

The young woman stood, dropping the mask and stumbling off before Josselyn could respond or stop her. Beginning to choke on the fumes engulfing the area, Josselyn picked up the mask, put it on, and pressed forward again, feeling even more helpless than she had when she started toward the towers. She wondered about the ever-thickening miasma pervading the air. It was such an odd color, almost pink; she'd never seen anything like it. She was still mercifully ignorant of the cause of that weird-colored haze, that it arose from the force of the bodies slamming down to the pavement as they catapulted from the tower's windows. She was still innocent of the scientific details of this horror, still feeling and living it raw and unmediated, not yet plagued by the indelible nightmares that would inevitably etch themselves in her mind … and haunt her forever.

"Here, lady," an emergency technician called out, thrusting a pile of rags into her hand and motioning to an open fire hydrant. "Wet these and hand them out."

Galvanized, Josselyn began to wet as many of the rags as she could, passing them out quickly and keeping one for herself. Seeing more rags inside one of the ambulances, she pulled out another armful when she'd finished handing out the first batch. For what seemed like forever, but couldn't have been more than a few moments, she kept grabbing, wetting, and handing out rags.

Suddenly the roar of a jet engine rumbled above the ensuing scene of destruction. *"No!"* Josselyn heard herself cry out. She was screaming, denying what was already unfolding. This plane came in low, dipping one wing and then deliberately flying toward the South Tower. Time stopped as she watched the plane crash head-on into the tower. The smash of concrete and steel was punctuated by another sound, weirdly similar to the thundering roar of rushing water: the simultaneous shattering of thousands of panes of glass.

It wasn't surreal any longer, just gruesomely, inconceivably horrible. New York—America—was under attack. That spire of sky between the towers—always taking her breath away because it looked as if somehow the towers created that piece of sky; sometimes blue, sometimes pink and violet, sometimes velvety black—now was filled with vile smoke so thick that it seemed the sky had been destroyed.

People on the street screamed, cried, and gasped, but also gaped in a silent horror worse than any sound. More-distant screams from the victims in the burning, smoking towers mingled with those of the onlookers in a soul-piercing cacophony that would echo through all their nightmares for as long as they lived … if they survived this Armageddon.

Against her better judgment, Josselyn pressed on. If this was an act of terrorism, as it most assuredly must be, she would go down fighting. She would not abandon her fellow New Yorkers—fellow Americans, fellow human beings—to an unspeakable fate. If she could save or help one person, she would. God must have brought her here today at this moment to do something. She had lived her life to be useful and courageous, to teach through her words. Today it seemed her destiny was to teach and help through her actions, and she was not about to run away.

Turning to grab more rags, she realized she'd used them all. The rag covering her face was already covered with soot, as was every part of herself she could see. The stench was overwhelming, and the screams were deafening; she didn't know which of the two was worse. The images of carnage and destruction were too heinous to even be processed, let alone comprehended; but the odors and sounds could not be denied. Now more than ever before, she could not fathom how anyone around the Nazi death camps could have ignored the odor of burning flesh. She'd long ago decided it was worse to feel utterly sickened than absolutely terrified because terror could be abated by taking action. As always when in the face of fear, she responded by channeling all her energy into her purpose, which filled her consciousness all the more now, actually overtaking her: *How can I help?*

Perhaps she had helped the young woman she'd tried to comfort, but that wasn't enough. She had no time to ponder further. A mass exodus was flooding the streets outside the towers. People thronging from everywhere, not just the flaming towers. Those in the surrounding buildings—across the street and on nearby streets—who had thought the first crash was accidental now thought otherwise. Some were screaming; others were too shocked to utter a sound. They headed in different directions: uptown, toward Brooklyn, toward Jersey. All of them sought nothing but safety. A group of people who had come to work on an ordinary Tuesday, their minds filled with business concerns, or even office gossip, now were running for their lives. Whatever each and every one of them had thought about during the morning commute, including even the most elaborate financial deals, was now quite undoubtedly a triviality. In an hour's time, more or less, the world had been wrenched upside down and inside out, irrevocably changed.

These thoughts raced through Josselyn's mind as she searched for some other way to help. She caught sight of another ambulance and made her way toward it, moving against the masses of fleeing people. Her coverage of the 1993 bombing of the World Trade Center again flashed across the screen of her mind's eye, just as it had earlier when she suggested an airlift roof rescue to the young woman. The '93 bombing had occurred a year or so after her return from Riyadh, where she'd covered the Gulf War and its aftermath. Was today's attack a diabolical reprisal that had been planned by the same perpetrators during the eight interim years? She shuddered, despite the enormous waves of heat pouring out of the burning skyscrapers.

Thankfully, she found more rags in the ambulance and began to immerse them in the water gushing from another open fire hydrant. The emergency workers were so overwhelmed by the enormity of the daunting mission before them that she might as well have been invisible. Probably she was. Like a turbo-charged automaton, she grabbed rags, wet them, and pushed them into the hands of the people rushing past her. She saw lacerated skin, bloodshot eyes, heads and shoulders covered in ash and soot ... and yet, what she saw did not register. She couldn't let it. She'd run if she did. If she survived this—if God meant for her to survive—it would not be merely to be plagued by the guilt of having escaped without trying to save others when she had the chance to. No, she was here for a purpose. Besides, she would not consign herself to suffer her mother's fate. It didn't matter that her mother's recriminations all had been self-imposed, that she could not have saved her family from the Nazi apocalypse and should not have blamed herself for having escaped the camps—her mother's guilt had been no more rational than her own would be. Josselyn knew she'd be haunted forever if she didn't heed her conscience's prodding in the moment; she would have to live with the same survival guilt that had haunted her mother. And it would poison her just as much. Not to mention that she'd inherited her father's commitment to fulfill the soul's true purpose. She would die here if that was her fate, but she would not run away.

And then began the worst part of the nightmare, the horror of it beyond description. No human being not witness to it happening live could ever truly grasp how it felt to have stood there watching helplessly as the South Tower began to collapse.

As she saw the mighty steel frame buckle and heave, and what it contained begin to crumble, Josselyn felt herself running. Survival mode must have taken over because she didn't remember starting to run, only felt herself suddenly running. Her foot caught on something, and she stumbled and fell. A pair of strong arms wrapped around her in the next instant, lifting her up and carrying her to safety. Pushing her against a wall, he covered her body with his. For seconds that seemed like an eternity, they breathed together—she shakily, he more strongly. As the crash of the collapsing tower roared, vomiting a tidal wave of smoke and debris from its guts, her only thought was, *I'm going to die.*

She must have whispered it aloud without even realizing she had. The fireman holding her squeezed her even tighter—she knew he was a fireman now because she saw his jacket sleeve where he had wrapped his arm around her. "You are not going to die." He said it as more of a command than a promise. "You need to write about this."

He must have seen her press badge. In the next instant he started to move her along again, half dragging and half carrying her.

"Yes," she promised, suddenly focused and determined by means of a weird, inferno-annealed clarity, though the smoke and hunks of debris they were inhaling made breathing feel like torture.

"Dylan Burke."

She flinched at the last name, even after all these years and in the midst of catastrophe. *There must be more than one Burke in FDNY.* She chided herself at the lunacy of her reaction. All she said was, "Josselyn Jeffrey."

"I recognized you from your photo. I read your books and everything you write in the paper. Turn this into something that will ... I don't know ... *mean* something."

"What makes you think I can do that?"

"If you can't, who can?" After seeing her safely out of danger, he turned to head back toward the disaster.

"Stay safe," she said. "I owe you my life. Thank you."

He waved off her gratitude. "It's what I do. Do what you do. And get the hell out of here." As he disappeared into the opaque cloud of smoke and debris, she prayed he was not heading toward a hero's death.

She was relieved she couldn't see him once he penetrated the smoke, even though she knew Dylan Burke would haunt her for the rest of her life, just as the memories of another Burke had haunted her for years and always would. Turning quickly, she headed toward Brooklyn. She vowed that she would find out what happened to Dylan, would not rest till she did, would pay tribute to his bravery as a symbol of all the brave men and women who would die this day fighting to rescue innocent people who should never have needed to be rescued in the first place. With that thought, the mélange of Josselyn's emotions ignited into rage.

Margaret Burke thought of her grandmother, dead and buried the previous Christmas, who had prayed for the police and firefighters every morning of her life. Her grandmother would be offering novenas in heaven today—count on it. And her father. Where would he be? Margaret would not let herself think of the Pentagon. She was glad her father never shared details with her, not that she would have listened even if he had. All the domestic-policy issues they fought over, and that she fought for, now seemed so inconsequential. Margaret was ashamed of herself. She felt the shame in small bursts that struck her in the midst of her other cresting feelings of rage, violation, helplessness, and grief. She had to get word to her father. She had to find out what happened to her firefighter cousin, Dylan. She had to do so many things, but all she could do was stand in the street with her neighbors, staring at the not-too-distant smoke rising from the flaming rubble that had once been the Twin Towers. As recently as the day before, Margaret might have ranted about the appropriate ugliness of structures that symbolized American imperialism and capitalism. Now all she could do was think about how beautiful they had been. She supposed it was sort of like fighting with a person all the time but then remembering him as perfect after he died. And missing him forever.

Margaret and the other onlookers choked on the noxious cloud of smoke and pulverized debris that ballooned and wafted over the city in the wake of the attack on the towers and their ultimate collapse. All of them sobbed and gaped in horror, knowing the fragments they could see flying through the air were too unspeakable to name. The media reported that people had jumped out of the towers to escape the flames; thousands of people must have been trapped when the buildings collapsed.

Margaret sobbed and sobbed, unable to muster her characteristic sardonic self-deprecation for the thoughts she considered absurd even as they flitted through her brain. A man standing next to her, who would have been just another stranger to avoid eye contact with a few hours before, put his arms around Margaret as she cried, unabashed and unchecked, against his shoulder. They never exchanged a single word.

At some point, Margaret found herself back in her apartment, not fully aware of how she'd gotten there. She felt like she was on autopilot. Noticing a streak of paint across the still life of tomatoes and avocados she had been working on when the first plane hit, she recalled the moment. Looking out the window to the south, she had seen a plane flying dangerously low, and then gaped in horror as she watched it fly straight into the tower. In her helpless shock, she'd flung her paint-dipped brush against the canvas. It looked appropriately blood smattered now.

Margaret set the canvas aside and picked up the phone. There was no dial tone of course. She had been trying to call her father since just after nine when the South Tower was hit, but to no avail. All Manhattan circuits were down. Why had she railed against cell phones, pagers, and every other twenty-first-century convenience? If she had kept the cell phone that her father had begged her to take and use, even if only for emergencies, she might be able to reach him now. For the first time, she understood her family's irritation—tempered by love and tolerance though it was—at her "holier-than-thou starving-artist mentality," as Dylan referred to it. *Ouch.* The next time she saw or talked to her father and Dylan, she would humble herself with an unqualified apology. No matter what.

The daughter of a war-zone denizen, Margaret wasn't going to waste time waiting for the area to be evacuated—or not. For all the times she had fought her father on issues of safety, arguing that they impinged on civil liberties more often than not, now she was grateful that he'd let her express her views but then had seen to it that she learned what to do in an emergency. She grabbed some essentials, threw them in one of her father's old duffel bags, and beat a hasty departure. Glad, at least, that she didn't have a lot to pack, even if she'd wanted to.

Cameron Burke slammed shut what seemed like the thousandth report he'd read that day. It was not long past noon, and he wondered how much more stupidity he would have to immerse himself in before all this was over. During the past twenty years, he had frequently warned that significant acts of terrorism were inevitable, but even so, he could not have imagined that the worst of his warnings would become reality in the course of a single day.

He picked up the phone, glancing at his watch as he put the receiver against his ear. He was trying to reach Margaret every couple of minutes. All the circuits in Manhattan were overloaded. Patricia had already called—and called, and called— the more time that passed, the greater the opportunity to blame him; the ineptitude of intelligence operatives (translation: him, personally) being the sole cause of this tragedy.

"Damn it, Margaret. When this is over you're getting a cell phone," he muttered, adding, "Maybe I can reach Dylan." Knowing it would be futile to call his cousin's cell, he dialed his home number in Brooklyn. The ring startled him after having heard rapid busy signals and digitized voice messages so many times.

Dylan's wife, Erin, answered. "Cam! Thank God you're safe. I've been so worried. Jesus, the Pentagon …"

"I was at Langley this morning," he told her abruptly. As usual, he was not interested in talking about himself. "Did Dylan answer the call?"

"Of course. He was among the first."

As if he hadn't guessed. He'd needed confirmation, though. Images of the now-collapsed towers all but overwhelmed Burke. What if Erin hadn't seen or heard about that outcome? Impossible. Before he could respond, she added, "I know what happened to the towers, Cam. But Dylan couldn't ever have been anything but a firefighter. You know that. I put him in God's hands every day when he leaves for work. Today is no different."

"Well, if ever the Burkes needed to be grateful for my mother's novenas, I guess it's today." If he didn't keep it light he would lose control.

"He's fine, Cam," Erin said, the strength of her conviction surprising him, even from the veteran firefighter wife and daughter that she was.

"Erin—"

"No, Cam. Hear me out. I've been through this with Dylan and with my father. When you love someone, you can't pull out of him what makes him who he is. Sure, it would be easier for me if Dylan didn't want to fight fires, but then Dylan wouldn't be Dylan. When I said that he's fine, what I meant was that he's accepted his fate. Whatever happens, he's out there doing what he's meant to do. What he loves to do. That is a gift and a blessing."

"Yes, it is. Forgive me. I don't know what I was thinking. You've lived this life long enough to know what's what."

"Forget it. I'm sure you're worried about Margaret too."

"I can't get through to her."

"If she gets in touch with me, I'll call you right away, Cam."

"Thanks. And also if you hear from Dylan."

"Of course."

19

"You guys take care of yourselves. I'll look into things on this end and see what I can find out. I'll keep in touch."

"We love you, Cam." Erin understood that what he'd said meant he loved them.

Burke hung up. Dylan had lucked out marrying Erin. Patricia never would have even thought about what Erin had obviously known and held fast to for a long time. He was amazed. How did a woman who had to sacrifice so much every day stay in love with her husband, the reason for the sacrifice? Maybe love was not feeling that it *was* a sacrifice. He supposed that was the difference between Erin and Patricia: Patricia felt that everything she'd done for him was a sacrifice, although he hadn't known it until she told him so a little more than a year before; Erin couldn't, and wouldn't, ever feel that way about Dylan. If Patricia had ever indicated how she really felt over the years he might cut her some slack now, but to go from "everything's fine" to "I want a divorce"—with no warning—that was what he refused to abide.

No time to think about that now. He had to put out feelers to find Margaret and Dylan. Always being in the midst of some crisis of gigantic proportions made a handy excuse for not dealing with day-to-day problems in his relationships. Maybe Patricia had been sending signals all along, but in his ongoing vigilance for looming red alerts, he had simply missed her less-urgent signs. Without all the sirens and flashing lights, anything she might have done would have been invisible. Patricia herself had eventually become invisible. Nothing gained by laying all the blame on her.

Burke picked up the phone and dialed again. "Come on, Margaret."

But all he heard on the other end was the rapid busy signal that greeted almost every person calling Manhattan that day.

Once in the street again, Margaret was absorbed into the mass exodus. Veering into the part of the crowd heading toward Brooklyn, she let the human tide pull her along. It was too hard to think for herself. If she got to Brooklyn, she could go to Dylan's apartment and stay with his wife, Erin, while she waited for word from Dylan. Erin would probably be glad for any company—even hers. Margaret almost smiled at the look of surprise she imagined on Erin's face when she, Margaret, didn't launch into her typical antiestablishment tirade. Margaret was far harder on herself than her relatives would be. They viewed her litanies as typical of a young, temperamental artist who, nevertheless, was a Burke. Burkes stood together, even when one of them was deserving of a "sound thrashing," as Margaret's grandmother had told her frequently, albeit lovingly, even in her last days.

Margaret couldn't even bear to look in the direction of the disaster scene. She let the sheer momentum of the crowd propel her. *God, let us all be safe. Let us all live, and I promise I'll do whatever you ask of me,* she prayed silently and then whispered three Hail Marys. That was the usual number she'd been given in the confessional—when she still went to confession, that is—and she hoped it would be enough this time too.

Suddenly she thought of her growing-up years, when, after he'd been hurt in the line of duty, her mother would tell her father that God was sending him a sign to stop doing such dangerous work. Her father had always replied that God needed to send a clearer message.

After her parents' divorce a little less than a year before, her father had asked whether she thought this was God's clearer message. Margaret had unequivocally told him that it was not. After all, the work he did defined her father; he could never do anything else. Even though she and he battled about politics, deep down she respected him for what he did. He knew it, and she knew that he knew it. Otherwise, he would have written her off long before now.

"I'm safe, Daddy," she whispered, as if she were a little girl. *I'll never again give you a hard time about what you do or what it means to live in this country.*

Cameron Burke finished reading the report and flipped the pages over.

"Clear," he said to the Chairman and Vice Chairman of the Joint Chiefs of Staff sitting before him.

The three of them were alone in the situation room that had been filled with upper-echelon personnel until just seconds before.

The chairman and vice chairman were seasoned, decorated military leaders who had seen most every form of atrocity. Burke himself was equally seasoned in military intelligence, as well as being trained as both soldier and rescuer. Yet all three of them had been humbled and forced to accept their own vulnerability. In so doing, they had no choice but to acknowledge their own humanity as well. Both reactions ran counter to the training that had prepared and sustained them, and that had enabled them to do their jobs effectively throughout their entire careers. All three men now nodded to each other in tacit recognition of all that.

"God bless," the chairman and vice chairman said in unison, each clapping Burke on the shoulder and then pumping his hand. Both of them knew there was no man better than Burke to head up this mission.

Cameron Burke squared his shoulders almost imperceptibly, as if unconsciously bracing himself to bear the weight that had just been set upon them.

Josselyn Jeffrey had made her way home across the Brooklyn Bridge. Now, safe in her brownstone, she sat before her laptop screen, numb. She, who fought all her battles with words, who healed herself and others with words, now could find none. Her pain and sorrow were too deep, too enormous. The powerful rage that had filled her that morning as she stood in front of the towers—the south already collapsed, and the north destined to soon follow suit—had turned to grief. As white-hot and oddly energizing as the rage had felt, the grief felt cold, enervating; as if it had incapacitated her will, her energy, her very soul.

Now the cursor blinked like a weird, mocking mantra: write, write, write. But no words would come. "It's what I do," reverberated in her ears. With a weariness devoid of emotion, she thought, *Typical Burke.*

"It's what I do," she typed, and then she began to tell the story of one of New York's Bravest as a tribute to them all.

After all, she had promised. And Josselyn Jeffrey never broke a vow.

An incongruously bright ray of sunshine fought to pierce the smoke-laden sky as Josselyn Jeffrey finished her tribute to New York's Bravest. She typed a succinct message to Luke Lanvin at the Times office, attached the file, and clicked SEND. Lanvin was her longtime friend, as well as her editor.

Not long after, Lanvin received the message. Alarmed to discover she'd been at the scene when she hadn't been sent there, he opened the file and read it.

"It's What I Do":
A Tribute to New York's Bravest
Josselyn Jeffrey, exclusive
to the *New York Times*

When the fire alarms began sounding shortly after 8:46 a.m. on September 11, those who rushed to answer the call never hesitated.

The alarms continued to ring, beyond 9:03, progressively increasing in the levels of danger that they heralded. Still, no firefighter hesitated. No firefighter ever hesitates. They are called New York's Bravest because that's exactly what they are. Day in and day out, week after week, month after month, year after year. They serve us and save us, asking in return only for our respect. We, eternal cosmopolitans that we are, self-confirmed cynics and egocentrics, adore them without reservation. They deserve nothing less. Especially after today.

I was at the World Trade Center this morning. I saw the apocalypse, from the planes crashing into the towers to the collapse of the South Tower, but that's not what I'm going to tell you about. Over the coming days and weeks, you will see those horrifying images countless times. The horror, rage, grief, and hopelessness will fight with one another to claim your attention and peace of mind. I will not fight with them. Instead, I offer an alternative image—one of hope, courage, compassion, and grace. You may not be able to feel any of those today or tomorrow or next week, but I pray that someday not too far away you will be able to, and that you will call to mind the portrait I'm about to paint for you.

A woman who considers herself inured to danger races to see if she can help in the midst of the ensuing chaos, the horrors she can't believe are unfolding before her. She stumbles and falls, suddenly terrified and furious for having knowingly placed herself in danger when she should have known better. In the next instant, just as she is convinced that she will not survive this horror, she feels a pair of strong arms lift her up, and then the man the arms belong to carries her to safety. In his actions, this man selflessly saves the woman, never thinking of himself. Once she is out of harm's way, he heads back toward the site of destruction and chaos.

As you've probably guessed, I'm the woman I just described. The man, of course, is a firefighter. I say "is" more as a prayer than a fact: I don't know what happened to him. His name is Dylan Burke, and I survived to write this only because he was there.

I promised him that I would write about what happened today, but as I've already indicated, I will not do so as a glorification of tragedy. Nor will I give in to the fear that those who did this want each of us to give in to.

I will write about September 11 only as a tribute to the heroes who died so that we could live, so that we could stand together, united in our fight to preserve the freedoms we hold so dear—never more so than when they are brutally violated.

Let us honor these heroes by becoming the best we each can be. Let us honor them by showing as much courage, compassion, and grace as I received today—and am still alive because of. We may never be among the Bravest, but may we be as brave as we each can be.

God bless our Bravest. God bless New York. God bless America.

Lanvin e-mailed back that he had wept reading what he, a hard-boiled newsman, would have derisively called hackneyed hooey the day before. He made no bones about telling her, either.

Josselyn smiled grimly. As if "hackneyed hooey" wouldn't have made *her* laugh the day before. It just so happened that she adored Luke Lanvin, but as she told him all too often, he was the only newspaper guy who still even thought of himself as a "hard-boiled newsman." Last Christmas she had even bought him a fedora with a tab labeled PRESS stuck in the hatband next to the feather.

Still, she loved the guy. Only in New York would you find anyone who wouldn't feel ridiculous about being such a living, breathing cartoon character. She was just such a sort of character herself, and she loved that too. It was possible only in the city—the only place in the world where tolerance was the common denominator. New Yorkers had the biggest hearts in the world. Where else on earth would people rally like this? Only hours after the disaster, and those equipped to help with the rescue efforts were already heading downtown to what had come to be called Ground Zero. Yes, New Yorkers might fight one another for a seat on the subway—undoubtedly would be back to doing that again once the shock of this catastrophe had abated—but they were there for one another in times of real crisis. They had proved that time and time again. The tribute to heroism she had just turned in would be but one of many.

She sank back in her chair now, too depleted to think. The radio's dire newscasts continued. Where and when would all this horror end? Looking out the window toward where the mighty towers had speared the sky just a few hours before, she realized that she was already growing accustomed to the haze that had descended upon the city. Her reddened eyes still burned, tears oozing out of them continuously from the effects of the smoke and flames, as well as from sorrow; the rank odor still filled her nostrils and burned her throat and chest, she could taste its acridity on the back of her tongue. She would not allow this to appear to be normal to her, not now and not ever. That smoky miasma arising from the smoldering remnants of the once-proud towers was not normal. The architectural vista of the towers was normal. Those monuments to American ingenuity, delighting and inspiring and awing her for years, were gone. Destroyed. Nothing would ever be normal again. *Thine alabaster cities gleam undimmed by human tears,* suddenly echoed in the recesses of her mind, and Josselyn gave in to the sobs that overwhelmed her, knowing that no American would ever again be able to feel that those words were true. The World Trade Center. The Pentagon. Flight 93's heroes, who brought down the plane in a Pennsylvania field rather than let it reach its destination: The White House? The Capitol? All of it was unthinkable, impossible to really digest at this point—if ever. Snapping off the radio, unable to listen to any more of the news, Josselyn shuddered but could not shake off her despair.

All the horrors she had witnessed in various parts of the world while serving as a foreign correspondent over time— Vietnam, Israel, Saudi Arabia, to name a few—never could have prepared her for how she felt now. In all those times and places, she had gotten through what she saw by feeling that America was there fighting for peace and liberty, however divided the nation might be regarding the conflict back home. Truthfully, though, she hadn't ever given it much thought. Regardless of the source of those conflicts, her job had been to write what she saw and tell it to the world. She wrote her novels the same way. She "saw" the story in her mind, stepping aside so it could pour through her and onto the page. How many interviewers had she told, "The stories write me, not the other way around"? And she'd meant it. Now she felt as if every word she'd ever written was meaningless and hollow because mere words were powerless in the wake of real disaster. She had never even considered that she could feel that way—that she would find herself in a circumstance that would cause her to feel that way. And that was why she felt so awful now: not only had her way of understanding and relating to the world become impotent, but her hope and strength also seemed to have been incinerated in the inferno, or else they had evaporated in the explosion. Regardless, they all were gone.

On another level, of course, she felt awful because she was an American and her country had been attacked. But it was more than that. She wondered about the young woman she'd encountered on the sidewalk, utterly bereft of all hope. She wondered, too, whether people had felt their hope depart upon learning of the kamikazes' attack on Pearl Harbor. Most Americans hadn't been eyewitnesses to that. Not to mention that they also hadn't discovered that their own commercial jets, bearing fellow American civilians, had been used as enormous missiles of premeditated murder and destruction. Would she ever again feel the way she had at 8:45 that morning, a minute before the world changed forever? After witnessing the atrocity, how *could* she ever feel the way she had before?

She wished she herself could muster the hope she'd tried to conjure up in readers with her tribute to FDNY, but she supposed she would just have to be patient with herself for a change. It would be a long haul, but she refused to do other than believe that something positive would come of all this horror. It had to. Without that hope, not only would all be lost, but the perpetrators of these heinous acts would also be victorious. That was unthinkable. She could never allow it, not while there was breath in her body.

The phoenix must rise from the ashes. Long ago, she had pledged to always remember that. If ever there was a time to prove that she would fulfill that pledge, it was now.

Josselyn kept walking from room to room in her brownstone, touching the things that were most important to her, realizing that these were all she had. First and foremost, the lifetime achievement award for literary excellence that she'd won—for her "evocative portrayal of the resilience of the human spirit as juxtaposed to inhumanity and heinous evil," as the awarding board had put it. Those words would always pierce her heart after what she'd witnessed that morning. She swallowed hard, continuing to touch various other treasures, including the individual awards she'd won for her books: *From Ashes to Hope,* her novel about the Holocaust, which was really a retelling of her parents' life story; *Lower than Heaven,* her novel about Vietnam. There were awards for journalism too, from her coverage during the Yom Kippur and Persian Gulf Wars. Next to those were things from her father, her role model as a foreign correspondent: letters he had written her from Korea, Indochina, and Israel; awards he'd won for war coverage; his journal from his days working with Raoul Wallenberg, the Swedish diplomat who had single-handedly saved a hundred thousand Hungarian Jews from the Nazis; and dozens of drafts of articles and short stories she had written and gotten her father to read and comment on—his penciled marginalia long faded by time and smudged by her fingers from multiple readings. He had loved her writing, though he hadn't lived to see her become a published novelist or an acclaimed writer and journalist.

So many memories, most of them sad.

"In the end, love is all we have, all there really is," her father had always told her. She heard his voice repeating the words again, thought about all the different interpretations she'd given to them at various points in her life. At one time, her father's words had made her wonder why her mother could not let go of the past, could not love Josselyn and her father in the present. At another, her own driving ambition, stubbornness, and fear—if she admitted to the last one—had caused her to forget those wise words. As a result, she had lost the love of her life. Now it made her realize that perhaps she had never lived at all, except in her all-too-brief time with Cameron Burke. What did the awards and acclaim matter if in the midst of the nation's greatest tragedy she had to come home alone? She chastised herself, remembering the young fiancée she'd met and all the others who must have lost loved ones.

Her finger reverently caressed her father's papers. And then she opened the lid of a velvet jewelry case and pulled the tab on the pad that held the strand of her grandmother's pearls—her grandmother had hidden them in the bag her mother carried when Wallenberg and Josselyn's father smuggled her out of Hungary, saving her life. Letting her gaze fall upon the snapshot lying beneath it, Josselyn gazed at it for a long time; so long that she almost imagined the eyes in the photo were gazing back. "Oh Cam," she whispered. "I hate feeling and sounding like some bimbo on a soap opera. But even more than that, I hate having lost you. I hate not knowing what might have happened to you. Were you at the Pentagon? Why are you all I can ever think about? Damn you." She slammed the case shut, relieved that the fresh flow of tears this whole exercise had brought on did not spill on the treasured snapshot.

As the phrase "hackneyed hooey" popped into her mind, she smiled in spite of herself. As long as she could laugh at herself, she knew she would get through this, both the tragedy and the long-buried feelings—about Cameron and her mother—that erupted in its wake.

By early afternoon, the human tide had traveled across the bridge and into Brooklyn, sweeping Margaret Burke along with it. She made her way to Erin and Dylan's apartment, the second floor of a brownstone in Carroll Gardens. Erin buzzed her into the building when Margaret rang the bell at the stoop, and Margaret raced up the inside stairs. Erin was waiting with the door open, and Margaret fell into her arms, overcome by another wave of now-familiar sobbing. Erin wept too. Crying, they held each other, rocking back and forth for a long time. Finally Erin stepped back, wiped her tears with the back of her hand, and led Margaret inside.

"Call your father while I make us something to eat."

"You talked to my father?"

"I promised I'd call as soon as I heard from you. I'm sure he'd rather hear your voice himself."

Margaret rushed to the phone on the kitchen wall. "What about Dylan?" she asked, cradling the receiver between her shoulder and ear. She dialed as she waited for Erin to answer her question.

"He's there."

"Oh God," said Margaret, more in awe of Erin's serenity than surprised to discover that Dylan was where she had known he would be.

"Talk to your dad now. You and I can talk later," Erin told her, just as Margaret heard the line connect.

"Burke."

"It's me, Dad."

"Hi, me," he said, just as if she'd been calling to chat on a normal Tuesday afternoon. It was a standing joke between them: no one else called him Dad, so she didn't need to say "it's me," but she loved how he laughed and said "hi, me" every time, so she kept doing it.

"I'm so sorry, Daddy," she said, breaking down all over again.

"You're safe, Muffin. That's all that matters. What are you sorry for?" All the irritation he had ever felt in connection with Margaret's strongly held liberal views became immediately inconsequential. She was safe. The rest of it didn't matter. It never really had.

Margaret felt the same sense of safety that she had felt when she was six and a fire broke out in the house next door to theirs. Her father had walked Margaret and her mother a safe distance away, carrying Margaret in his arms the entire way, and then he'd returned to don a rubberized firefighter's suit— "turnout gear," he'd called it—so that he could help put out the blaze. He'd done this despite the fact that he was no longer a firefighter, despite the fact that he had sustained terrible burns and injuries in an explosion during a mission in Israel early on in his intelligence career. Her father never cared about his own safety and comfort, only other people's. Everyone had gotten out safely that night, and the engine company that had battled the blaze then made her father an honorary member. Which, in turn, had resulted in a ride on the fire truck the following Saturday for Margaret and her teddy bear, another grateful rescuee.

"I'm sorry for making you worry, Dad. I'll never do that again."

"Sure you will. It's your job, remember?"

Margaret winced. "How can you joke about that? All those horrible things I've said and done over the years. I'm so ashamed, Daddy."

"You've got strong convictions, and you stand up for them. Horrible is what barbarians did this morning, not anything you've ever said or done."

"You fight to keep this country safe, and all I do is give you a hard time."

"I fight to keep this country safe so that you *can* give me a hard time, if you want to. But you never do. Not really."

"Oh Dad. I do so."

"Fine. You do. I didn't mean to burst your bubble," Burke chuckled. He needed the release of joking with Margaret, needed to feel nothing had changed between them, even though the world had changed forever, and the two of them along with it. "Listen to me, now. This is serious."

"No kidding, Dad. You're the one who's been cracking all the jokes."

"You take care of yourself. When things settle down a bit, I'm sending you a cell phone—no arguments. I want to hear from you every day till I tell you otherwise. Until you get the cell, you e-mail me or call me from Dylan and Erin's. Are we clear on this?"

"Yes," she answered softly. "Daddy?"

"What, Muffin?"

"Thank you. I wouldn't have known what to do today if it hadn't been for the way you taught me to handle a crisis. I … I'm proud to be your daughter. I'm proud of you and all that you do for this country. I'm proud to be an American."

"I know. I've always known that, but thanks for telling me. And I'm proud of you. I'm proud you understand what's important."

"But all our disagreements … I just feel so bad about all that."

"Don't. You believe what you think is right. Someday we'll argue about it again. You've just realized that there's a time and a place for every fight. That's what wisdom means. Think about it."

"I will," she said. She hadn't ever thought of it that way, but he was right. "You take care of yourself, Daddy. I'll be okay. Do I call you at this number?"

"Same number and e-mail as always. I'll get back to you from wherever I am. Even if I don't contact you every day, you still—"

"I got the message, Dad. Promise me you'll take care of yourself."

"Margaret, please don't make this any harder than it already is."

But Margaret stood her ground, just as she had for as long as she could remember. If she made him promise, he was bound by his oath. They both knew it.

"Okay. I promise," Burke relented, as always. "Tell Erin I'll call as soon as I find out about Dylan. And call your mother."

Her mother. Margaret sighed.

"Margaret, she's worried about you. She is your mother."

"All right."

"That's my girl."

"I love you, Daddy."

"I love *you,* Muffin."

"Daddy—I'm going to do something to help people get through this. I don't know how or what yet, but I'm going to."

"Good for you, honey. My money's on you."

"God bless," Margaret whispered.

Hearing her say the words, Burke realized just how much this catastrophe *had* changed her. He was fighting for what he'd always believed in and never doubted. Margaret had been spun

180 degrees in a few hours' time and was already back on her feet and running. And she thought *he* was the brave one.

"God bless us all." He hung up.

Margaret silently prayed for his safety with more fervor than she'd ever mustered in her entire life.

"Keep the faith, honey," Erin said, putting her arm around Margaret's shoulders. "Come sit down and eat."

"I'm not really hungry."

"You might not have an appetite for a while. You still need to eat. You'll be wiped out if you don't."

Margaret sat down with Erin and obediently tackled the tuna fish sandwich on her plate, surprised to discover that her appetite returned as soon as she started eating.

Erin smiled to herself as she observed Margaret's gusto. "No matter how long it ever took to get word from my dad when he was out at a fire, my mother always made us eat. As soon as he got home, the first thing he asked was always, 'You kids eat while I was at work?' This is 'just work' for Dylan and all the other guys. Your not doing regular things won't change that."

Margaret nodded. "But this *is* a million times worse than any other call."

"It is. Life will go on, though. The sun is still shining. Look at how it's fighting to break through the smoke."

How do you do it? How do you do this every time he goes to work? Margaret wanted to know, but she wouldn't ask. At least not until Dylan was home safe.

The phone rang. Erin picked it up on the first ring. She was quiet for a few seconds after she answered, and then she said, "Oh thank God. Thank you, Cam." Another pause. "I will. I promise. You take care of yourself. We love you." She hung up the phone.

Turning to Margaret, she said, "Dylan's okay. He wasn't in the towers when they collapsed. He's on the rescue crew. I don't know when we'll hear from him."

"Thank God," said Margaret. No Burke ever questioned the source or veracity of her father's information. Of course, now that he knew she and Dylan were safe, her father would be off to whatever his own mission was. "He asked you to look after me, didn't he?"

"Are you surprised?"

"Only that you agreed," Margaret admitted, lowering her head.

"We were all young once, you know. Life is short. Don't take everything so seriously. Especially yourself."

Margaret all but jumped out of her chair and gave Erin a hug. Family was all that mattered when the going got tough. Why had she never realized it before?

Dylan Burke refused to think about the events of the day. The firefighters all knew that they had lost their chief and their chaplain—even before anyone would confirm it—along with hundreds of their guys, which no one could deny, even if they wouldn't say it aloud. Instead, he just did what he had to do, tackling the gargantuan task of this rescue one small piece at a time.

A battalion commander, he had cautioned his men to pace themselves just a few minutes before. He was finding it nearly impossible to practice what he preached, but he knew it was the only way.

If he hadn't seen Josselyn Jeffrey fall, he would have been crushed by the South Tower when it collapsed. On his way to the South Tower from the North Tower at just the moment that he saw her stumble, he had felt compelled to help her. She was just someone in need of his help; he hadn't noticed who she was until he was holding her and could see her face and read her soot-smudged press badge. Helping her had been no more than an instinct, and he followed his instincts in order to survive,

never questioning them. Never taking time to consider what-
ifs. He couldn't do this job if he did either of those things.

God willing, he'd have the chance to thank Josselyn Jeffrey
for saving *his* life.

∽◌

Toward mid-afternoon, Josselyn found herself outside, walking
toward the brownstone that housed Natalie Tevner's home and
office. Natalie, her closest friend ever since they were little girls,
was a psychiatrist who specialized in trauma recovery. Josselyn
knew thousands of people needed Natalie more than she did
right now, but her feet refused to acknowledge that fact.

Natalie came rushing out the door just as Josselyn was
lifting her hand to press the buzzer.

"Joss, you look dazed," Natalie said, closing and locking
the door behind her. "Oh my God! You were there." Natalie
clapped her hand over her mouth.

"I thought I washed all the ash off me."

"You did, sweetie. I could tell by your eyes." Natalie put her
arms around Josselyn. "I have to go over to a makeshift trauma/
crisis-intervention center that's been set up in the church. Come
with me."

"I'd only make people feel worse."

"No, you won't. Have you written about it yet?"

Josselyn nodded, following Natalie down the stoop.

"Well, you can show other people how to do that. Or you can
just be with them. Talk to them, listen to them, feel with them.
You have to learn how to feel *with* people, instead of *for* them."

"I don't know how to do that."

"I know you don't. You've never really tried. When do you
plan to make the attempt? You're fifty—"

"I know how old I am, Nat."

"It's not about how old you are; it's about how much you isolate yourself, considering how old you are. You have to let people in. This whole thing will destroy you if you don't."

The friends' eyes locked. As they walked to the church, Josselyn described all that had happened that day, from dawn to the moment when she arrived at Natalie's doorstep.

"So much for your inability to relate to people when you don't have the page between them and you," remarked Natalie, after Josselyn explained that she'd stayed to help, relating her conversations with the young woman and the firefighter.

"In the midst of all this, why on earth would I focus on Cameron Burke?" she demanded of Natalie once the tale was told. "Just because the firefighter was named Burke?"

Natalie gave her an "oh please" eye roll. "Well, aside from the fact that Cam was also a firefighter, he is the only man you ever loved and the only person aside from your father who ever made you feel completely safe."

"Do you really think I'm still hanging on to all that, in spite of all the time that's gone by? In spite of *everything*?" sputtered Josselyn, outraged because she knew that she had been doing exactly that, every day of her life for the past thirty years, and the tragedy had merely opened the sluice to the feelings she was normally able to keep at bay, more or less.

"You tell me. Better yet, don't tell me. Tell yourself." Natalie stopped in front of the church. She intuited what was going on with her friend and wished she could help her do the work, but she knew all too well that she could not. The best she could do was to be a clear channel for the wisdom and healing Josselyn needed to light her way. She couldn't be that if she let herself get pulled into the vortex of Josselyn's emotions.

"Feel *with* them," Natalie whispered fiercely as she pulled Josselyn inside, praying that her own most deeply held belief—that we heal ourselves by helping others—would prove to be true for her friend.

Josselyn worked alongside Natalie for many hours at the trauma center. Numerous people recognized Josselyn from television appearances or book-jacket photos, just as Dylan Burke had, and her presence seemed to comfort them—as if her being there somehow validated the depth of their own grief. It made no sense to Josselyn, but she was glad to be of help. Natalie kept casting sidelong glances at her, as if to say, "I told you you'd be glad you came."

When they had a few seconds' pause between patients, Josselyn said, "Who needs an I-told-you-so psychiatrist? Isn't that against the Freudian oath?"

"I'm not a Freudian; I'm a Jungian. And no such oath exists. Besides, you're not my patient," Natalie nudged her good-naturedly. "You already knew what I told you before we got here. It was just a refresher."

"A harsh one."

Natalie nodded, but her look said, "You needed it, and it worked."

Josselyn shook her head, more in self-mockery than denial, and turned toward the man approaching her. She would have plenty of time for the self-analysis she'd been postponing for years. She would have to get to it, but not right now. In the moment, people needed her. It felt good. And she knew that it would help her to discover what she needed to know about herself too. In the story of herself, she needed other people to be her pages.

Erin told Margaret about the psychiatrist who had really helped her through a crisis when even her fireman's-daughter upbringing left her at a loss. Dylan had been badly burned, needing skin grafts and lingering in a coma for twenty-four hours. She'd almost lost him. He'd received last rites. But he had come back. He'd *chosen* to come back, he'd told her when he regained consciousness. Although she'd been overwhelmed by her gratitude and relief—renewing her love for Dylan whom she'd never less than adored—she couldn't shake the feeling that he was with her on borrowed time. That was when the fire department had referred her to Natalie Tevner. Dr. Tevner had guided her to change her perspective, not her beliefs. Doing so had saved Erin's sanity, so now she suggested that Margaret get in touch with the same doctor.

Dr. Tevner's office was in Brooklyn Heights, not far from where Erin and Dylan lived in Carroll Gardens. When Margaret called the office, a recorded message advised patients that Dr. Tevner would be working indefinitely at a nearby church that was operating as a trauma/crisis-intervention center. The message gave the address of the church, advising patients in extreme need to go to the nearest hospital.

Margaret was not in "extreme need," and she knew she wasn't a danger to anyone except her iconoclastic friends, who would probably spit on her now if they knew what her revised thinking was. Hopefully, though, they'd revised their thinking too. Desperate times called for reconsidered opinions. *A time and a place for every fight … that's what wisdom means,* she called her father's words to mind, vowing to remain mindful of them.

Margaret jotted down the address of the church and decided that she would go there the following day. Maybe she could help. She had walked from the city to Brooklyn today; she could easily walk from Carroll Gardens to the church in Brooklyn Heights tomorrow. Just thinking about helping filled her with hope. Or was it faith? Maybe Erin was right about keeping the faith, after all.

Cameron Burke adjusted himself quickly to his new quarters. It had been decided, and he had agreed, that he was too well known to be a foreign operative in this mission. Instead, he was going to run it from secured quarters deep within the bowels of the Pentagon, with contact only by means of secured e-mail and phone lines until things settled down a bit, and a semblance of normalcy could be restored.

He welcomed the solitude, actually. It was a blessing. An opportunity to serve his country the best way he could and simultaneously search his own soul for the answers to questions he should have asked himself—and answered—long ago. In the quiet of his semidark room, Burke closed his eyes. The utter stillness drew him into itself. Long-ago memories began to surface. They called to him, in almost inaudible whispers at first, but then, as he allowed himself to listen, they grew louder, eventually insisting that he answer the questions they put forth—that he speak to his own soul and quench its deepest yearning, once and for all.

BOOK II
ALL'S FAIR

$\mathcal{V}$ietnam. The jungle, blazing hot and glaring by day, suffocatingly still and utterly dark by night. A living hell for every GI who lived through it. The tortures witnessed—and perpetrated—were the worst any of them ever imagined they would have to endure.

The war was different for Cameron Burke than it was for most of the others in his unit. He had chosen to come fight for his country, felt no resentment, no unbridled rage. The guys in his unit relied on him and respected him, even those who didn't like him, though most did. They knew that Burke was the guy to turn to if you had a problem, big or small; he was also the guy who would risk his life for you, no questions asked, no acknowledgment expected.

Burke, for his part, liked their knowing this and liked their knowing that he knew it. It gave him a certain tacit authority and reverence that he never would have had otherwise. As the son of a firefighter, and a former firefighter himself, it felt good to be so honored by these draftees, mostly college boys and pampered kids. He could see the guys at the firehouse laughing when he told them. He had left to enlist, but his father and his cousin, who was more like a brother to him, were still at the same firehouse, and Burke remained good friends with all the guys there—not a one of them ever thought of himself as a hero. Burke never had, either. Nor had his father or grandfather before him. Once a firefighter pledged to save and serve, it was his job—no more, no less, and certainly no reason to think of himself as a hero. Burke had heard that more times than he could remember. When he repeated it to the guys in his platoon, they had looked back at him in sheer wide-eyed wonder, not in disbelief but in awe. That was when he realized that he had earned a certain standing among them.

That had been forever ago. He couldn't remember the day, month, or year. All time was the same in the jungle. You watched day turn to night to day to night—and on and on and on—but you were frozen in time by the heat and the merciless stifling of the thick, heavy, wet air.

Despite all that, Cameron Burke loved serving his country. Loved it more than saving people from the searing tongues of flame. He couldn't actually say that he loved—or didn't love—fighting fires. He felt called to it, to be sure. Felt alive and purposeful as soon as he got on the truck. When he pulled someone out of a fire, an indescribable kind of love poured out of them, mixed with gratitude so deep that it was almost unbearable. His parents loved him, but their love for him—and his for them—was completely different from the love of someone he rescued. Serving his country somehow filled him with that same kind of love, that same outpouring of boundless gratitude. He couldn't explain it, even to himself, other than to say that it somehow felt the same. And he didn't want to live without that feeling.

Josselyn Jeffrey would never get used to the weather in Vietnam. She tried to look on the bright side: it was summer, so the rest of the year would not be this hot and humid. When she heard the summer was interminable, she had to force herself not to scream. What kind of reporter was she going to be if she couldn't endure terrains and climates of all sorts? She would get used to it; she'd force herself if need be.

Piling her long, thick, wavy dark hair on top of her head, she twirled it into a sort of topknot, and secured it in place with two pencils. That helped. A little. She enthusiastically convinced herself that keeping her hair up would make her feel infinitely cooler. A friend of hers in Haight-Ashbury had told her that thoughts were only things; in the mind resided the power to change anything, according to one's thoughts. That had been his parting wisdom as she'd boarded the plane bound for Southeast Asia. She'd have to acquaint herself with Eastern wisdom, he'd told her.

But her father, a veteran news correspondent who had served in World War II and countless other places, warned her against embracing the truths that arose on foreign soil. After all, had he done so, he might have become a Nazi instead of a collaborator of Raoul Wallenberg. She had argued with her father that she wasn't destined for greatness. He had argued back that everyone was destined for greatness: did God create any soul for it to never do anything but languish and despair? In the middle of this discourse—the kind of dialogue Josselyn so adored having with her father—her mother had called for her father, and that had been the end of it. Her father focused his care on the helpless in his midst, and that was always her mother, never Josselyn. That was her greatest gift to her father: that she could survive without him. Still, she wished she could have known the rest of what he wanted to tell her. Her cab had come shortly afterward, with time enough for good-byes to both her parents but nothing more.

She would search within for the answer, and then she could write to her father about it. That way it would truly be a discourse, not just her one-sided absorption of her father's considerable brilliance. Her father, who never considered himself anything close to brilliant, would enjoy that too.

Glad to have determined her course of action, Josselyn swept out of her tent in pursuit of a story, an image of herself as the next Hemingway already beginning to take shape, complete with the reporting, the correspondence, the adventure, the drama—and eventually, even the novels. Yes, she could see it all coming into sharp focus.

She was about to discover for the first time the principle that would come to guide her as a writer: her stories wrote her, not the other way around.

For as long as he lived, Cameron Burke would never forget seeing Josselyn Jeffrey for the first time. He knew that in an instant, even before he knew her name or whether she would be a part of his life, knew it deep within himself without knowing why or how he knew. It exhilarated and confounded him at the same time. He had never felt this confused before, and he was infuriated to feel so now. Still, he knew he would never forget her.

In the next second, she was approaching him, putting out her hand and smiling as she introduced herself. He did the same. Everything about it was absolutely ordinary, except that it was the most extraordinary moment of Cameron Burke's life. What was it about her? She was beautiful. That was undeniable, but it wasn't what held him hostage. She had a vibrancy about her—a zest for life—that made him just want to be near her. She was radiant, that's what it was. He always laughed when he read that about women. He would never laugh about it again. Wherever he went and whatever he did, seeing or hearing the word *radiant* would forever conjure up her image in his mind—her black eyes sparkling with sheer rapture at being alive, her dark hair shimmering in the sun, her hand cool and smooth in his. He had taken her hand in a gesture of civility, but it had felt more like an intimate embrace. Their eyes had locked in that instant, and he'd known that she, too, sensed this power between them. He couldn't help but wonder if it made her feel the same way it made him feel.

He knew he was not leaving this world without finding out.

Burke agreed to let Josselyn Jeffrey write a story about him. "A day in the life of one GI," was how she described it. Of course he agreed to it; he would have agreed to lie down in the dirt while she backed a jeep over him if she asked him to.

He didn't know where this would lead, but wherever she led, he would follow. That much he knew for sure. It seemed to be the only thing he *did* know for sure since first looking at her.

He was so caught up in the feelings she'd brought to life in him, he hardly paid attention to the thoughts that were arising rapid-fire in his mind.

He had to learn everything there was to learn about her, had to let her discover everything there was to discover about him. And he never willingly let anyone discover anything about him. He barely even knew the deepest parts of himself. Yet the landscape of Cameron Burke was now Josselyn Jeffrey's for the asking, for the probing—for whatever she wanted to do with him.

Burke realized he couldn't wait for her to probe the deepest parts of him—couldn't wait to bare the secrets of his soul. Suddenly he felt completely alive as never before, in fire or in battle.

Josselyn Jeffrey could not believe her good fortune. One step out of her tent, and she had immediately set her eyes upon the perfect soldier for her "day in the life of one GI" idea. That he was almost unbearably attractive was all but too good to be true. He had the kind of quiet strength that always appealed to her in men, a demeanor that bespoke his self-confidence and integrity without his feeling the need to hit anyone over the head with it. He was not really handsome—that wasn't it at all—it was his bearing; his voice, deep but warm; and something else she'd felt when they shook hands, like a current of energy surging through her entire body. It had made her shudder, not with fear, but with excitement and anticipation. She had never felt this way before, but she had dreamed of feeling this way, had known this was how she was supposed to feel with a man. She had waited for it to be this way, and now she was glad that she had. No matter how many men she might meet in this life, she would never feel this way again. And she was determined that Cameron Burke would know it before too long.

Days felt long in Vietnam, but lives didn't always last. She was not going to spend the rest of her life wishing she'd said or done something she would never have the chance to again. You did that, and you lost not only what you missed but also the time you spent regretting. She had seen her mother surrender herself to the past so completely that the present meant nothing to her. She, Josselyn, was not losing this moment to regret or anything else.

This moment was hers; hers and Cameron Burke's. She would make it count. *They* would make it count.

Pencil and notebook in hand—she had left them behind, not thinking she would find a lead *that* quickly—Josselyn Jeffrey swept out of her tent for the second time in the same hour, but this time she knew what her destiny was, and with whom. And she set off to claim it.

Burke dragged hard on the last of a cigarette. He stomped it out as he saw Josselyn Jeffrey approach him, and then he spread out a blanket for her to sit on.

"I don't mind if you smoke," she said, sitting down next to him on the blanket.

But he didn't want to smoke around her, didn't need to. Smoking settled him; drinking settled him. She made him feel alive. He just wanted to feel what she made him feel. No barriers, no pretenses. Just the two of them.

"Let's start by your telling me what a day in the life of a GI in Vietnam is like. A typical day." She rolled her pencil between her thumb and forefinger. Burke had to use every ounce of control to not become mesmerized by her movements, by the ordinary things she did, things he never even noticed in other people.

"There is no typical day in Vietnam, but today is even less so. On a typical day—whatever that means in this jungle—we'd be on maneuvers."

"Right," Josselyn said quickly. *Brilliant. He knows I'm seasoned now. What was I thinking?* She felt a flush spread across her face and prayed he didn't notice.

"We were beaten back pretty badly a couple of nights ago, so we're lying low for a while," he explained.

"Right," she said again, tucking the pencil behind her ear and clasping her hands together to keep them from shaking. She looked up at him. "Look, this is the first real assignment I've ever gotten. And I had to beg for it. I've never done this before."

"Neither have I."

Josselyn smiled. "So I could have pulled this off without admitting that?"

Burke shrugged, flashing a hangdog grin. "You kind of wanted to tell me, didn't you? It seemed like it."

"I guess I did."

"I never tell anyone things about myself."

"Neither do I."

"I want to tell you everything, though. Except I feel like you already know all there is to know about me."

That was how she felt, too, but she didn't know what to say. The self-confidence she had felt in her tent a few minutes before seemed to dissolve in his presence. In that instant, she was merely what she was—inexperienced, ingenuous, vulnerable. Although she felt genuinely attracted to Cameron Burke, she was at a loss as to what to do next. If only she had played those high-school and college games of flirtation.

"I didn't mean to make you feel uncomfortable," he added tensely, when she didn't reply after a beat.

"You didn't. I mean ... I don't know what I mean." Surprising herself, she put her hand on his arm. She started to pull back, but he reached over with his other hand, putting it over hers. *It's now or never.* "I've never felt this way before. I don't even care about the interview; I just want to be with you." She spoke softly and quickly, afraid she might lose her nerve.

"Do the interview. I'll be with you as long as you want me to."

Josselyn forced herself to breathe. A tide of longing swept over her, its surging sharp and fierce. She had never realized how much she longed to feel this way until Cameron Burke first clasped her hand in greeting. Up until that moment, she had only wanted to write. Although she had known in her heart what love should feel like, she had been unaware of how much she missed *not* feeling it until it seemed within her grasp.

"You need to do the interview," he said, forcing her to focus. She clung to his words as if to a lifeline, grasping at whatever she could to avoid plunging into the depths of these feelings. Delicious a plunge though it would be.

"Okay," she said.

"Vietnam isn't like other places. You never know what might happen the next day. The next minute, even."

"Other places are like that too."

"It's not the same."

"Only because you expect it here."

"No, that's not all of it. I was a firefighter before I enlisted. I started every day knowing that I might not survive to see the next. But here, it's … I can't explain it."

"It's like waiting for the other shoe to drop."

"Exactly!" Had she read his mind? She hadn't even stopped to think about it, just said aloud exactly what he was feeling. It was as if she just knew it somehow. "How did you know that?"

"My mother escaped the Holocaust, but her parents perished," she explained. "Waiting for unforeseen horrors that we can't control or escape is something my mother can't help but do."

"What about your father?" He said it to keep the conversation going, unable to imagine living in such a clot of fear—nonetheless growing up in it.

"My father's a foreign correspondent," she continued. "Certainly no stranger to horror, but it's different when you go into it knowingly, I suppose. That's what he always says. He covered the European theater during World War II. Korea and the French war in Indochina too. And the Six-Day War in Israel."

"Is Bartholomew Jeffrey your father?" He was relieved to have an excuse to get off the other subject.

Josselyn nodded. "When I'm not waiting for shoes to drop, I'm trying on ones I can never fill."

"My money's on you." He squeezed her hand. That odd but exhilarating current sparked between them, and their eyes locked, each knowing the other felt it too.

"It's so hard. I'll never be as good as he is. He worked with Raoul Wallenberg, for God's sake."

"Be the best you can be. That's all any of us can do."

"You sound like my father now."

"No, that was *my* father. That's what he told me at the first fire we went to together; he told me again when I enlisted to come over here."

"I'm talking too much. It's like *you're* interviewing *me*," she took the pencil from its perch behind her ear. "Tell me about waiting for the other shoe to drop. Tell me what it feels like … here," she said, touching his heart with her left hand. She had intended to touch her own heart, but when she moved her hand, it found its way to his heart instead, seemingly of its own volition. But she knew it was of a volition all her own, so deeply her own, in fact, that she did not question how right and natural it felt. Natural the way breathing was natural; so essential to living that it required no thought, no voluntary action whatsoever. That was how being with Cameron felt to her, how she knew it would always feel—she felt sure she was

51

falling in love with him, crazy as that might be. If she thought about it, rather than just feeling it and intuitively trusting what she felt, she would run.

Burke encircled her wrist with his fingers, pressing her hand against his chest more firmly. "It feels like death is the only thing I can count on for sure."

Josselyn exhaled, letting the pencil she held in her right hand fall to the ground.

Burke released her wrist, sliding his hand down hers and pulling her into his lap. "Aren't you going to write down what I said?" he teased.

"I won't ever forget anything you tell me. And I won't regret hearing any of it." She wasn't sure why she'd said that last part—she had heeded an instinctive impulse and was glad to discern it must have been something he wanted to hear, because in the next instant, he put his hand against her face, tracing the line of her cheekbone with the edge of his thumb, and then leaning her face back so he could look straight into her eyes. After an interminable few seconds, he tore his eyes away from hers, and then he kissed her. A soft, sweet, tender kiss. More the kiss of longtime lovers than new. Letting go of his hand that still held hers, she reached up to caress his neck, and he lifted her out of his lap and into his arms. His tenderness deepened, strengthened, but the passion already flaring between them ignited.

"If I go up in smoke, it might as well be with a fireman," she whispered, the velvety huskiness of her own voice surprising her, and thrilling him.

They were no more than a few hundred feet from her tent, and he carried her there, neither of them caring if anyone else was around to have seen them.

As he held back the flap and stepped inside, still holding her in his arms, she knew that the next time she came out of that tent she would be irrevocably changed.

He let the flap fall and set her gently on her feet, stepping behind her, pressing his lips against the back of her neck. She leaned back against him, fearing she would actually lose consciousness, the pleasure was so intense. He pulled the pencils out of her hair, letting it tumble over his face as it cascaded past her shoulders. Then he turned her around in his arms, kissing her full on the lips again, pressing her body hard against his. Locked against each other, he edged her back toward the cot a few steps away. They sank down together, barely aware of the cot beneath them, pulling off one another's clothing with hasty fumbling.

Their passion for one another was all-encompassing—so much so that it drowned out their awareness of everything except each other. They rode the intoxicating waves of it together, exulting in the crests and plumbing the depths, each knowing they would never be able to have enough of the other.

Moonlight crept around the edges of the tent, the only indicator that any time had passed, so lost had they been in the delights of one another.

Josselyn lay on her side, her head tucked under Burke's chin, her cheek pressed against his chest. She leaned away from him slightly, propping herself up on one elbow. With the fingers of her other hand, she gently caressed his chest, still amazed by the power of desire she could feel for this man she had only just met, yet felt she knew utterly.

Burke placed his hand over hers, in that endearingly protective way of his, and then drew it toward his lips. He kissed her fingers and the back of her hand, turning it over to kiss first her palm, and then the inside of her wrist where her pulse raced. Shock waves of pleasure and longing flooded her entire body every time he kissed her, every time he touched her anywhere.

He shifted his weight beneath her, pulling her on top of him at the same time.

"You all right, baby?" he asked, smoothing her hair back from her face, running his fingers through the silky coils of it.

"Of course," she smiled. She would have hated any other man's calling her "baby," wouldn't have allowed it, but she loved it when he called her that. "Why wouldn't I be?" She planted a velvety kiss on his forehead.

"I just want it to be good for you, that's all." He ran his hands over her shoulders and down her back. Her hair fell loose, the ends of it brushing against his chest.

He would never get over how soft she was—her hair was like silk, only thicker; her skin like satin. The delights of her were endless, more intense than he'd ever known with any other woman. He breathed in the scent of her—lilacs or gardenias, he could never keep those scents straight—deep and sweet, but not heavy.

"It will be, as long as I'm with you," she whispered in his ear, kissing his neck, mounting his passion to a fever pitch again.

He put his hands around her face, and they looked deep into each other's eyes. Her eyes were unbelievably dark, luminous, fathomless pools, but in them he could see his own soul, and he felt as if he had never really seen himself before.

She felt the same way looking into his eyes.

They had discovered some deep truth about themselves that they could not have discovered without the other; as if loving each other provided the key to unlocking the truths of their own souls.

"Whatever else happens, Joss, I want you to know that I love you. I'll go to my grave loving you. This wasn't just—"

"I know it wasn't. I'll always love you too. No matter what."

"But no talking of tomorrow. There's no tomorrow here. We have to just trust one another in spite of the insanity around us. Say that you trust me."

"I will if you will."

"I'm serious, Joss."

She smiled at him. "I do trust you, Cam. I wouldn't have given myself to you if I didn't trust you." The last part she said softly, pressing her cheek against his afterward.

"Of course you wouldn't have. That was stupid of me." He held her closer.

"And I agree," she continued. "There is no tomorrow for us; there's only the time we have together now."

"Okay."

"Kiss me again. But don't stop this time."

Passion claimed them again. They lost themselves in each other until the moon went down. Burke kissed her, promising to be back as soon as he could, and then he slipped out of her tent.

Josselyn knew that she'd been right; of course she was irrevocably changed. Cameron Burke had penetrated more than just her body. He had reached all the way into her heart and her soul, and she knew she had done the same for him—in that, it had been the first time for both of them. She had always imagined that when she lost her virginity she would feel smaller, perhaps even bereft; instead, she felt expanded, exultant. Before, she had lived only to put words on the page, to be the woman she believed her father saw her as being. Now she knew she would live only in the moments when she was with Cameron. She would still write, of course. Writing was in her blood; was the air she breathed. But being with Cameron—not just the lovemaking itself, but the soul-to-soul oneness they shared—was more powerful than anything else she had ever experienced, like a life force she couldn't live without, and wouldn't want to even if she could.

For seven more days, there were no maneuvers. It was a record. At least for Burke's tour. Were it not for Josselyn, he would have jumped out of his skin in response to his own restlessness.

Instead, he decided that the time was a gift, and she agreed. Rather than worry about how long it would last, they chose to live as if it would last forever. Each knew it wouldn't, but acted as if it could for the other's sake.

When Burke found her crying softly, he held her in his arms until she quieted, neither of them saying a word. When Josselyn caught him sitting on a rock and staring off into space, she came up behind him and wrapped her arms around his neck, pressing her cheek against his until he turned and took her in his arms. Again, not a single word exchanged. Their pact of optimism was bound by love, in its truest essence, and quite beyond any words they could ever speak.

During the day, Burke would contrive to steal time to be with her. Sneaking away to a quiet corner somewhere, they would talk about everything: every dream, fear, desire, experience either one had ever had—or at least the ones that seemed important to them, which meant the ones that their passion for each other, in its all-encompassing force and breadth, had not obliterated from their consciousness. The importance of other things in light of their newfound importance to each other surprised them both, but it also gave them perspective on the remainder of their lives. Subconsciously aware that they would have to go on living outside of this time warp their love had created, they valued the perspective, though it was impossible to admit that to each other, or even to themselves. Admitting that would have been tantamount to admitting that their parting was inevitable. Neither of them could do that outside the safety of their own unconscious realms.

Still, their love was so powerful that neither of them consciously felt any sense of denying reality or the inevitable. All they felt was that love was the only thing that was real in the truest sense, the only thing worth living for. Cleaving to that truth, they could move forward without falling into despair over the likelihood of losing one another.

As the sun descended, their voices would hush to whispers almost involuntarily, as if quieting at the behest of the end of day. The sunset sky would glow vermilion and pink, slowly cool to lavender at the edges farthest from the horizon, and then darken to violet all over. As the twilight deepened, Burke would stand up and take her hand, leading her back to her tent. He would hold back the tent flap, ushering her inside but standing with the flap resting on his shoulder for a few seconds so that he could catch a glimpse of her before the last of the light gave way to dusk. He never showered her with compliments, just drank her in like an elixir that sustained his very life. She much preferred it that way, and he knew it. They knew everything about each other, it seemed. Everything that mattered anyway.

When Burke had sated himself with looking at Josselyn, he would let the tent flap fall abruptly, as if he couldn't stand another second apart from her body. They would entwine effortlessly— one body, one breath, one soul—but with sensations that miraculously belonged to each other separately and together at the same time. Every nuance of their lovemaking was as magical each time as it had been the first time. So much so that they might have made love one time or a million times. When they came together, skin against skin and hearts beating as one, each time before and yet to be merged into a single mystical union ... ever new, ever magical, ever intense in its singular pleasure.

Neither of them would have wanted it any other way. If that mystical quality had been absent when they made love, it would have been impossible to convince themselves that their love could endure all things, even the hell of war. Only the paradise of being together, suspended in time and space through their physical and spiritual connection to each other, could eclipse the reality of hell long enough to make the endurance of love credible. And without it, those hellfires would have destroyed them.

Josselyn lay in Burke's arms, just on the edge of sleep. He was awake, staring straight ahead, a long coil of her dark hair snaked through his fingers. He stroked her hair attentively, almost as if he held a lifeline.

"Don't fight sleep, baby." His voice rasped against the soft night air. She wondered whether he was trying to make himself sound gruff on purpose. It didn't matter; he could never really sound harsh to her.

"There's plenty of time to sleep. Anyway, I'm not tired," she lied, stifling a yawn.

"So I see," he teased.

"Well, if I am tired, it's your fault," she teased back.

"Let's see if I can wake you up then," he stopped stroking her hair, moved his hand to the curve of her neck, easing her toward him and kissing her deeply. Josselyn surrendered herself to him completely, losing and finding herself simultaneously in the miraculous way that happened whenever she was with him. He pressed her tight against him, and they melted into one another, flowing into and around each other like liquid light, fluid and radiant and beautiful. Currents of passion and pleasure flowed through her, filling and surrounding her with such intensity that it seemed she was losing consciousness, but she had never felt more alive or aware in her life. Every cell of her body and being was electrified by Cameron's love for her, by the exquisite way he touched and caressed her. Parts of her came alive that she never even knew existed before he came into her life. Suddenly every inch of her became erotically charged just because he was near her. When they lay this way, no room for even air between them, nothing existed except her sexual awareness, her longing for him, and her desire to quench his desires. Not that she felt she was just an object for his pleasure. Cameron always made sure she knew that their lovemaking was as special to him as it was to her, not just in the words he whispered while making love to her, but in the way he looked at her, touched her, held her, released himself inside her. He made her feel cherished, exquisite, precious—not just when he was making love to her, but all the time.

Burke shifted his weight slightly, coaxing Josselyn's body beneath his. He was so used to the darkness that he could see her clearly in the alabaster shaft of moonlight that streamed through the gap between the tent flaps. Her porcelain skin gleamed in the ethereal cast of the moon. He kissed and stroked her everywhere, over and over again, and she returned each one, kiss for kiss and caress for caress. She was so smooth, so infinitely satiny and sweet. He drowned in the sheer sensual delights of her. In the beginning, he had felt almost unworthy of touching anything so soft and beautiful with his rough, callused hands, but she continually assured him he was beyond gentle—he was tenderness itself. He never lost his sense of amazement over the magic of loving her so much and wanting her so much, and being loved by her and wanted by her in exactly the same measure. Whatever God demanded of him, up to this point and afterward, he would gladly take on—and pray he lived up to—for the gift of her love for him and his for her.

He arched his back, and she began to curve against him, reflexively. Ever so gently, he pressed her shoulders back against the cot. "No, don't move," he whispered.

She lay still, using every ounce of her will to not follow the movements of his body, to not press herself against him. The few inches between them felt like a chasm. She saw the longing in his eyes, in the set of his jaw, and realized he felt it too.

"I'm memorizing you," he said at last. It had only been a matter of seconds, but it felt like hours. His hands still touched her shoulders.

"Can you only do that with your eyes?" she asked, looking up at him, holding his gaze in that deep way that bore into his soul, exposing the core of him. The core he let her alone see.

He leaned his head down, kissed her forehead and then her lips, and she arched her back, her desire pulling her closer to him, the way the sun pulls a plant toward the light. She had not willed her body to move, only felt it respond to a pull that was so strong it was beyond her control—like gravity or magnetic attraction. In the instant she moved up, he shifted forward, moving inside her more deeply than ever before. The pleasure surged through her in cresting waves, so intense she could scarcely bear it, almost as if it were pain rather than delight. Because she couldn't keep from crying out and didn't want to be overheard in the otherwise silent night, she pressed her mouth against his shoulder to muffle the sound, overtaken by involuntary shudders as the pleasure rippled through every muscle and nerve of her body.

He held her tight in his arms, the velvety softness of her filling and surrounding him.

Waves of pleasure crashed over her, exploding in surges of passion, the last of which reached a thundering crescendo that vibrated through her in delicious shudders, and she felt him shudder too.

Together, they gave themselves over to these exquisite pulsations, one after another … after another. … And then they both lay still in the absolute ecstasy that washed over them, leaving in its wake a sea of bliss and serenity.

Burke eased Josselyn back against the cot again, pulled back slightly, and turned on his side, coaxing her against him again.

"Didn't you have enough?" she asked softly, her voice low and husky.

"Never of you," he said lightly.

"Hah! Even *you're* too exhausted for more right now."

"Never of you," he said again, but this time he said it with a reverence that brought her to tears.

"Oh Cam." She buried her face against his chest, turning slightly so she could feel his heartbeat against her cheek.

"I meant for it to make you happy," he said, almost desperate at the thought of having caused her pain.

"It does make me happy, darling." She brought her face up close to his, so he could look in her eyes. "I will never be happier than I am at this moment. I swear it."

He wiped away her tears with his fingertips, kissing her tenderly. "No matter what happens," he said, more to himself than to her, but she nodded in response.

"Cam?"

"Hmm?"

"Promise me something."

"Anything."

"You won't forget me."

"How could I forget you? I just memorized you. Remember?"

She brushed her fingertip across his lips. "Please don't tease me. Just promise."

"Joss, that's crazy. You mean more to me than any—" He stopped. "We know how we feel about each other."

"Of course we do, darling. Please promise me anyway. Please."

"All right. I promise. I will not—and could not—ever forget you." *You're the love of my life,* his soul all but screamed, but he couldn't say the words aloud.

"Thank you, my love. I adore you beyond words."

"My promising meant that much to you?"

"I'd adore you even if you hadn't promised ... but, yes, it did."

"Why?"

Josselyn drew in a breath, holding it for a second or two before exhaling. She somehow sensed that this was the only love she would ever share with a man—this passion born and fomented in the Southeast Asian jungle, too hot, too exotic to be sustained anywhere else. Just like she was. She would never be able to sustain love in everyday life. Station wagons and grocery shopping and PTA meetings and …

He looked at her, surprised by how long in coming her answer was. "Why?" he said again.

To avoid the full-blown panic she felt was about to flood her, she said quickly, "Because you're a man. You'll have other women, even if they never mean as much to you as I do, even if it's never this way for you again."

"I won't."

"Of course you will. I want you to—unless we find one another again back in the States. You'll ruin your life without a woman. You'll work yourself to death without a woman to tell you to stop. Remember me, Cam. That's all I'm asking you to promise."

"All right, I promised you that, but I'm not giving you my blessing to be with another man. Ever."

"Do you have any idea how adorable you are? I didn't ask for your blessing, and I know you can't give it to me. That's all right. If we don't find each other again, I'll live like a nun. Coffee, pen, paper, and me," she said softly, almost beatifically, as if she would have been disappointed if he *had* given her his blessing.

"Can we end this conversation now?"

"Yes, darling. Thank you for promising. Please don't be angry with me. I'll never ask you for anything else. I promise."

Burke held her tight in his arms. "I'm not angry. I just don't understand why you needed me to promise."

Sighing, she kissed his cheek. "If we find one another after all this is over, the promise won't matter, Cam, and you can laugh at me and say you told me so every day for the rest of our lives."

"Promise?"

She smiled. "Yes. But if we don't, I have to live on that promise for the rest of my life. Do you understand that? Your promising that you'll never forget what I am to you—what our days and nights together will always mean to you—are all I'll have of you. Just my memories and your promise. That's all I'll have," she emphasized the last part by looking into his eyes and pronouncing the words more slowly than the rest of what she'd said.

Burke said nothing, just held her gaze.

"I'm not asking you for anything else," she continued. "I don't want the blessing I know you can't give. I'm sorry I had to ask you to promise, but I ... I just had to. Good night, darling."

"Good night, baby."

Sorrow filled him suddenly, because he knew she had surrendered not just her body and soul to him, but also her future—if he could not share it with her. He wished he had told her she didn't need to apologize, that he wasn't angry with her; he was angry with himself because she was stronger than he was, and that was the one thing he had never been prepared to accept: his own weakness.

Burke crept outside and back to his own tent, crawling into his cot and letting himself drift in and out of sleep as he waited for reveille to sound. All the while, Josselyn filled his dreams, every beguiling, delectable aspect of her. He allowed himself to relish the sheer delight of her, of being with her. It wasn't just making love to her that filled him with this unbridled passion—this pleasure that utterly consumed and transformed him—it was the whole experience of being around her. Hearing her laughter, drinking in her scent, feeling her hair or her skin brush against him—these simple, ordinary things became erotic encounters for him. Everything between them was charged with passion—with love. And, because he loved her so much, he wanted to be worthy of her love. He wanted that—needed that—more than he had ever thought he would or could.

He had never felt this way about a woman. Not that he had been with that many women—his Catholic upbringing had hammered home the sin of sex out of wedlock, and although it might not have precluded him from experimenting, it certainly made him think twice every time. But he knew he would never again be with anyone like Josselyn. He would never want to be with another woman. He felt as if he had spent his life with half a soul up until he met Josselyn because she was the other half.

Why hadn't he told her that? Why hadn't he promised, without hesitating, when she asked him to promise not to forget her? And then he could have just told her how much she meant to him, all the things he'd just realized. Now, even if he did tell her, it would seem like an afterthought. His dreams of her subsided in response to his self-recrimination. All he could think of was his own selfish reluctance to make the simple promise she'd asked him to make.

The edges of dawn began to creep up out of the treetops, and once again Cameron Burke found himself waiting for the other shoe to drop, filled with the foreboding he had long grown used to, but which now was mixed with a sense of despair that he was completely unaccustomed to. Both congealed in his gut, along with the self-disgust he'd been feeling for the last few hours, ever since discovering what he considered to be his own weakness. He hated these new feelings.

"If you want to be the strong one, be a man, for God's sake. Tell it to her now. Just say, 'I couldn't put it all into words when you asked me to promise.' She'll understand," he whispered these words to himself quickly in the darkness, half praying and half reproaching. Still, he knew it would never be the same as if he'd said it straight out, and he would have to live with his regret for a long time to come. Maybe forever.

By the time reveille sounded, Cameron Burke was wide awake. He had put his dilemma over Josselyn back in a corner of his mind, where it would have to wait until he could deal with it. He was all too aware that, despite the complete and unalterable reconfiguration of his inner world, his outward surroundings were the same as they had been the day before and the day before that. They would be the same throughout this day and every other day in this interminable conflict in this unknowable place. He needed to focus on what was in front of him: fighting for his country, seeing through the commitment he had made to serve it.

Burke remained proud to serve his country. Patriotism was the only response he could muster toward America. Anything else was completely unthinkable to him; alien, even. Still, he couldn't help but wonder what had made the powers that be think that they could actually win this war, defeat an enemy whose powers of covert maneuvering were so great, their men might just as well be invisible. They *were* virtually invisible, in all honesty. He wouldn't mind being a fly on the wall in some big-brass meeting. It would be fascinating to find out what they were thinking. Maybe they had some elaborate, brilliant scheme already in the works, and he was but a cog in the military machinery that would ultimately bring it about. He wished it were so, but his instincts told him otherwise. Deep in his gut, he knew that they were just posturing, really had no clue how to win this war or even get out of it. That made the day-to-day hell of it all the worse. When he was fighting for something he knew was attainable, he could always bear the worst of it, no matter how bad it got. Once he knew he had no chance of winning, though, he lost the will to keep fighting.

Or perhaps the will to fight just left him. It didn't really matter which. If the will to fight was gone, it was gone. He imagined it was pretty much the same for other men too. The battle would always overtake the man who had no will to fight.

He had learned that fighting fires and then witnessed it proved true again in war. Perhaps it was different in wars that had an enemy a man could keep in his sights. When a visible front stayed in a man's line of vision, real or imaginary, his will to fight remained keen for a long time ... or at least a longer time. When the enemy crouched in the darkness—movements shrouded by inscrutable shadow and impenetrable jungle, and true intentions veiled by an ideology equally inscrutable and impenetrable, perhaps even more so—victory as he and other Americans thought of it did not seem attainable. Even if they did attain victory, by some miracle, the enemy would not feel vanquished. The enemy in this war could remain in hiding in the jungle underbrush indefinitely—forever if need be—and not ever mind. To them, victory was an inward knowing, the same as the bliss of the perfect consciousness to which their native religions taught them to aspire. Diametrically opposed to the American concept of victory, an outward display of glory that was a hairsbreadth away from joy. Burke, who viewed joy and bliss as far removed from one another—the former coming in sparkling bursts; the latter, in radiating calm—recognized that this ideological difference regarding the conception of victory lay at the heart of why this war had devolved into such a quagmire.

Burke shrugged as he lifted his binoculars to scan the outlying territory. He was just a GI, a cog in the military machine; what he thought didn't make a bit of difference. Nor did he think that reading a book on Buddhism or Taoism made him a philosopher, not even close. But he did think it was important to know what made a man tick, particularly when you and he were engaged in mortal combat—and having a clue as to his mind-set could mean the difference between life and death. His musings forged improved survival skills, nothing more.

He had never given such things much thought before coming to Vietnam. Up to that point, his opponents had never been men, just smoke and flames. With a fire it wasn't that complicated. One tongue of flame was essentially the same as another; it was the way each fire fed that was different. Like every other firefighter, he learned how to tell the moment when a fire turned, when it became unbeatable. When that moment came, continuing to fight meant death. Suddenly the heat felt unbearable; the smoke and fumes, overwhelming. Up until that moment, though, a firefighter kept fighting. When the force of the fire took over, the flames and heat absorbed all the energy and power of the blaze, and that absorption claimed the firemen's will to fight too—incinerating their hope of beating it back.

The first time Burke railed against a fire that won, he had felt that turning-point moment. He had known it without needing a veteran to tell him, even though he couldn't explain *how* he had known. It had been as if he could feel their hope—their will to fight—go up in the flames. The force of the fight had shifted, almost imperceptibly; the blaze had belonged to the men, but then the flames had taken over. It had been instantaneous. He'd been about nineteen then, and he hadn't yet fought more than maybe a dozen fires. That was the fire he would never forget. Not just because he had learned how to tell when the fire gained the upper hand, but also because his uncle had been lost in that blaze. Having safely brought a little girl out of the burning building, terrified but unburned, his uncle had succumbed to the smoke.

Burke recalled what his father had said that night. "My brother sensed the shift of that fire. But when a fireman knows he's going to his grave, he makes sure no civilians go before he does." Burke had nodded solemnly, suddenly far older than his nineteen years. He understood then and now that the soul of a rescuer could never have peace otherwise, in life or afterward.

Burke's father would become a surrogate father to his brother's son, Dylan. That was fine with Burke, who had always felt Dylan was more his younger brother than his cousin. But they never talked about that fire or Burke's uncle again. Burke knew the depth of his father's love, it just wasn't his way to be demonstrative or to talk much. What was done, was done; talking about it rarely served any purpose. For the most part, he shared his father's opinion on this. It had helped him be a better firefighter, and now it helped him be a better soldier. Burke had always tried to live up to the example his father set—in fighting fires, living a life of integrity, and loving with sincerity.

Burke took a breath, his thoughts shifting from war and firefighting to love. Of the many lessons his father had taught him by example, the greatest one was that a person proves that he loves another by what he does, not what he says. He hoped his actions, as well as his words, would prove his love to Josselyn—especially his admitting his own vulnerability to her, without any pretense, which he intended to do the first chance he got. Because of this war, he didn't know how much time he would have to prove his love to the woman he loved, which made it all the more critical to prove it by saying what he needed to tell her while they were together, by baring his soul and confessing his weakness ... and even his fear. Even if she already knew it intuitively, as well she might, he needed to know she'd heard him say the words to her. There wasn't a blessed thing he could do about the outcome of this war, but at least the woman he loved would know how much he loved her. That much he could control. And he hoped that by laying it all on the line that way, he would feel worthy of her love, after all.

His resolve sharpened his focus. He saw clearly exactly what he needed to do. To start with, he had to get Josselyn out of this place. It was no place for a woman, reporter or otherwise. Even if it meant that they never saw each other again, he had to do it the first chance he got, before tonight if possible. He continued to peer through the binoculars, searching every last inch of the surrounding terrain, while all the musings he'd immersed himself in earlier—about life and love—coalesced in his mind in an unsettling clot.

Cameron Burke was used to fighting hard, but he'd always fought the good fight that he knew how to win, knew he could win. He didn't like not knowing how to win this one—or if it even could be won. More than that, he didn't like having to admit his own weakness, didn't really know how to. But he realized that only by admitting his own weakness would he find true strength.

Yet again, Josselyn Jeffrey spent an entire morning attempting to write her day-in-the-life-of-one-GI story. Several drafts lay at her feet, in shreds and crumpled balls, testaments to her frustration.

Just capture Cameron—that's what the story is. Stop trying to capture your feelings for Cameron! This is a soldier's story, not a romance.

Her heated instructions to herself did nothing to resolve her frustration. She knew she couldn't separate her feelings for Cameron from Cameron himself. If she couldn't do that, how could she think of him separately from her feelings for him? If she couldn't think about him objectively, how could she write about him objectively?

Dejected, she pushed away the shaky makeshift writing table, turned her body in the chair, rested her elbows on her lap, and lowered her head into her upturned palms. Her entire focus had changed, utterly and irrevocably, in the span of just days. She had come to Vietnam determined to become a great war correspondent, committed to proving her worth as a reporter and writer, only to find herself dedicated to nothing other than the man who had become her lover, whom she had known for barely a week, and whom she feared would not remain a part of her life—not just because he might not survive the war, but also because she would not be able to handle ordinary life with him or anyone else.

She wondered how her father had been objective when writing about Wallenberg. Of course, her father had never been passionately in love with Wallenberg, but intense admiration a hairsbreadth away from worship—"glorification," her father called it—was almost the same as being in love, especially when the glorified one disappeared from your life and view, so that he all too quickly became flawless, existing purely in your cherished memories of him, not in your living reality. If that wasn't being in love, what was? It was just that most people didn't feel comfortable thinking of it that way, but she had long since grown accustomed to thinking differently from the way most people did. "The gift of a brilliant mind blessed with a loving heart," was how her father described it. His bits of wisdom still filtered through her confusion pretty regularly, but they seemed to have lost their customary power to clarify all for her. "More like a curse than a blessing," she mumbled to herself as she thought of the way he'd always described her "gift."

Raising her head slowly yet deliberately, she forced herself to breathe evenly in order to regain her balance, figuratively speaking. She recognized that she had two choices: give in to fear and doubt and worry over what might happen in the future, or embrace the present and have faith that she could endure whatever was in store for her. She thought of all the times she had vowed to herself that she would never live her life the way her mother had, and yet she realized she was doing just that. The circumstances were entirely different, but the behavior pattern was exactly the same. She had no intention of living her mother's life all over again, and she also understood that her mother had doomed herself to that fate: simply put, misery and happiness were each a life's choice, and she, Josselyn, had to choose now.

Choosing happiness meant keeping the promise she had made to herself time and time again: that she would not waste her life the way her mother had. That meant that she had to embrace the present, not surrender it—whether by living in the past as her mother had, or by fearing the future as she herself was now doing. And she simply refused to waste her life. The present—this time now with Cameron—was all she might ever have; she wasn't about to relinquish it. Not for the sake of her writing; not for anything. Whatever happened, writing and the pursuit of her truth would wait for her.

Besides, so what if she never became a great writer? So what! Maybe her father had become a great writer because he had never felt a love as deep as what she felt for Cameron. Who was to say which was better or more important? Certainly not she. She didn't want to write instead of loving Cameron, and she didn't want to convince herself that she'd rather write than love him because she was afraid of what might happen. Even if she chose writing now, the love she felt for Cameron had already chosen her, and the force of it was far greater, far stronger, than the pull of any words could ever be.

Josselyn surrendered to love in that instant—to its power and its joy. The words began to flow effortlessly, almost immediately after she surrendered, and she discovered for the first time that her stories wrote her, not the other way around. When she let love take over, whether it was her love for a person or her love for writing itself, magic always resulted. She was beginning to learn about the other force and strength that dwelled in love: sustenance. "Love abides all things," she heard herself say. It surprised her, but it would prove to be true in a deeper sense than she ever could have known.

Burke's relief came not long afterward, and he set out to find Josselyn.

Too many days had passed without any sign of a single enemy encroaching. This would be the tenth consecutive day of no activity. Cameron Burke was not a man to fight fate. He accepted whatever fate brought, and he faced it bravely. But he could not accept a cruel fate for Josselyn; he could not live with himself if any harm came to her.

When he arrived at her tent, Josselyn was finishing up her story.

"You ought to take that into Da Nang or Saigon," he said sharply.

"I'm glad to see you too."

"No time for niceties today."

"So I see," she remarked, looking at him over her shoulder, one eyebrow arched.

"You need to get out of here, Joss," he said, his tone a bit softer.

"What is going on with you, Cam?" she wanted to know. She rose from her chair and took the few steps between them. Standing in front of him, arms akimbo and black eyes flashing, she waited for his answer.

"You're not safe here."

His toneless voice maddened her. "Is that so? You didn't seem all that concerned for my safety the last few nights," she shot back.

He hadn't counted on her getting angry. But then again, he hadn't counted on his going about it all wrong. So much for proving himself worthy of her love. He wasn't giving up until he had proved it to her … and to himself. "Will you hear me out, please? This is hard for me."

Why is he doing this? She felt a knot of pain clench around her heart. "Say what you came to say." She made her voice frosty, more to stave off her own tears than to hurt him.

"You aren't safe here. I love you, and I want you to be safe."

"I'm a reporter. I go where the stories are, Cameron. You won't be able to protect me from every bad thing in this world."

"I know," he said so tenderly, she could barely keep herself in check. She turned away from him.

"Don't turn away from me, baby. Please." He stepped up behind her, wrapping his arms around her.

"Do you have to make this harder? What happened to there being no tomorrow?"

Burke leaned her back against his chest, locking his arms around her and bending his head toward hers so his cheek pressed against her temple. "Being away from you will be harder for me to bear than anything I've ever borne. But knowing harm had come to you would be even harder."

She rested her hands on the arms that held her. "All right, Cam. I'm sorry if I sounded cold before. I was angry and hurt."

"Don't apologize. I'm the one who needs to apologize."

"For wanting to protect me?"

"No," he said, turning her around to face him, "for what I didn't say last night … but should have." He took her hand and led her to the foot of the cot. She sat down, and he knelt in front of her, still holding her hand.

"You don't need to kneel, darling."

"I want to. Last night, you said you needed me to promise you something, so I did. There's something I need to tell you. Please just listen. Okay?"

She nodded.

"Last night was the first time I should have said you didn't need to apologize." Burke squeezed her hand. "I wasn't angry with you. I was angry with myself … because you were so strong, so strong for yourself and for me … for us. I should have been the one to be strong—for each of us and for both of us. I don't want that to fall on you. Let me be the strong one."

"All right," she whispered, knowing she would still have to be strong for herself, but recognizing that he needed her agreement now as much as she had needed his promise the night before.

He pressed his lips against her palm, drawing her hand to his heart and holding it there. "There's something else I want you to know: I never want to be with another woman. I feel like

I spent my whole life with half a soul up until I met you. You're the other half. The half that I love the best."

Josselyn let herself drop from the cot to where he knelt in front of her. Pulling her into his arms, he held her close.

"I adore you, Cam. Whatever else I do, no matter what happens, I came into this life to love you and be loved by you."

"I feel the same way about you."

She pulled back slightly, smiling and touching his face.

He stood up and then pulled her to her feet. "You pack, and I'll get you a ride to Da Nang. You'll have to get to Saigon from there. Unless I can get a pass and take you myself."

"No tearful good-byes," she said.

He took her in his arms again, kissing her deeply. "No. We'll part just like this. No regrets."

"Good." She slipped out of his embrace, pain shattering her solar plexus at the mere thought of separation. Opening a duffel bag, she began to toss things inside, barely aware of what they even were.

"I'll go talk to the captain," he said, crossing quickly to the tent flap.

"Cam?"

"What, baby?" He turned back, his hand on the flap.

"Thank you."

"What for?"

"For what you told me, for what we mean to each other, for loving me. Most of all, for being you."

"I couldn't have done any of it without you," he winked at her. "So, thank *you*," he finished solemnly.

Captain Swinton, Burke's commanding officer, gave him a three-day pass to Saigon. Scarcely believing their good fortune, he raced to his own tent, threw his gear into a duffel bag, and then hurried back to Josselyn's tent. They were headed for Saigon within a half hour of the captain's granting Burke the pass.

Between them lay the unspoken yet completely understood pledge that all talk—even thoughts—of parting was done. When the time came to part, they would; until then, they would live only to love each other, to enjoy the precious hours that they still had to be together.

Josselyn called the Associated Press office from a bar in Saigon. Burke heard her beg off coming in with her story, saying the travel in-country had wiped her out. He knew she was only doing it to spend more time with him, that it could very likely have lasting repercussions on her career as a journalist. She didn't hesitate, though; he watched her jaw set and her eyes turn hard as she listened to whomever she was talking to. Catching him looking at her, she turned away, finished the conversation, and hung up.

When she joined him a few seconds later, she was all smiles.

"Everything okay?"

"Couldn't be better," she chirped, taking his arm and leaning her head against his shoulder.

"No, it couldn't." He kissed the top of her head. If AP had given her a hard time and she was waiting until after he'd gone to deal with it so as not to waste their time together, that was her gift to him—to them both. He wasn't going to spoil it.

Josselyn knew she'd have to mend some fences at AP, but it didn't matter. She'd work it out somehow. She was Bartholomew Jeffrey's daughter, and if she had to point that out to them, so be it. She would never rest on her father's laurels without earning her own—being worthy of his legacy as a writer was a demon she wrestled with constantly—but if subtle reminders paved a smoother way for her in a cutthroat business, she'd be a fool not to avail herself of those benefits. That was how she'd convinced AP to give her this assignment in the first place. It would all work out. Besides, if hedging could buy her irreplaceable time with Cameron, she would do it. She would do anything for a minute more with him now.

"I got a room through AP," she told him. "Do you want to drop our stuff there?"

"Sure," he said.

She handed him the scrap of paper that she'd scribbled the address on while on the phone with the AP office.

"I'll ask the bartender how to get there," he said.

"Think the room will have a nice view?" she asked, smiling.

"*I* will. I can't say about the room."

The room was in a hotel where the AP kept some rooms for correspondents when they came into Saigon. Or, more precisely, a hotel of sorts. Burke, alarmed by how much more dangerous Saigon seemed since he'd last visited, was a bit reassured when he saw Josselyn's face fall at the sight of the place.

"It's typical writers' lodgings, I'm sure," she said, more to convince herself than Cameron.

"I wouldn't know. It's a fire trap; that much I do know."

She stole a sidelong glance at him as he assessed the quickest access in case of emergency. "Cam—"

"Never mind. For all the benefits of being with a firefighter, you have to put up with this."

"Hmm."

"I'm glad you agree." He led her into the hallway. "That door at the end of the hall is the quickest way out. A building like this would go up like that." He snapped his fingers. "Are you paying attention?"

"Of course. A building like this would go up like that," she repeated his phrase, snapped her fingers, and kissed him on the cheek.

"Don't mock me. This is serious." His tone was gruff, but he kissed her back.

"I wasn't mocking you. Besides, right now I have my own personal firefighter to look after me. Weren't you telling me about benefits in that regard? What was that you were saying?"

"It'll be clearer if I show you."

They walked back into the room, locking the door behind them and shutting out the dingy surroundings by losing themselves in each other.

The moon was down, but Cameron Burke was wide awake. Too accustomed to rising before dawn, he supposed. Josselyn slept peacefully, cradled in the circle of his arm, her head resting on his chest. What wouldn't he give for more time with her? But he knew that whatever time they could steal from fate would never be enough.

Stirring, she opened her eyes.

"I didn't mean to wake you," he said. "Go back to sleep."

"I don't want to be asleep if you're awake."

"It isn't even dawn yet."

"Good. We can watch the sunrise together," she purred, snuggling against him.

"Can you see the sky from there?" he teased.

"I don't need to see the sky to know the sun is rising," she stroked his face. "What could be better than dawn breaking while you make love to me. ..." She didn't say it as a question. Her voice trailed off at the end, so he knew she was thinking, "maybe for the last time," even though she didn't say the words aloud.

"As you command, my lady," he bowed his head toward her in imitation of knightly gallantry.

Josselyn laughed.

He stroked her shoulder. "You'll always be my lady," he said, his tone serious. "My love."

"I know. You're the only one for me, Cam. There aren't enough ways to tell you."

"You've already shown me. That's all that matters." He turned, taking her face in his hands. "I've got you memorized now."

He kissed her, letting all the love he felt for her pour through him and flow into her. She wrapped her arms around his neck, returning his kiss with equal passion and tenderness.

She wished they could exist in this moment forever, but she knew the best they could do was live it as if it would last forever. Perhaps their limited amount of time together was a gift, after all. It made them treasure every second; they would never have the regrets of time squandered.

She was lost in Cameron now, letting herself go deeper and deeper into his kisses, no longer aware of where she ended and he began. His caresses were exquisitely slow and tender, with passion blazing just beneath the surface, spiking her desire for him to an all-but-unbearable peak. She met his passion with her own, answering kiss for kiss and caress for caress, thrilling him as always.

Her tenderness and love were so open, so giving, his heart filled to bursting. He could never hold her close enough, never get enough of her, never cease to be amazed by her endless love for him.

They matched each other's tempo perfectly, keeping their rhythm intoxicatingly slow, delighting each other and reveling in feeling each other's pleasure.

Burke bent his face close over hers, drinking her in with his eyes and letting his other senses absorb every inch of her too. "I love you, Josselyn." *I vow I will come back to you. I will not leave this life without making love to you again.* Again, he found himself unable to say out loud everything he felt, but he prayed that she intuitively knew what he felt but couldn't articulate.

He felt her love for him, far more deeply than he ever had with any other woman—or ever would again.

"And I love you, Cameron." *How I love you. Even if I never see you again, I'll live on your love for the rest of my life. Just as I told you I would.* She drew him down toward her, opening herself to him completely.

Their shared love filled them both completely, the familiar waves of passion cresting and then rolling, over and over again. At last, their desire peaked and then released. And in the serenity that came in that release, they each found the strength to let the other go, knowing that there can be no true separation where love exists.

"So, what do you think of daybreak lovemaking?" he asked, leaning back against the pillows in delectable exhaustion.

"Not bad."

He drew her close to him, holding her tight.

They laughed together, the low, sweet laughter of a shared secret. Their joy in each other had banished all sorrow. Having shown each other the depths of their love as best they could, they each rallied to be strong for the other.

"Cam, will you do something for me?"

"Name it."

"Leave me here," she whispered. "I mean, I want to remember you ... us ... together this way, not saying good-bye in front of strangers in the street. We did agree: no tearful good-byes."

"Your wish, as always, is my command."

"Did you want me to—"

"No." He touched her lips gently with his. "If I have to leave you, I'd rather do it like this too. But I ... I didn't want to say it, in case you didn't want me to leave you this way."

"There's no easy way, darling."

"No. No, there isn't, my love."

They held each other for what felt like a long time. After a while, they eased away from each other slightly.

"There's something else I want you to know, besides that I love and adore you and always will."

"Knowing that is enough for me, Cam."

"But it isn't for me. I want you to know that I have never let anyone know me the way you know me. And I never will."

"I do know that. It's the same for me with you. ..." She let her voice trail off, afraid that if she said any more—if she said all she felt, all she longed to say—her emotions would overwhelm her. Besides, no matter what they said to each other now, it would never be all that they wanted to say. It couldn't ever be, and they would have to just live with that somehow.

"I'm glad."

"So am I."

They resumed holding each other in nurturing quiet again. This time, Josselyn broke the silence.

"Do you think something good comes of everything? Even of evil?"

"I think what's meant to be is what happens," he measured his words. "It just isn't necessarily within our ability to comprehend. More often than not, it isn't."

"Hmm."

"Journalist's conscience?"

"I wish that's all it were. That would be simple. Ever since I was a little girl, I've had to think about the existence of evil."

"Because of your mother?"

"Yes. She's the one who escaped the Holocaust, but I've always felt that I was the one who was forced to live with the effects of that evil."

"How do you mean?"

"She stopped living when her family was captured. Wallenberg could only save one more person, so her parents gave her to him. My father promised Wallenberg he'd assure her safety. So, she survived, but without the desire to live. She lives in the past, with no interest in the present or hope for the future."

"Maybe it's the best she can do," he offered gently, but his words still stung.

"I ... I guess I never considered that," she admitted, horrified at her own self-absorption.

"Well, it's easy for me to say, baby. I didn't lose my childhood to her grief. You did."

Josselyn inwardly pledged to help her mother when she got back to the States. If her mother let her.

"Besides, I've seen more grief than I ever want you to. I've seen it raw and terrible. It's worse than the fires ever are, and far more deadly."

Josselyn nodded. It was sweet how he was trying to make her feel better. Why had she brought this up? To have something else to feel miserable about besides his leaving?

"I'm going to add to my answer. You know, to your question about whether something good comes of everything."

"Go on."

"I think maybe it does, but we have to look for it."

"Look *hard,* you mean."

"No. Sometimes we look too hard. More like, look in the right place."

"In that case, I hope we each have an angel."

"I have mine." He squeezed her.

She snuggled against him. "I meant to point the way." She considered a moment before adding, "Maybe it isn't about looking at all. Maybe it's about letting the good that comes of it find *us.*"

"Maybe that's all you need to reach your mom."

She kissed him. "Maybe."

"It was all you needed to find me," he added, kissing her back.

She nodded wordlessly, holding back tears.

"You know the story of the phoenix, don't you?"

"Sure. The mythical bird that rises from its own ashes to be born again."

"It's no myth to me. I've seen people rebuild their lives from the ashes, time and time again," he smoothed her hair back from her face. "If anyone can rise like that phoenix, it's you."

Josselyn smiled, shaking her head slightly.

"Yes, you can."

"For my mother, you mean?"

"I don't know your mother, so I can't say. I meant for yourself. And for me."

"For you. And for me."

"Till we're together again. I love you."

They kissed and then embraced.

Burke eased himself out of her arms, putting on his clothes without a word.

"Take care of yourself. I love you too," she said it all in a single breath, willing herself not to break down in front of him, not to make what was already scarcely bearable even worse.

He stopped at the door, his hand on the knob and his duffel bag over his shoulder, and blew her a kiss with his free hand. "Remember me too," he winked.

She smiled back. "I promise."

He opened the door, walked out, and closed it behind him.

"It could be worse," she whispered to herself. Although that seemed impossible, she believed things could *always* be worse—another of her mother's successful inculcations, one that she appreciated, especially because she knew it had sustained Jews throughout century after century of suffering. Her own pain was nothing compared to that.

Still, as soon as she heard his footfalls on the stairs at the end of the hall, she collapsed into tears, realizing that no matter how much she might acknowledge the magnitude of any collective or universal suffering, it could never make her own pain hurt any less. So she just let herself cry, let God's mercy come to her through her tears. At last, she fell asleep from sheer exhaustion.

All the way back to camp, Burke forced himself to think about the war, about the missions that might come up—anything to keep his mind from wandering back to Josselyn.

He had enlisted to serve his country, but now he felt like he was stagnating in the frustration of guerrilla warfare. Oddly enough, it had not seemed to bother him so much before he met Josselyn. Up until he met her, he had felt he was doing his duty merely by serving his country. Now, because he loved her, he felt that he had to do something meaningful; otherwise, the risk was too great. He could lose her, and yet never have made a difference to his country. If he participated in some grand mission, volunteered to put his life and limb on the line for his country, his service would mean as much as he needed it to mean.

Josselyn would understand why he did what he did. That was why he couldn't speak aloud his pledge to return to her. He couldn't make a promise when he knew that keeping it was beyond his control. It was selfish of him to put all that on her, he knew, to expect her to just accept that he had to be a hero, had to prove his heroism and worthiness to her and to the world ... but mostly to himself. She loved him for wanting to be a hero, of course, but she loved everything else about him too; wouldn't change a thing about him, even if given the opportunity. Aside from that, she already thought he was a hero, but if he didn't see himself as a hero, he would begin to question his worthiness of her love all over again. Her love—and his continuing to feel worthy of it—was his life's elixir. And he doubted he could survive without it now. More to the point, he didn't want to.

He chuckled to himself; even with his concerted effort *not* to think about her, all his thoughts centered on her nonetheless. Fine. He would make that work to his advantage. When images of her filtered into his consciousness—which happened every other second, it seemed—he would use them to focus on his combined primary goal: to emerge a hero in service to his country, and to return to her still deserving her love and admiration. With that two-pronged objective firmly in place, he didn't see how he could fail. Serving his country and loving Josselyn, and being loved by her, were all that mattered to him now.

Fueled by his rededication to his country and his love, he rode the rest of the way to camp with a quiet mind. Purpose always brought him a sense of contentment that bordered on serenity; although, without Josselyn, it was bittersweet in a way he'd never experienced before. He would have to get used to that: the nagging feeling that something was missing because she wasn't there. But he would get through it. He would remind himself that he had to fight the good fight, do what he'd come here to do, and remain secure that he would be with her again soon.

The jeep jolted to a halt in the camp, and Burke swung out of it, hitting the ground and heading straight to his CO's quarters without even stopping to drop off his gear.

Cameron Burke entered the captain's quarters, announcing himself with a salute.

Captain Swinton was an informal, no-nonsense type. He and Burke shared a mutual respect.

After Swinton had returned the salute, he offered Burke a shot of bourbon.

"No thank you, sir." Burke set his duffel bag on the ground, and then he moved toward the captain.

"Forgot. You're a whiskey man," the captain said, proffering a different bottle and a clean glass.

Burke smiled. "Thanks, Captain." He took the drink.

"To the US of A," said the captain.

"To the US of A," repeated Burke as they touched glasses.

"How was Saigon, soldier?"

"Saigon is Saigon, sir."

"You went with that reporter, didn't you? She's something else." He let out a low whistle.

"Yes, sir, she is."

Swinton was about to say more, but he caught the look in Burke's eyes and thought better of it. Instead, he clapped Burke on the shoulder and said, "Glad you enjoyed your leave, soldier."

"Thank you, sir."

"You want to tell me something?" Swinton asked, with the straightforwardness Burke so admired in him.

"Yes, sir."

Swinton nodded.

"I'd like to volunteer for the next recon, sir."

"You're one of my best men, Burke. I'd send you on recon in a heartbeat, you know that."

"Thank you, sir."

"You'll get your orders after reveille."

"Thank you, sir."

"That's all."

"Good night, sir."

They exchanged salutes.

Burke picked up his gear and set off for his tent, leaving Captain Swinton to wonder why a man who had a girl like that reporter would volunteer for a recon mission. He shook his head, tossed back another bourbon, and prayed that this war would be over soon—one way or the other.

The morning after Cameron left, Josselyn headed for the AP office. She got there at about eight and waited for her boss, Carlton Quiggley, to arrive. Sitting in the anteroom with a Styrofoam cup of bad coffee, she mulled over the telephone conversation she'd had with Quiggley when she and Cameron arrived in Saigon. She hadn't thought about it since then, having been consumed first by Cameron's being there and then by his leaving, but now it worried her. Quiggley was definitely going to make life difficult for her. It wasn't anything he'd said specifically, just his tone, and even more important, what he *hadn't* said. She could tell that he had no respect for women. He categorized her as a spoiled girl who was where she was purely because she was the daughter of an illustrious journalist.

Men like Quiggley made her blood boil. She knew it was only a matter of time before they locked horns, and she felt her emotions whipping into a frenzy of anxious anticipation. Her friend, Natalie, termed that "frothing," in honor of the Italian coffee they always loved to linger over with *sfogliatelle* pastry at their neighborhood Italian restaurant, Trattoria Barese. When the waiter steamed the espresso, foaming the milk on top (he called it "cappuccino," which the girls had never heard of until the first time he made it for them), Natalie always said it reminded her of Josselyn when she whipped herself into a frenzy. Josselyn preferred "frothing" to "whipped into a frenzy," so it had stuck. She couldn't help but smile at the recollection of times not so long ago when the future had seemed so clear and unencumbered. The barriers she had established for herself to safeguard against being overwhelmed by her mother's pain and isolated by her father's larger-than-life greatness made her view most other people—and her relationships with them—as encumbrances, without even realizing that she was doing so. Josselyn saw the pain and loneliness she felt at Cameron's absence as being what encumbered her, not recognizing that the love she was allowing herself to feel was encumbering her too, simply because she was so unaccustomed to allowing herself to experience any love but her father's.

Josselyn couldn't let herself dwell on her feelings now. It was time to focus on her career again. She had no intention of withering just because Cameron was absent, and she knew he wouldn't want her to. Nor did she have any intention of letting her emotions swamp her and cloud her focus and judgment. She had originally come here to do a job, and she was still determined to do it—brilliantly. When the assignment was over—and she returned home the seasoned correspondent with accolades galore, as she fully intended to—she could think about Cameron and her mother, and even her father, and her feelings for each of them. There would be more than enough time for all that later.

Mid-reverie, one of the other correspondents approached her.

"Never drink bad coffee alone," he said with mock solemnity, extending his hand. "Luke Lanvin."

"Josselyn Jeffrey."

She extended her hand, and he shook it. His grip had a firmness that conveyed sincerity and integrity, but no aggression. Her father had always counseled her to look for that in male colleagues. "Those are the ones who'll be true friends to you," was the way he'd put it. She smiled at the thought of it, and Luke Lanvin smiled back.

"We should start an alliteration club," he said.

Her smile deepened into laughter, and Luke Lanvin knew he'd found a friend too.

"You're right about the coffee," she remarked. "Who makes this stuff?"

"No one. It spawns overnight in Ichabod's office."

"Who's Ichabod?"

"It's *I.* Carlton Quiggley, my dear." Luke smiled wickedly.

"What kind of person would name a child Ichabod Carlton?" Josselyn wondered aloud. *That explains a lot.* She kept the last thought to herself.

"The kind you'd expect would. But then again, I was christened Luc Lanvin," he pronounced his name with perfect French enunciation. "My mother spelled it L-U-C, not L-U-K-E, but I changed it when I entered the world of journalism," he added with the same deliciously witty smile.

"But that's elegant, not cruel."

Lanvin bowed. "I just wanted to give you a glimpse of what's in store for you with Mr. Q. Don't take it to heart."

"Thanks. He's already given me a bit of a hard time. I think it's because I'm a woman and Bartholomew Jeffrey's daughter. I'm used to getting flak about both."

"Hmm." Lanvin paused and swigged some coffee, grimacing. He set the half-empty cup aside. "Want some advice from a seasoned journalist?"

Josselyn nodded.

"Break that habit. Immediately. Do not remain used to it. Fight it every time. You'll never earn the respect of men in this business if you don't. Start with Quiggley."

"All right." Her post-frothing resolve fortified her.

"Incidentally, I've read some of your stuff. You're a top-flight writer. Remember that. It's the unbiased opinion of—what did I just call myself?—oh yes, a seasoned journalist." Lanvin winked at her and then headed back to his desk.

Josselyn smiled. She instinctively liked Luke Lanvin—would have even if he hadn't passed her father's handshake test with flying colors—and it felt good to know she had someone in her corner. Just as she was about to mentally script her opening remarks to Carlton Quiggley, he walked into the office.

Lanvin looked up from his desk. "Hello, Carlton. Fine weather we're enjoying this morning in Saigon. The coffee is splendid as always too."

"Are you here for the coffee and the weather, Lanvin?" Quiggley retorted. Josselyn detected the same self-righteous indignation that she had sensed during the telephone conversation. Perhaps

Luke was right about Quiggley's bestowing his obnoxiousness equally upon all.

Quiggley turned in Josselyn's direction, not waiting for Lanvin to reply, but Lanvin called lightly, "No."

"It was a rhetorical question, Lanvin," Quiggley said, not turning back to face him.

"Oh."

Quiggley bristled at Lanvin's mock incredulity but did not respond. Josselyn could practically see the smoke curling out of Quiggley's ears.

"Good morning, Mr. Quiggley," she said firmly, extending her hand and keeping it steady.

"Well, if it isn't Josselyn Jeffrey. Miss Jeffrey, I'm gratified to see that you are finally ready to join our ranks."

"Thank you, Mr. Quiggley. Although I must warn you that I share Mr. Lanvin's low opinion of the weather and the coffee." She kept her voice as firm as she had upon greeting him, pulling her hand back when he made no move to extend his own.

"Terrific. Now I have two comedians, and one of them is also a princess."

"I seriously doubt any princess would drink this coffee or stay in the room you sent me to without complaint. If you want a princess, you'll have one. If you want a journalist, you'll have one. The choice is yours, Mr. Quiggley, but be advised that whichever you choose, you'll get more than you bargained for."

"That sounds like a threat, Miss Jeffrey."

"No, but it is a promise." Handing him the story, she turned on her heel. Over her shoulder, she added, "If you'll excuse me, I'm going to scout some leads. Let me know which choice you've made tomorrow. Nice meeting you, Luke," she said to Lanvin.

"Same here," he winked at her again.

Josselyn swung out of the office, shutting the door behind her.

Once outside, she couldn't help but grin. Whatever the outcome, she had set the stage, and she was glad for Luke Lanvin's advice and encouragement.

I. Carlton Quiggley, on the other hand, far from shared Josselyn Jeffrey's ebullience. In fact, he was livid. Who did that girl think she was, speaking to him with such insolence? "Does she know that I am the one who runs this office?" he asked aloud.

Lanvin quipped, "I'm quite certain she is aware of exactly of who, and what, you are, Carlton."

Quiggley glared at him, poured himself a cup of coffee, and practically retched at the first sip. Determined not to give Lanvin any satisfaction, he affirmed, "Not a damn thing wrong with this coffee."

"There's one place for coffee like this: the sewer."

"Of course, I'm not a sophisticated New Yorker like you, Lanvin."

"Of course you're not."

Quiggley fumed at himself. No matter how clever he thought he was being, Lanvin always topped him. And he never even missed a beat doing it. "We drink coffee like this in Detroit every day."

"That's what it tastes like! Gasoline. You're supposed to put it in the cars, not drink it, Carlton."

Quiggley stomped into his office, leaving Lanvin chuckling. So now he had two prima donnas who thought they were the greatest gifts to writing since the printing press! He slammed his fist on his desk, remembering that his own last thought, clever though it was, was no more than a direct quote of one of Lanvin's favorite witticisms. Quiggley, a portrait of mediocrity at best and a miserable little man at worst, decided that he was not about to be shackled with these two self-proclaimed geniuses for too long. Lanvin was bad enough. This Jeffrey girl was the last straw. Fortunately, Carlton Quiggley had a plan. A brilliant one. With any luck, the Saigon climate would get to both of them before they got to him. This was the extent of the "plan" he considered brilliant. Smiling smugly to himself, he dialed the number of the café around the corner to order a Vietnamese coffee. After all, he did need a potable beverage to begin his day.

Cameron Burke prepared for his third recon mission in as many days. Captain Swinton had been as good as his word, giving him his orders directly following reveille the morning after their conversation. Burke had accepted the orders, requesting that the company clerk wire Josselyn Jeffrey in Saigon to let her know that she shouldn't worry if she didn't hear from him for a while. The clerk, raising an eyebrow when Burke hastily explained that she was working on a story about him, had sent the wire nonetheless and without any audible comment.

As soon as he knew the wire had gone out—he stayed to watch the clerk send it—Burke forced himself to put Josselyn out of his mind. That is, except for the nighttime thoughts of her that he indulged in—that kept him going through nights that otherwise would have been endless. His nights still belonged to her, but his days he surrendered to the task before him: doing what he could to help his country win this God-forsaken war—conflict, folly, quagmire. He didn't know what to call it anymore, but he settled on hell.

Burke crept out of the underbrush where he'd been waiting and watching. He saw the signal: a single flashlight beam piercing the darkness three times at seven-second intervals. He crawled along the ground toward where the beam had appeared. In less than seven seconds, he joined Loomis, another GI assigned to the mission, and they waited for the next signal, which would direct them to their rendezvous point for the reconnaissance.

The two men breathed shallowly, the humid darkness that surrounded them so oppressive, it would have been hard to fill their lungs even under ordinary circumstances. The men on this mission entrusted their lives to one another, yet each barely knew the others' names. That confounded Burke. Fire-rescue succeeded primarily because the guys loved one another like brothers, never even stopping to think about risking their own lives if another firefighter was in danger. He had always thought that war was that way as well. It was for John Wayne. He bit his tongue to keep from laughing at himself. So what if he'd idealized fighting for his country? John Wayne wasn't the only one. Vietnam just wasn't like the other wars American GIs had fought in. But Burke had requested this mission, and he would prevail.

The next signal flashed, and the two men picked their way to a slight clearing in the underbrush. A split second later, a chopper was overhead, and two ropes dropped down from it for them to use to climb. In less than ten seconds, they had to grab the ropes and swing up and into the chopper. If they were lucky, the Vietcong would not yet have kicked into action to shoot them down.

Burke grabbed one rope; Loomis, the other. They swung up in a few long, hard pulls, hauling themselves into the chopper. Breathing hard from the exertion, they took their positions in the chopper, manning the guns ready to return fire. The pilot hightailed the chopper out of there. The VC hammered at them but missed, and Burke and Loomis returned equally impotent fire.

With their adrenaline still pumping, the recon squad sped to the next destination point, the chopper all but swallowed up by the blackness of the jungle night.

Josselyn entered the AP office. Delighted to see that Quiggley was absent, she decided to sort through the notes on her latest story lead: an exposé on Vietcong infiltration of US military intelligence via Saigon prostitutes. She would have to do some undercover reporting to pull off the story, and she wasn't sure she would be credible as an American expatriate hooker in Saigon. Not to mention that even if she could, it wasn't exactly in line with her promising Cameron that she'd be careful. Breaking promises always entailed moral dilemmas for her. As she read over her notes, she attempted to justify to herself that she was not breaking a promise, because Cameron had not been specific in his "be careful" instructions. She knew it was lame, that she was playing semantics on a tenuous technicality, but she was so torn between her hunger for breaking the story and her moral conviction to keep her promise.

Setting down the notes, she rubbed her temples. She had never experienced such intense and constant headaches as she now suffered from in Vietnam. Luke Lanvin assured her it was the weather, not the work. Although Carlton Quiggley had to be a contributing factor, Josselyn did agree that the heat and humidity were the primary cause. Just as she was about to resume reading her notes, Luke walked in.

"How goes the war?"

"With Vietnam or Quiggley?"

"Take your pick." He stopped at her desk, removing a piece of paper from his shirt pocket and setting the paper on her desk.

Cocking one eyebrow, she asked, "What's this?"

"Telegram. It came for you this morning. I intercepted it before Ichabod could get his paws on it."

"Thanks," she said. "I really appreciate your not letting IQ get a hold of it." She'd come to think of their boss as the "inaptly initialed IQ."

"No problem. Hey ... 'IQ' ... good one." He winked at her.

Josselyn smiled, taking the telegram and scanning it quickly. After she read it, she was grateful for Luke's tact in not mentioning its content.

Luke Lanvin smiled back, and then he moved quickly toward his own desk. After all, he *was* a seasoned journalist, a foreign correspondent who had seen more of people's private affairs than he cared to remember. One girl's telegram from her lover was hardly newsworthy to him, but he felt sort of fatherly toward Josselyn. He just hoped she wouldn't get hurt, that was all. He'd walked away to give her some privacy, knowing that the telegram would be creased with rereading and refolding before the week was out.

As soon as Luke returned to his own desk, Josselyn read the telegram again, more slowly this time.

J STOP might not hear from me for a while STOP don't worry STOP will wire again as soon as able STOP as ever STOP C STOP

Josselyn traced the C tenderly with the tip of her index finger, supposing that "as ever" was as close as a soldier could come to "I love you" when dictating a telegram to the company clerk. She laughed softly, picturing Cameron dictating the message, the daggers in his eyes alerting the clerk that he'd better not say a word.

All right, darling. I promise I won't worry.

She wondered how she could use this latest bit of information to resolve her dilemma. Of course, Cameron's accepting a dangerous mission—which she surmised was what this was about—was not the same as her willfully deciding to do undercover reporting by posing as a hooker. There were other stories. Besides, doing this one would only give Quiggley more ammunition to fuel his propaganda about no woman ever becoming an ace reporter just on the strength of her journalistic talents. She should set it aside for that reason alone. If only it weren't such a fantastic story. ...

Telling herself there would be other great stories, Josselyn collected her papers, patting the notes into a neat stack and tucking Cameron's telegram into her pocket.

She crossed to Luke's desk, perched on the edge of it, and asked, "Want a hot lead?"

"Is this your way of being kind to an old guy?"

"You're not old, and I'm not kind."

"Of course you are. But you're right, I am in my prime."

"Indeed you are."

He grinned. "What's the lead?"

"VC infiltration of our intelligence through Saigon hookers' liaisons with GIs."

Lanvin whistled. "That's some story, kid."

She nodded. "I'd hate to think of IQ's smirking that the only way I could get a story was to pose as a hooker."

"True. Besides, I really shouldn't let you do it. It's too dangerous. I hate your giving up such a great lead, though," he scratched his head. "Tell you what: I'll take this lead and give you mine, that way you stay safe *and* get a great story that has no ammunition for Quiggley."

"And they say nice guys finish last."

They both laughed.

"Thanks, Luke."

"Sure, kid." Lanvin had a daughter around Josselyn's age. A peacenik graduate student at Berkeley. He wouldn't want her doing a story like this either.

"You be careful too, though. It's dangerous, even for you."

"You're telling me. You should see me in a pair of fish nets."

She shook her head at him. "I should have figured you would listen to me as much as my father ever does."

"Fathers give advice. *Daughters* listen to it."

She gave a short laugh. "Indulge your fantasy. What's the lead you're giving me?"

"Intermittent fighting in a village between here and Da Nang. It could be something, or it could be nothing. This is the only war I ever covered where nothing is what it seems to be. Someone who smiles at you on the street in the morning might try to kill you in your sleep that night." Lanvin grew uncharacteristically somber. "I wonder how—or if—this war will ever end."

Josselyn patted his shoulder.

"Here's a map," he said, pulling a pencil from behind his ear and drawing an X to mark the place.

She took the map he'd marked, folded it, and stuffed it into her bag.

"You be careful, kid. Every place here is dangerous."

"Hey! I thought you wanted to give me a lead," she said lightly.

Just as Lanvin was about to say that he figured he'd be as successful talking her out of a career as a foreign correspondent as her father had been, a messenger arrived with another telegram for Josselyn. This one was from her father, telling her that she had to return stateside at once: her mother was in a coma.

"I guess you've got both leads, Luke."

"I'm sorry, kid. Look, you just get yourself out of here. I'll square it with Quiggley when he gets back."

She hugged Luke and then dashed out of the office. "You be careful. Thanks for everything," she called over her shoulder in parting.

Luke Lanvin waved good-bye, deciding that he didn't feel like finagling a ride almost as far as Da Nang, so he might as well just go look for a hooker.

Josselyn raced back to her room in a daze. Operating on pure adrenaline, she shoved everything into her duffel bag, running right back out of the room within minutes. She hurried to get herself on the first available flight stateside. Saigon to Tokyo to Honolulu was the best she could do. She would get to Honolulu the following morning. Take it or leave it. She had no choice. The flight left in an hour. With just enough time to send two wires—one to her father and one to Cameron's company clerk—she got on the plane by the skin of her teeth.

As the adrenaline ebbed, the reality of what was happening hit her full force. Eyes squeezed shut, she prayed: *Hold on, Mom. Hold on till I get there. Please. Don't leave before I have the chance to tell you what I have to. I love you, Mom. Please hold on.*

Josselyn opened her eyes. The clouds slipped beneath the plane as it banked its initial ascent, and she realized that she was unequivocally changed, not just because of Cameron Burke, but also because she would never again feel that she had all the time in the world to do and say what she needed to.

She watched that childhood myth evaporate into the stratosphere.

Josselyn arrived in New York weary and bedraggled after two solid days of practically nonstop air travel. From Honolulu, she had flown to Los Angeles, with a few hours' layover, and then on to Chicago, with another layover, until she reached her final destination of La Guardia.

When the cab pulled up in front of her parents' brownstone in Brooklyn Heights, Josselyn's insides lurched, acid and fear and grief coagulating into a knot that she doubted would ever loosen. She paid the cabbie, giving him a generous tip so he would haul her bags up the stoop and leave them at the front door. Squaring her shoulders despite the ever-deepening pit in her stomach, she fished the key out of her purse, opened the door, and shoved and dragged her bags inside. Closing the door gently behind her, she cast one last look through the frosted-glass pane, wondering why, at every crisis of her life, the sun persisted in shining with maddening brightness. Was it derision or just an attempt to show her that life would go on? Life would go on, she knew, no matter how unbearable events might seem—whether personal or collective. She prayed that someday soon she'd have the wisdom and grace to always remain mindful of that, instead of constantly letting her emotions overwhelm her, even though most who observed her saw her as incomparably cool and collected.

Leaving her bags in the foyer, she hurried back to the kitchen, knowing she'd find her father there. When she called him from La Guardia, he'd said that she would have time to drop off her bags and change her clothes before the next cycle of visiting hours began. Her mother was at NYU Medical Center in Manhattan, where the ICU hours were from ten to noon, three to five, and seven to nine. The ICU only allowed two visitors at a time in the room, for a maximum of twenty minutes. Her father had explained all this over the phone, further indicating that he went to see her mother every morning and evening, but went home in the afternoon.

"Dad," she called, as she hastened down the hallway.

Sure enough, he emerged from the kitchen, standing in the double doorway between it and the dining room, the late-afternoon light streaming through the windows and framing him in an incandescent radiance. For her, he always possessed that, even without the sunshine. He was the sun to her.

"Hello, angel," he said, moving toward her and clasping her in a bear hug.

"It's good to be home," she said, hugging him back.

"Good to have you home."

She pulled away to look at his face, wanting to ask when the last time he'd slept had been. Instead, she said, "I'm here now. You don't have to bear this alone any longer."

Her father smiled at her, kissing her forehead. "Of everything I've ever had to do for your mother, this is the easiest. She's finally at peace. I think she's been waiting just to see you one last time."

"Come on, Dad. You're the one who's always told me that when it's your time, it's your time. God's will always prevails." She broke away, the pit in her stomach easing and giving way to hunger.

Her father nodded. "But he also gave us each free will."

"But that is never stronger than His will," she argued, crossing to the refrigerator and opening the door to see what was inside. She pulled out a peach and a plum.

Her father sat down at the kitchen table. "It is when He lets it be. Sometimes God's will is for us to rise up, to use the free will He granted us. Although I wager He has probably questioned giving us that free will more than once over the millennia."

She smiled over her shoulder at him from where she stood at the sink, washing off the fruit. "I'm glad to see you haven't lost your sense of humor," she remarked, moving toward the table, holding a dish bearing the fruit and a small knife. She set the dish on the table, patting his hand and sitting next to him.

"I never shall. Neither should you. A sense of humor keeps all of life in perspective."

She nodded. He'd long ago inculcated that in her. She was better about staying mindful of it at some times than others. Thinking about how well her father's philosophy on humor fit with her mother's insistence that things could always be worse, she smiled. Pity her mother couldn't have seen it too. Had she viewed the wisdom with a sense of humor, she might have moved beyond her interminable grief. Sighing, Josselyn cut both peach and plum into quarters, giving her father a piece of each.

He peered at her, wondering what she was thinking, what the sigh signified specifically. "You changed the subject. I want to know your thoughts on free will."

She reflected for a moment. "I don't know. I need to think about it."

"Good. You learned something while you were away. Before you left for San Francisco, you would have just agreed with whatever I told you." He took a bite of the piece of plum she'd given him.

"Yes, I guess I would have," she admitted, nibbling the fruit. "Was it a trick question?" she asked, arching an eyebrow at him.

"No," he chuckled. "I do believe what I said. But you don't have to believe it just because I do. God gave you a magnificent brain, meaning for you to do much more with it than echo my sentiments."

"How many times have I heard that?" She munched the rest of the fruit.

"Enough to believe it, I hope," he smiled. How much he had missed bantering with his daughter, delighting in the rapid-fire output of her nimble mind and unfettered imagination. He had engaged her in this exchange to divert her mind from her mother, hoping she wouldn't detect the subterfuge, however futile a hope that might be. Josselyn never missed a thing. She had been born with the acumen of a journalist and the heart of a poet; would become a far greater writer than he'd ever had it in him to be.

She stood up and went back to the sink to wash the dish and knife. Setting them in the dish rack, she dried her hands. "Do I have time to wash up and change?" she asked him offhandedly, allowing him to feel that he had managed to divert her, as she knew he'd intended to.

"Sure. We'll head out when you're done."

He followed her out to the foyer, helping her haul her bags upstairs to her third-floor bedroom. "Don't rush, honey. We'll get there in plenty of time." Her father kissed the top of her head, lingered for a moment, and then left the room.

Josselyn walked into the bathroom, tearing off her clothes, tossing them in the hamper, and practically leaping into the shower. The water felt so warm and clean—delicious, even—

after the time she had spent in Vietnam, taking showers in bursts of cold water. *Plenty of time to delight in the creature comforts of home later,* she scolded herself, adding, *when Mom's okay.*

But deep in her heart, she knew that was not to be. As she rinsed the last of the shampoo out of her hair and shut off the water, her heart felt heavy, and she wished she didn't know what she knew. Her father was right: her mother was waiting for her; always had been. Josselyn could feel her mother's tortured soul beckoning to her—pulling her, really. And in that instant, she understood that her mother would never be free until she, Josselyn, let her go.

Burke and Loomis woke up during the night, hearing rustling in the underbrush. Connor, the third man on the mission and the chopper pilot, was on that shift of the night watch. The rustling came from Connor's watch post. Crawling noiselessly to the spot, Burke and Loomis saw Connor, frozen in fear and face-to-face with a VC. In the ensuing scuffle, Loomis managed to get Connor away, while Burke took on the VC.

The two of them struggled, wrestling on the ground beneath the underbrush, Burke and the man both losing their weapons. With a sharp right cut, Burke gained the upper hand, pinning the man beneath him and delivering a series of swift, hard pummelings. He'd intended only to knock the man out, thereby buying Loomis and himself enough time to hightail it out of there, dragging along Connor, who would hopefully come around and be able to fly the chopper. But the VC surprised Burke with a stomach punch that knocked the wind out of him, and Burke knew he had no choice but to fight to the death. The man locked Burke in a choke hold, and he saw the flash of a steel blade in the moonlight. When he was finally able to get out of the man's grip, Burke pinioned him, knocking the switchblade out of his hand and choking him until he was dead.

Burke saw the VC's eyes roll up and back, and then he heard the air in the man's windpipe whistle once before it just stopped. Everything stopped. The violence of it shocked Burke. He had never killed a man up close before; it was far different from throwing a grenade or firing a weapon—even if you knew in the back of your mind that the screams that followed were in response to what you'd just done. You could keep it in the back of your mind when it happened that way, rationalizing that it might not have been the grenade you had thrown or the gun you had fired, even though you knew it was. That was "dispatching," as the big brass termed it. But this—up close, seeing the other man's eyes bulge—was not dispatching. It was killing. Burke could not—would not—deny having felt the life force abruptly leave the man's body, knowing that he had been the instrument of the man's death.

He had thought that seeing death in fires would prepare him for anything; now he felt stunned by how wrong he had been. Death in the fires he'd battled was always horrible and senseless, but never deliberate. Of course, he realized he had been fighting for his life, but that could not render the taking of another's life any less devastating. He was relieved that it hadn't; it proved that he still valued the sanctity of every human life as much as he always had. He prayed that if he ever found himself in hand-to-hand combat again, he would feel just as devastated upon killing his foe as he did now; prayed, too, that if his foe emerged the victor, the man would at least feel awe at taking Burke's life, just as Burke now felt awe at having taken the VC's.

Burke murmured a hasty Hail Mary over the man's body—a prayer for the sanctity of the man's soul, as well as Burke's own—and hurried to the safe spot Loomis, Connor, and he had scouted and agreed upon at the start of the mission.

Can there be any heroes in this war? he wondered bitterly, deciding he'd been right to attribute "God-forsaken" as the perfect descriptor for the whole situation. God-forsaken, indeed, was this hell.

Burke returned from the reconnaissance mission, reporting straightaway to Captain Swinton. The captain listened to the report in silence, his brow furrowing at the mention of Connor's freezing in the face of the VC, and the barest traces of a grimace appearing at Burke's description of his own to-the-death struggle with the VC.

"Well done, soldier," Swinton pronounced when Burke had finished.

"Thank you, sir."

"Other wars weren't like this one, son," said the captain as he clapped Burke on the shoulder, leaving the younger man to wonder whether he had said it as an apology, or to assure himself that he could never have known what this guerrilla fighting would be like when he'd been sent to Vietnam. Perhaps Swinton hadn't even meant to say the words aloud.

Burke only nodded in reply, and Swinton dismissed him.

Dropping off his gear in his tent, Burke headed to the company clerk to see if Josselyn had responded to his telegram. In place of the long letters he was hoping for, a telegram from Saigon waited for him:

C STOP returned stateside STOP mother ill maybe dying STOP
Will wire again as soon as able STOP love as always STOP J STOP

Burke folded the telegram and stuffed it in his shirt pocket. He had wished she would leave Vietnam, but never for such a reason. His grandmother's constant warning throughout his growing up years—"Be careful what you wish for, it might come true"—haunted him. A truth so simple and so endemic as to appear to be a prediction, even when he knew it wasn't. He rolled his shoulders as if to shake off the feeling.

He had to get word to Josselyn. A telegram would no doubt scare the wits out of her; a phone call would be better. That would take some doing: getting her number from the AP office, wangling an international line, negotiating the time difference. He would not be deterred, though. He *would* talk to her. As he began to plan the logistics of placing the call, he remembered the conversation he and Josselyn had about her mother, and he hoped she would have the chance to share what she'd discovered. It didn't seem likely, given her message, but he still hoped.

Consoling himself with the assurance that Josselyn was safe, Burke set out to gather the necessary information.

Josselyn sat at her mother's hospital bedside, the monitors beeping and blipping at the appropriate intervals, more monotonous than morbid. It struck her that this setting, with its sterile white walls and emotional silence, was a more appropriate place for her mother than any other. She chided herself but couldn't help thinking it. All the things she'd planned to tell her mother, all the hopes she'd had that she might renew their relationship and establish some rapport, had evaporated, leaving behind an emptiness in her heart that she had never felt before in connection with her mother. Before, she had felt only anger and resentment … and pain. Once she acknowledged her own responsibility—her own destiny to reach out to her mother, to love her mother even if her mother could not show her love in return—the anger and resentment gave way to desolation. She felt as if she were suddenly living with the feelings her mother had lived with for almost her entire life, as if her mother had transferred her own feelings to Josselyn.

Josselyn pressed her eyes shut, blinking them open a few seconds later to take note of the reassuring red flashes on the various monitors. She reached over to stroke her mother's hand, reflecting that her mother looked serene. It was the first and only time she could recall her mother looking that way.

"Cast your burdens on me, Mom. I will take them up if it brings you peace," she whispered, continuing to stroke her mother's hand, while leaning closer to kiss her forehead. "All my life, I couldn't understand you; couldn't reach you. I suppose I should have tried harder. It doesn't matter now, Mom. I know you love me, and I love you. I feel how it feels to be you somehow, and I'm grateful. You will live on in my love for you, always. Just as your parents lived on in your love for them. I understand now, Mom. I forgive you for not being the mother I wanted you to be. You did the best you could. And I've come to see that you were the mother I needed. I can't explain why, but I know it's true. Forgive me, Mom. I love you. ..." Her voice trailed off into tears of sorrow, not despair.

Bowing her head, she kept hold of her mother's hand, stroking it tenderly.

After a few seconds, her mother squeezed her hand, taking Josselyn so by surprise that her head jerked up, and she saw her mother's eyes flutter open.

"There is nothing to forgive," her mother said softly, her contralto voice as elegant as ever, stamped with the inflection of the part of Buda along the Danube where she had spent her childhood. "I have always known that you loved me, Juditka, and always wished I knew better how to show you my love for you. Calling you by the name of my beloved mother—may she rest in peace—was the only way I knew."

Stunned, Josselyn berated herself for never having realized that before. "I know you did the best you could, Mom," she repeated.

Her mother smiled. "You must promise to take care of your father. He has cared for me for so long now, he will be lost without the duty."

"I promise," Josselyn assured her, smiling at her mother's perspicacity; wishing she had noticed all this—any of this— before.

"Listen to what I have to tell you. I won't be able to talk for long. While I lay here, I seemed to learn things—I don't know how. What you said, that I am the mother you needed, I think is true. You perhaps would not have discovered your words with another kind of mother. You were the daughter I needed. I knew it but could not accept it, because so long ago, I promised myself that I would never let myself need or love anyone ever again. I was wrong to have done that to you. I waited to tell you. I pray you forgive me."

"I forgive you, Mom, but only because I know you need me to, not because I'm holding on to any bitterness. I only want you to have peace … at last."

"Thank you," her mother whispered. "Something else … lean closer."

Josselyn put her ear practically against her mother's lips.

"Remember … it is not how much time you have to love one another that matters … all that matters is how much you love one another in the time you have."

"I didn't love you enough, all those years."

"Yes, you did, my love … my little one."

Josselyn could barely hear her mother's answer, but she felt her mother's love—as if all the bonding she'd missed throughout her life was now filtering through to her in a condensed form, a sort of elixir of nurturance. She could feel her mother's life force slipping out of her body and filling the room. It surrounded Josselyn's body like a veil of spun silk. Soft. Warm. Comforting.

"Rest in peace, Mom. I love you."

She felt her mother's hand begin to grow cold, and she slipped her own hand from its grasp. The essence of her mother stayed in the room, making Josselyn feel safer and more completely loved and at peace than her mother's living presence had ever made her feel. She cried quietly, in awe of what she had witnessed and been part of, grateful and humbled. Gradually, the "veil" lifted, leaving her with the unequivocal feeling that she would never be alone; that her and her mother's love for one another was eternal. Their love had existed since time began; it would endure forever. All that had kept them from feeling it was themselves—their own fears and doubts.

Josselyn prayed she would remain ever mindful of this. Even if Cameron disappointed her in the future, she would never let her love for him harden into bitterness.

She stood and walked out of the room, seeking her father so that she could tell him that her mother had found peace—at last.

The paperwork at the hospital completed, Josselyn and her father headed home to Brooklyn. On the subway, they sat shoulder to shoulder, communing in comforting silence, as they each reflected and recollected. The images flashing past them rapid-fire as they looked out the windows of the train punctuated the journey perfectly. The train pulled into their stop, and they got off, climbing the stairs to the street and walking the couple of blocks to their brownstone.

A few doors away, her father broke the silence. "Let's go get something to eat. How about some cioppino?" He referred to the seafood stew served with linguine that was a house specialty at his favorite restaurant, the same Trattoria Barese where she and Natalie had discovered cappuccino.

"Sure," she said. Really, she just wanted to stay close to him, but she hadn't eaten a thing since the peach and plum, and little else in the hours before that. She suddenly felt famished.

Grinning, he took her arm and steered her in the opposite direction, toward the adored trattoria.

Trattoria Barese was owned by a couple who had immigrated to America after World War II. Giovanni Barese and Bartholomew Jeffrey had hit it off immediately, as a result of Bartholomew's commiseration with Giovanni's outrage over the immigration officer's having changed his surname. He had been born Giovanni Chierichetto. In his rapid Southern Italian, he had mentioned something about being Barese (that is, from Bari), and that was the only thing the officer could understand—or spell—so Giovanni Barese he had become. Bartholomew's compassion had earned him a double espresso on the house, as well as the best available table and plenty of gratis delectables whenever the Jeffreys dined at the trattoria.

When the door chimes rang, Rosa, Giovanni's wife, came to greet the customers, delighted to see Bartholomew and Josselyn. She embraced them both.

"*La signora?*" she asked hopefully, using the term of respect she always reserved for Magdalena Jeffrey.

Bartholomew shook his head. Something in the sadness in his eyes told Rosa he meant "dead," not "still in the hospital."

"*Mi dispiace.*" Even after all these years, Rosa Barese still spoke in her native tongue when gravely upset or under duress. She knew that Bartholomew and Josselyn knew enough Italian to understand her and not take offense.

"Sit. Your regular table," Rosa continued in English, ushering them toward their favorite spot. "I'll be right back," she assured them, rubbing Josselyn's shoulder. No woman was ever ready to lose her mother, and this one was barely more than a girl. With a sigh to herself at Josselyn's sad eyes, Rosa set out to do what she always did whenever people were hurting or in need: lovingly prepare food to nurture them.

Her father reached across the table, taking Josselyn's hand in his and squeezing it tight. She squeezed back.

Seconds later, Giovanni emerged with a rich Chianti and some potent grappa, both of which he aged in the cellar himself. Wordlessly, Giovanni poured two full glasses of the wine and four shots of the grappa. By the time he finished pouring, Rosa reappeared with an overflowing basket of her fresh-baked rosemary-olive focaccia. Setting down the basket and two bread-and-butter dishes, Rosa took a grappa while Giovanni passed one each to Bartholomew and Josselyn, keeping the last shot for himself.

"Maddalena, *requiescat in pace*," he intoned.

The others raised their glasses.

"*L'Chaim*," said Bartholomew.

Josselyn tossed back the grappa without a word, and the others followed suit. Rosa hastened back to the kitchen, stroking Josselyn's hair as she passed. Josselyn smiled up at her, touched by her mothering.

"Leave it to me, Bartolomeo," Giovanni said, meaning their dinner order. "Nothing but the best for you and *bellissima*," he cupped Josselyn's chin in his hand. He'd called her that for as long as she could remember.

Her father nodded, and Josselyn smiled again. She loved the Bareses. Childless, they had sort of adopted her and Natalie years before.

After a feast of caprese salad and a cauldron overflowing with steaming cioppino, Josselyn sank back in her chair, staring at Giovanni in mock horror when he asked about dessert.

"What? No tartufo? No tiramisù?"

"Giovanni, I haven't eaten this much in months—maybe in my entire life!" she exclaimed.

"What does that have to do with dessert?" She loved the way he pronounced it: "day-sart."

"No room, Giovanni."

"Okay, *bellissima*. You take it home. Later, when you want sweet, you will be happy."

He and Rosa returned several minutes later, bearing two cartons apiece, each one filled to capacity with food, and a small box of pastries on top.

"Giovanni ..." her father started to protest.

"Else I come cook in your kitchen," Rosa warned.

"Thank you both," her father said, knowing it would be no use to argue. He pulled out his money clip to pay for their meal.

"Bartolomeo—what is this? I cannot take your money tonight." Giovanni stood with his arms folded across his chest, as if accepting Bartholomew's money were an offense he needed to protect himself against.

Bartholomew stood firm. "Giovanni, you and Rosa have been more than kind with these care packages. You have to let me pay for our meal. I won't accept the extra food if you don't."

Giovanni and Rosa exchanged a glance.

"*Va bene,*" Giovanni acquiesced, knowing that Rosa would be sick with worry if she could not send the Jeffreys off with food prepared by her own hands.

The two men hugged. "*Grazie,* Giovanni."

Josselyn stood up, hugging first Rosa, and then Giovanni. "Yes, *mille grazie* to both of you," she said.

The Bareses handed over the cartons to the Jeffreys, bidding them good night and watching from the doorway as their friends headed home, the aroma of Rosa's cooking wafting on the evening breeze. The Bareses believed that regardless of how deep the pain of any grief might be, food prepared with love could heal it. Rosa prayed with all her heart that the food she had given the Jeffreys would nurture and comfort and heal them in exactly that way.

When they arrived home, Josselyn set about unpacking all the food Rosa Barese had prepared for them.

"God bless Rosa. She must think we aren't going to eat for a week."

"She was thinking of the shivah, probably," her father remarked, referring to the seven-day mourning period Jews observed after the death of a loved one.

"I suppose so." After she set the box of pastries on the counter, Josselyn pulled out a roll of masking tape and a pen so she could mark each item before she stocked the freezer and refrigerator. "Did Mom tell you what she wanted?"

"Of course. To have died in Mauthausen with her parents." He said it softly, giving her a smile that was so sad, it tore her to pieces.

Josselyn turned to face her father. Had he not seemed so overwhelmed with sadness when he said it, she would have been furious at his sarcasm. "I'm serious, Dad. The burden of Yiddishkeit does fall on me, you know." Her mother had inculcated in her the importance of remaining mindful of her Jewishness. Having a Jewish mother made her Jewish according to Jewish law, not to mention what a maniacal despot rising to power might consider her—her mother had always emphasized that. Josselyn had never been sure which part of the message her mother wanted her to remember more: piety or fear.

To soften her chastisement of her father, she added, "Besides, I'm only trying to help."

"Indeed. Forgive me, sweetheart. I've been taking care of your mother for so long—trying to muster her will to live—now that I no longer have that responsibility, I'm not quite sure what I'll do with myself." Exactly as her mother had predicted, and he said it with a feigned brightness that was almost worse than the sorrow he'd shown a moment before.

"Rabbi Tevner will help you. If you let him."

Her father nodded. "He's a good man. A true spiritual guide. He was the only person who could ever really reach your mother."

"She and I reached each other. Today. Right before she died."

"She was waiting for you."

"Did Rabbi Tevner tell her that?" Josselyn asked, dismayed. The mystical connection she had felt with her mother meant so much to her; if she found out that some third party had intervened—even Rabbi Tevner, whom she truly loved and respected—it would crush her.

"He helped her see how she … failed you. But also that she had the chance to ask for forgiveness and make peace, so she could go on to wherever she's gone to, and you could have a life unencumbered by bitterness." He put his hands around her face. "He did not show her how very much she loved you—always— she never needed anyone to show her that."

She nodded, fighting back her tears. This was not the time to break down. After all the times she had been strong and resilient for him, now was not the time to fall apart—when he might actually need her.

He gathered her into his arms, tucking her head under his chin. "You are the only person in the world who ever completely loved me without needing me," he said softly.

"Of course I completely love you. And of course I need you."

"No, I'm the one who needs you. I always have."

"That's silly. You don't need anyone," she pronounced, pulling back so she could look at him.

"I'm able to foster that illusion only because in the back of my mind I know you're there, loving me so completely. Without that, I'd be a hollow shell."

Arm in arm, they walked to the kitchen table and sat down.

Josselyn chuckled. "You're only saying that to make me feel better. Besides, it's ridiculous to think that you don't automatically need the people you love."

"Is it?"

"Yes. I need you because I love you."

"Only you would see it that way, angel."

"What about Mom? She loved you and needed you."

"But it was reversed: Your mother loved me *because* she needed me. You see the difference, of course."

She merely nodded, unconvinced that her father was right about her mother's feelings. Her mother had been so imprisoned by her own inability to feel her feelings—let alone accept and deal with them—that Josselyn doubted whether her mother had ever even understood them herself. She wouldn't tell that to her father, though. He needed to see her mother the way he needed to, and Josselyn accepted that.

"To answer your original question, I did speak to Rabbi Tevner. The funeral is set for tomorrow morning. We'll sit shivah here."

Josselyn smiled. Even if her mother had been ambivalent about her own Judaism—resenting the obligations of observance but compelled to carry them out nonetheless—her father needed the rituals for closure. In so many ways, her Presbyterian father was more Jewish than her mother had ever been. Rabbi Tevner understood that too, allowing her father to participate in certain rituals that strict orthodoxy would never allow because he had never officially converted. As the rabbi put it, her father was a mensch, and he had a real Jewish soul.

"It's been a long day, following many longer days. I'm going to bed."

"Good night, Dad."

"Good night, sweetheart." He kissed the top of her head, leaving her alone with her thoughts. She could hear him moving around the brownstone, ensuring all the doors to the outside were locked for the night before he climbed the stairs.

She reflected that regardless of whether her father was right about why her mother had loved him, she never wanted to love Cameron that way. Need should follow love, not the other way around.

Bartholomew Jeffrey sat in the Windsor chair he had set facing the bedroom window, his slippered feet propped up on the windowsill. The drapes were open and the shade was up, and he had not turned on any lamp, letting the moon and the cast of the streetlamps illuminate the room instead. Every so often, the headlights of cars and cabs would gleam. The only sounds were the intermittent screams of sirens—police, fire, or ambulance—sometimes punctuated by the more resonant wail of the fire truck Klaxon. Such sounds always elicited the same response from him: a mixture of hope and dread. Years of living in war zones had failed to numb him.

He shrugged this off, smiling to himself. He had never wanted to be numb—to be numb was to stop living. A lifetime devoted to Magdalena would have proved the truth of that to him, but he had known it long before. Even as a boy. Perhaps his knowledge of it, his certainty of it, was what had enabled him to devote himself to Magdalena without hesitation, without regret, without bitterness.

He had loved her of course, but in the way a man loved a frightened child or a wounded puppy. It had been a love born of pity, strengthened by the resultant compulsion to protect the pitied one. It had never been a love of passion or even respect. Passion had never kindled in either of them, though she had respected him from the very beginning; she had trusted him too. More than anything else, she had needed him, and he needed to be needed. That was what had drawn them together and kept them together. Over time, he'd grown to respect her, to admire the energy she forced herself to summon just to live each day. It was wearying to go through life with so much guilt and grief and resentment and misery. His pity for her never abated.

Long before, he had come to accept that Magdalena and he had been destined for each other. He could see the finger of God guiding each of them along their individual paths, with Raoul Wallenberg at the crossroads. Wallenberg: their first common denominator.

How well he remembered Wallenberg informing him that a family of three—father, mother, and young daughter—were in need of their services. Wallenberg had done everything in his power, but in the end, he could save only one. Of course, the parents had chosen their daughter, Magdalena. It never ceased to amaze Wallenberg that the parents of these children never wavered: saving their children was as automatic to them as breathing. In the face of such courage and selflessness, how could a man not help? It was that sentiment that had forged the bond between Wallenberg and himself. Bartholomew was magnetized, then and now, by that deceptively simple adherence to goodness. There was wrong, and then there was WRONG. That was the essence of what Wallenberg's example had taught him, proving to him that life's most meaningful lessons were simple, easy to understand at first glance, but the greatest challenge to live up to every day. Still, he strove to do exactly that, never stopping to consider whether he was worthy of carrying on Wallenberg's legacy. Quite simply, not attempting to carry it on was unthinkable. How lucky he had been to work with and be befriended by so great a man. That was a gift he was forever mindful of and eternally grateful for. No matter all that he had endured and suffered as a result, he would not trade it. Not even with hindsight. Bartholomew would always be glad he had helped Wallenberg save as many people as possible.

He recalled how Magdalena had arrived with her parents, who had told her all three of them were escaping. Her parents had known that Wallenberg could only save her, but they had also known that she would never have agreed to be the only one of them who was saved. All three of them had been doomed of course, but Magdalena persisted in believing that her parents had died to save her, that she survived only at their peril. Nothing ever swayed her on that until the last several days, so many years later, when the specter of her own death loomed so close.

Bartholomew could still see her face when she'd been ushered onto "Wallenberg's train," as they'd called it, while her parents had been held back by the SS. Clutching the paper Wallenberg had given her, she had stared straight ahead, betraying no sign of emotion. Beyond inscrutable, she had appeared lifeless. It had chilled Bartholomew to the bone; it still did whenever he thought of it.

Wallenberg had approached him then, asking him to take care of her. He'd never explained why, but Bartholomew, seeing the anxiety etched in every feature of Wallenberg's face, had agreed without hesitation. This great man, whose entire life had been a series of monumental sacrifices and towering courage in a time and place where humanity and mercy seemed to have been extinguished, had never asked him for anything. How could he have refused?

As things turned out, that was the last conversation he and Wallenberg ever had. And taking care of Magdalena was the last task he ever carried out for the friend who was also his hero. Magdalena for her part was torn apart by her hero-worship of Wallenberg, who had saved her life, and her guilt for having survived. Nightmares of Mauthausen, the concentration camp where her parents had perished, haunted her night and day for the rest of her life. She once told Bartholomew that she had never expected a person could have nightmares in the middle of the afternoon, with her eyes wide open.

Yawning, Bartholomew stretched his arms above his head, drawing his feet down from the sill. If only Magdalena and

Josselyn could have had more time together in understanding and commonality. But then again, he acknowledged that far too many people never even had the chance to experience that kind of empathy. To feel it at all—whether for a moment or a lifetime—was a gift and a blessing. It brought Magdalena the serenity that had eluded her for almost her entire life. He could only hope that it would spare Josselyn the wasting of her own life. The clarity gained in a mystical moment was so fragile, so easily dimmed by the daily cares and woes of life.

Bartholomew pulled down the shade, closed the drapes, and turned on the bedside lamp. Sitting on the edge of the bed and bowing his head, he prayed that God would always guide his daughter, always abide with her and sustain her. The path she had chosen could be filled with wonder as easily as with desolation. "Let her always find the light You showed her with her mother. That way, even if the desolation comes, it will not overwhelm her. Amen."

Raising his head slowly, Bartholomew turned off the lamp. Folding back the covers, he slipped beneath them, exhausted, but filled with peace and gratitude.

Rabbi Tevner delivered a beautiful eulogy, describing Magdalena Jeffrey as a woman of courage and perseverance, which both Josselyn and Bartholomew appreciated deeply, albeit for different reasons and from disparate perspectives. Josselyn had never understood her mother, but through her mother's imminent death, she had gained some awareness that was a kind of understanding, and as a result had found peace. Bartholomew had always understood his wife, but through her death, he had come to better understand himself, and as a result had found peace. Both Josselyn and Bartholomew would have to journey farther to see how lasting that peace would be.

After the burial, the Jeffreys returned home to sit shivah. Rabbi Tevner and his wife and daughter were waiting for them at the base of the front stoop. Rachel, the rabbi's wife, had placed at the front door a pitcher of water for them to use to rinse their hands: a ritual that symbolized the washing away of death after a burial. To emphasize that new life springs from death, hard-boiled eggs, symbolizing the earth's fertility and the circle of life, waited on the table. Rachel Tevner had prepared these too.

"Thank you, Rebbitzen," Bartholomew said to Rachel, "and you too, Rabbi. For everything."

Rachel smiled, picking up the pitcher and pouring water over all their hands except her own. She had not been at the grave, having gone directly from the temple funeral service to the Jeffreys' to set up the house while everyone else had gone to the cemetery.

The rabbi, in his typically affectionate nature, patted Bartholomew on the back. Offering one arm to Josselyn, he put his other arm around his daughter, Natalie. "Best friends should be reunited for happier occasions, girls," he said, echoing their own sentiments. They had not seen each other since the day that Josselyn had flown to San Francisco, headed for Vietnam.

All five of them entered the brownstone together, heading to the kitchen to eat the hard-boiled eggs. Rabbi Tevner said a brief prayer before they ate the eggs in silence.

"May we remain ever mindful of the sanctity and blessing of life," the rabbi said in English, after they finished eating.

A chorus of "Amen" echoed.

"May I also say that Magdalena, in her own way, recognized that sanctity and blessing, even if it might not always have appeared so," the rabbi added.

"I agree, Rabbi. Thank you," Josselyn replied, knowing he had addressed the added comment to her, without specifically saying so. He had counseled her on her despair-ridden relationship with her mother many times over the years.

Rabbi Tevner smiled, ushering them all toward the front parlor where the shivah would take place. As the others moved ahead, the rabbi placed his hand on Josselyn's arm, holding her back. "You and your mother had a chance to talk?"

"Yes, Rabbi. We had a good talk. The kind of talk I wish we could have had many times over the years."

"It's wonderful to have many talks like that with those we love, you're right. Most of us aren't that lucky."

Josselyn nodded. "I'm so happy and grateful that we had that one talk at least. So many people never have even that. I shouldn't complain."

"Of course you should. When you feel like complaining, complain. If you don't, you'll only bury it. Learn from what your mother did and didn't do. That was what she prayed for in the end, once she saw her mistakes," said the rabbi. "Besides, I wasn't saying it for you to feel guilty."

Josselyn arched an eyebrow at him, but then she smiled.

"Sometimes we only need one moment like that with one we love; other times, many. God grants us what we need. That's what I hope you'll take from this."

"That's very deep. I'll need to ponder it a while. It does sound true, though." She squeezed his forearm affectionately. "Thanks, Rabbi. You're always such a wonderful friend to me. And a wonderful guide too."

"You're welcome. I'm glad to be both."

He took her arm and led her into the parlor. Two mourners' seats, which looked like small cartons, were next to the sofa, in front of the windows that faced the street. As part of the shivah ritual, Josselyn and Bartholomew would sit on these special seats when they received those who came to pay their respects and offer condolences throughout the coming seven days. Josselyn took the seat next to her father. The Tevners sat beside them on the sofa.

Soon after, the first round of visitors came. Never feeling comfortable in large groups of people, Josselyn steeled herself for it. She was glad, though; her father loved large groups. If this would make it easier for him, she would find a way to endure it for his sake. While her parents' acquaintances and neighbors—her mother had never made any real friends aside from Rachel Tevner—and her father's friends and colleagues came and went, Josselyn focused her thoughts on Rabbi Tevner's last words of wisdom: *Sometimes we only need one moment like that with one we love; other times, many. God grants us what we need.*

A sense of foreboding filled her all of a sudden, as if he had predicted a trend for her life—too few moments with those she loved most. Despite the warm sun streaming through the front windows, she shivered. The rabbi didn't know that she had told Cameron that she would live on the memory of the brief time they spent together, but she knew that she had. She could not deny feeling that her promise and the rabbi's advice were somehow linked. Nor could she help feeling that she had jinxed herself and Cam.

Rachel and Natalie Tevner were preparing dinner in the Jeffreys' kitchen when the phone rang. They exchanged puzzled glances: No one called a shivah house. No one who understood how sacred and healing the mourning period was to the family, that is. Natalie hurried to answer the phone before its ringing would cause too much of a disturbance.

"Hello?"

"Overseas operator. Collect call for Josselyn Jeffrey. Will you accept the charges?"

"Who's calling, operator?" Natalie wanted to know.

"Cameron Burke," came an unfamiliar male voice over the phone line, his faraway location making it sound like he was in an echo chamber.

"Cameron Burke," Natalie repeated aloud, wondering who he might be.

Josselyn had walked toward the kitchen when the phone rang, reaching the doorway just as Natalie spoke his name. She practically lunged for the phone. "Accept the charges, Nat," she said.

Natalie did, and then she handed Josselyn the phone.

"Cam?" she strained to make out his voice over the static.

"I can barely hear you, baby."

"I can't really hear you either. Are you all right?"

The static cleared. "I'm fine. I got the wire about your mother."

"She's dead."

"I wish I could be there. I wish you were in my arms right now."

"I am, darling," she said, actually feeling his arms wrap around her as his love came over the phone line.

"In my heart, you always will be." He paused. "Listen, I only have another minute or so. I can't tell you where I'm going. I won't be able to communicate regularly. Do you understand what I mean?"

Of course she understood: Danger. Being a hero. Glory. "Just take care of yourself, darling."

"You do the same. You're not coming back in-country, are you." He didn't ask it as a question.

"I don't know. I'm not sure where I'm going. I'll wait to see what my father wants to do. See if he needs me. ..." Her voice trailed off. "I'll write to you."

"I'll write back. Send it to Captain Swinton. He'll see that I get it." He knew she had Swinton's address from when AP had posted her to the original assignment.

"All right, darling."

"I love you, baby."

"I love you, darling."

The line went dead.

Josselyn pressed the receiver against her heart, willing herself to keep her tears in check. After a few seconds, she hung up the phone.

"That was a soldier I met in Vietnam. He heard I'd come home because my mother was dying."

"And he called you from Vietnam. Sounds like a wonderful man," Rachel remarked.

"He is. He really is."

Rachel smiled. "Well, dinner is in the oven. I think I'll go sit in the living room for a bit."

As soon as her mother left the kitchen, Natalie pulled a chair back from the table, practically shoving Josselyn into it. "Well?" she demanded.

"We haven't had five minutes for a conversation since I got home, you know." Josselyn felt surprised by her own reluctance. She and Natalie had always told each other everything. For some reason, she wanted to guard not only Cameron but also the way she felt about Cameron.

"And now we do. Who is this guy?"

"I interviewed him for this story I was working on, and we just … fell in love. I can't explain it, Nat. Everything is different when you know you might be dead before the next day dawns."

"You don't have to justify it to me. What's he like?"

Josselyn hadn't been trying to justify anything. She knew Natalie would psychologize everything she said. Better to just tell it to her and be done with it. Natalie would not let up until Josselyn told her everything. Or what Natalie would think was everything, at any rate. Josselyn wouldn't dream of just telling Natalie that she didn't want to talk about it—that part of her wanted to keep the most important thing that had ever happened to her private, at least for the moment—she couldn't tell that to Natalie, didn't know how to say it. Besides, Natalie always had such wondrous insights, and another part of her didn't want to miss out on them.

"He's the man I've always dreamed of. I know that sounds ridiculous and completely corny."

"If you justify or apologize one more time …"

"I'm not."

"Yes, you are."

"Can't you stop being a psych intern for a second?"

"No. I was born a psych intern."

"Fine. Just stop analyzing me. I don't need analysis."

"You're right, you don't. What you need is a smack in the head," Natalie pronounced.

"How compassionate."

"Do you love this guy?"

"I'm crazy about him."

"So what difference does the rest of it make? If you love each other, who cares if you were in a war zone or not? You found the man of your dreams, Joss. That's what matters."

"I don't know if I'll ever even see him again," Josselyn said, the part of her that wanted to keep Cameron all to herself losing dominance in her conflicted psyche.

"You sound relieved," Natalie said tartly.

"Don't be ridiculous! I feel like I've been hit by a truck. Knowing I'll probably never see him again … and then my mother dying."

"I think you're relieved about that too."

Josselyn was too enraged to even answer her friend. Mostly because she knew Natalie was able to say these things to her because she never told her not to.

"Feel as mad at me as you want to. Stop speaking to me. Hate me. But at least think about what I said. No one but me could say it to you."

"You got that right."

"You wouldn't be so angry unless you felt there was some truth in it. Besides, did it ever occur to you that if you really didn't want to hear me say these things to you, you would tell me to shut up and mind my own business?"

Josselyn looked at her friend, aghast. She could feel her mouth form a perfect O. "Nat ... I ..." she sputtered. Her anger and indignation evaporated in the wake of her utter shock.

Natalie had her pegged all along. Typical. It was maddening how well she knew her. How well they knew each other. But Natalie was so in touch with her own feelings and her own inner life that Josselyn never had the chance to share any observations about her that Natalie had not already realized about herself. That was even more maddening.

"I'll think about it," Josselyn said, completely humbled.

"Think about it soon," Natalie urged with a wink. "Don't worry. I have thick skin. I won't shrivel up and die if you tell me to mind my own business."

Josselyn flushed. Natalie's intuition was uncanny. She wondered if it was that way with everyone or just her. If it was that way with everyone, she would single-handedly cure every mental-health patient someday.

"And I'll still love you," Natalie finished.

Josselyn hugged her. But she couldn't find the words to explain to Natalie why she needed her insights and wisdom, even when she sometimes resented them. Predictably, Natalie didn't press for an explanation, didn't even seem to want one. It was enough for her to know that she had helped Josselyn because, more than anything, Natalie needed to help others, especially the people she loved. Josselyn knew that. When she wasn't completely bound up in her own conflicted emotions, she admired that quality tremendously.

"Joss, don't push all your feelings aside, don't stuff them all down. Don't do any of the things you usually do with your feelings. Which is some method or other of not feeling them."

"I got the message, doctor," Josselyn said with a grin.

"Good. I'll finish this session later. Now tell me all about him."

"You want to analyze Cameron too?"

"No. I want to hear the good stuff." Natalie laughed. "The girlfriend stuff."

"I can't tell you," Josselyn said, surprising herself. "I need to keep that just between him and me."

Natalie nodded, putting her arm around her friend's shoulder as they went back out to the living room. "He's lucky you love him that much."

"We love each other that much."

Natalie squeezed her shoulder. "Good." She hoped it was true, for her friend's sake. Josselyn could survive never loving a man, but loving a man that much and being betrayed or abandoned by him—even if only in her own perception—would destroy her.

Later that night, Josselyn lay awake. Despite trying to put it out of her mind, she couldn't help but focus on what Natalie had said about her feeling relieved. A part of her *did* feel relieved. Relieved that she might escape having to discover whether she and Cameron could sustain their love in everyday life; relieved that she wouldn't have to discover whether she and her mother could embark on a relationship based on their newfound peace and understanding. Forgiveness was an awful lot easier when the forgiven had died. Love was an awful lot easier when the beloved existed in your heart and mind, more imagined than alive.

She wondered why it had to be this way for her, why the journey had to be so fraught with challenges, why peace and serenity had to be so elusive. She thought that the serenity that had come to her with her mother's death would be enduring. How wrong she was. The struggle she had felt with her mother would continue, only it would be not between her and her mother, but between her and the part of her mother that lived on in her own psyche. Between her and her own demons.

Lasting peace and serenity would not be hers for a long, long time—if ever in this lifetime.

Josselyn sighed, knowing she could not fight fate or her own destiny. Only by accepting and embracing that destiny could she hope to succeed in finding any measure of peace.

When Josselyn awoke she felt more tired than when she'd gone to bed. Nothing was more exhausting than a sleepless night. She went downstairs to put up the coffee and make breakfast for her father. She had no appetite. While the coffee percolated, its aroma wafting through the air and lifting her spirits, she assembled the ingredients for pancakes. Pancakes and waffles were all her father ever ate for breakfast. After years of making do with "morning field tripe," as he called it, he insisted on a hot and hearty breakfast every day. For whatever reason, he was less finicky about lunch and dinner, although he insisted upon only the highest quality food for their table. Given her mother's life experience, this was a tacit understanding more than an agreement; so seamless, in fact, that Josselyn had never thought about it growing up, except when she ate at friends' houses.

Her mind wandered as she mixed the pancake batter, watching the mixture turn with her stirring, and her thoughts eventually centered on her mother. She saw her mother's hands mixing the batter for thousands of pancakes, waffles, cakes, cookies, pastries, breads. … Josselyn let the mixing spoon drop against the side of the bowl, its heavy wooden handle hitting the glass bowl dully, and she backed away in a combination of horror and grief, realizing that she would never see her mother's hands baking, cooking, or doing anything ever again. This realization, simple as it was, shook her to the core, hurting her too deeply for her to even cry. Reflexively, she stroked her own hands, and then, taking a few deep breaths to settle herself, she stepped back toward the bowl, taking the spoon in hand and resuming the mixing. The rhythmic action soothed her, and she soon felt grounded again.

As soon as the batter was smooth, she heard her father's footsteps on the stairs and then on the hardwood floor heading toward the kitchen.

"I smell coffee."

"You're chipper this morning," she said, returning his kiss on the cheek. "Ready for pancakes?" She was already greasing and heating the griddle.

"Do you have to ask?" He grinned at her. "Want some?" he asked, gesturing toward the now-brewed coffee.

"Do you have to ask?"

Her father chuckled, filling two large mugs with the steaming brew. Handing her one, he sipped from the other.

"Thanks." She took a scalding sip and then checked the griddle to see if it was hot enough. "It'll be a few minutes, Dad."

"Did *you* sleep last night?"

"What does it matter now?"

He peered at the deepening dark circles under her eyes.

"I'm fair-skinned. I always have these circles under my eyes," she said quickly.

"So do pandas and raccoons," her father quipped.

Turning away, she sipped more coffee, willing herself to wakefulness. The griddle was hot now, and she poured the batter onto it to make four pancakes.

"Did you sleep?" she countered.

"Like a baby."

"You're lying."

"I am not. I was dreaming about your pancakes. I could smell the maple syrup in my dream." He grinned at her again, walking to the pantry to get the maple syrup, his favorite kind, dark and heavy and sweet, but with a hint of woodiness. He kept the syrup in its original metal container, purchasing it by mail order it from a farm in Vermont whenever he needed to replenish his supply.

Josselyn watched the pancakes, giving him a quick smile over her shoulder. "I didn't know you had those kinds of dreams, Dad."

"Well, don't let it get around. I'll know who leaked it." He set the syrup on the table and then sat down.

"Your secret is safe with me."

They both chuckled.

Josselyn flipped the pancakes and then downed the rest of her coffee. She immediately poured herself another full mug, setting it aside to cool.

Bartholomew unscrewed the cap of the syrup container, the heady maple-sugar aroma filling the air, mixing with that of the coffee and the pancakes. Bartholomew inhaled deeply. "Quite intoxicating."

Josselyn nodded, sniffing appreciatively. Both sides of the pancakes now an inviting golden-brown, she flipped them from griddle to plate, took silverware from the drawer, and brought it all to her father.

"Thank you, sweetheart," he said, cutting into the stack of pancakes and then pouring the syrup over them. "You outdid yourself," he told her, after chewing and swallowing his first mouthful. "Nothing like a good breakfast." He tore into the rest of the stack.

Josselyn already had more on the griddle. "Let me know when you're ready for the next batch."

Now that she'd gotten some coffee into her, she felt herself come back to life, complete with an appetite. Thank goodness, the depths of grief she'd felt earlier had evened out. She didn't like falling victim to her own emotions, refused to give in to the wisdom that emotions ebb and flow, and riding the roller coaster was just part of life.

She brought her father another stack when she saw that he'd cleaned his plate, and then she made herself a portion with what was left. She had mixed only enough batter for that many, never liking to save it from one day to the next. Joining her father at the table, she ate the first bite, which dripped with the syrup she adored as much as he did. The pancakes were delicious, if she did say so herself.

"Your mother would be proud of how you made these."

"Dad ..."

"She would be."

"You don't have to say that Mom would have been proud of me."

"I didn't. I said she'd be proud of these pancakes you made. And she would be. Of course she's proud of *you*. She was always proud of you."

"She was?" Her voice was barely a whisper.

"She was. She is. She always will be." His voice was firm and clear, as reassuring as ever. He put his hand over hers. "This, too, shall pass, sweetheart. You'll be able to remember her without the pain. It takes time; let it." He pushed back his chair, bent down to kiss the top of her head, and turned to exit the kitchen.

"I love you, Daddy."

"I love you, sweetheart." He went back upstairs to get dressed.

Josselyn finished her coffee, put the dishes in the sink, and filled it with hot, soapy water. She looked up when she heard a light tapping at the kitchen door that opened to the alley. "It's open," she called, her hands dripping suds.

"Good morning, sweetie," Rachel Tevner bustled inside, her arms filled with food, as usual. "I'll do that!" she scolded, setting the provisions on the counter. Mourners were not supposed to do any work.

"It feels good to make breakfast for my father."

Rachel rubbed her back. "Leave the cleanup to me."

"Okay. I'll go get dressed."

"Don't rush. It's early." Rachel let her eyes settle on the smudges under Josselyn's eyes, saying nothing.

"Can I ask you something?" Josselyn asked, yawning. "I'm sorry. I just can't wake up this morning."

Rachel gave her a you'd-be-able-to-if-you'd-slept-last-night look. "What did you want to ask me?"

"I ... when will I stop seeing her in everything? Missing her all the time? I thought that when she and I talked that last time, that I'd found peace. But now ..."

Rachel stroked Josselyn's cheek. "When my mother—may she rest in peace—died, I thought about her all the time. Missed her all the time. The more I tried to stop thinking about her, the more everything reminded me of her."

"I saw her hands mixing the batter when I was making the pancakes." Tears coursed down Josselyn's cheeks.

Rachel gathered her into her arms. "You have to just let the feelings come when they come. Once I stopped fighting it, my mother's being gone just was what it was: a fact of my life, not my whole life."

"The rabbi said that sometimes one moment like I had with my mother is all a person needs. That she and I finished our business in this life with that one talk," Josselyn paraphrased what the rabbi had told her. Even though it wasn't exactly what he had said, it *was* what she had extrapolated from what he'd said.

"But you're not so sure he's right."

Josselyn pulled away. "I meant no disrespect to the rabbi," she said quickly.

"Disagreeing doesn't mean disrespecting."

Josselyn went on hurriedly. "It's just that ... it shouldn't be that way. I mean, when you love someone, you should have time together. Lots of time. Lots of conversations. A lasting connection."

"When you love someone the connection is there forever, but the time and conversations aren't always. One memory can shine light through a lifetime, and then one moment is much more than just a moment. You have to make the most of the time you have."

The last part was almost exactly what her mother had said. But all Josselyn said to Rachel was, "My mother and I didn't."

"You did the best you could. Both of you."

"We can't get back the time we wasted, though."

"That's true. But life isn't about doing things over. It's about moving forward and growing wiser as a result of what you've learned."

Rachel squeezed Josselyn's shoulders, smiled, and then gently steered the conversation back toward Josselyn's ambivalence over the rabbi's remark. "My husband is a wise man, a great scholar, a wonderful rabbi. Sometimes he forgets we're not all Talmud scholars like he is." She chuckled, shaking her head, inviting Josselyn to recognize that for all his wisdom, Rabbi Tevner was merely a man, a human being, replete with imperfections like the rest of the human race, although he might be a more enlightened and more compassionate person.

After letting all that she'd said sink in for a moment, Rachel asked Josselyn, "Can I tell you something my mother always told me?"

Josselyn nodded.

"'We have to wake up in this world every day, no matter what happens.' That's the rough translation anyway."

"What does that mean?" Josselyn asked. It seemed deceptively simple.

"It means that we can learn and learn, but life is still just life. We still have to live it every day. Just live each day the best you can. One day, you'll wake up and feel wiser because of your experiences. Then you'll understand what I mean."

"I think the rabbi meant that I have to let go of things more. That peace is a gift I have to accept."

"First you let go of the old. And then you accept the new. You can't do both at the same time. Don't listen to men so much.

They don't understand what it means to be a woman. We're born to yield, to accept, to nurture. It's hard to let go when you're made to receive. Learn to accept who you are; that's the best you can do and the most you can do. And if you don't do it, you'll never do anything else … not really. And then, one day, you'll realize you never grieved, never let go, never accepted, never moved on. Listen to me: grieve, let go, accept, move on."

"It's so hard, though."

"The other way will be harder. Trust me; I know."

Josselyn bent her head.

"Just let yourself be." Rachel patted Josselyn's shoulder, and then she turned toward her work at the sink.

"I don't think I can."

"Don't think about it so much," Rachel said over her shoulder. "Just leave it alone for a while. Give yourself a rest."

"Natalie always tells me that."

"Well, she's not adopted," Rachel smiled. To be sure, her daughter was a born healer, far more intuitive than Rachel herself had ever been, but she hadn't grown up in a vacuum. Rachel took pride in the nurturing that she had given Natalie, which had nourished her daughter body, mind, heart, and soul, helping her not to become all that she was meant be but to do so more easily. Being a mother was Rachel's most significant contribution to the world. When she told someone, "I'm Natalie Tevner's mother," it was always with dignity, pride, joy, and love. An acknowledgment of, "Oh you're Natalie Tevner's mother!" was the greatest compliment she could receive. Even when such a statement was made perfunctorily, intended merely as a point of fact, Rachel still took it in as a compliment, and her pride and joy overflowed. She mothered Josselyn by extension, loving her sincerely and responding involuntarily to Josselyn's need for mothering ever since the girls were small.

Josselyn smiled. Natalie had a head start at caring and understanding with Rachel as her mother. Not to take away from Natalie herself, but she'd be the first to admit it.

"Nat always says that too," Josselyn told Rachel, and then she turned on her heel to leave the kitchen. Pausing in the doorway, she turned back and said, "Thank you." She walked out softly and headed upstairs before Rachel even had a chance to respond.

Letting herself be was precisely what Josselyn didn't know how to do. How was she supposed to rest from being herself? Did everyone find pursuing the answers to these deep questions as exhausting as she did? The only times she ever felt true solace were during the moments she spent utterly engaged in her writing—which was how and why she had come to write in the first place. Yet she knew everything Rachel and Natalie had said was right and true.

At the top of the stairs, she paused, leaning against the wall and closing her eyes. "Will you help me, Mom? Please. I'm so … lost. I don't know how to just be. Please help me, Mom," she whispered. For an instant, she could have sworn she heard her mother call her name. It had taken no longer than a split second, but it was enough. Josselyn smiled. Perhaps she and her mother were more connected than she had ever realized; perhaps she would not fail in her effort to find peace and grace, after all. Perhaps, too, her love for Cameron would become more than just a few precious moments treasured in her memory. Only time would tell.

She hurried to get dressed, feeling lighter and more hopeful than she had since returning home. It might take her a while to find what she sought; her goal might remain elusive, fluttering into her grasp every so often, only to inevitably slip away. It didn't matter: as long as she could feel herself succeed some of the time, she would endure. No, prevail. Triumph. She was the daughter of two heroes, after all.

The seven days of shivah passed quickly. On the last day, Josselyn and Bartholomew sat until the required ten o'clock in the morning, and then they rose and walked around the block, as a testament to the circular nature of life. They would continue to mourn, but life would go on even as they did so. And that was exactly as it should be, exactly as God willed: the circle of life—no beginning, no end. Which was why love, dwelling within that circle, was eternal.

Josselyn remained outside after her father went in. She sat at the top of the front stoop, watching a lone bird ascend the heavens. It soared high above her, a small V etched against the azure vault of the sky. It reminded her of Cameron's description of the phoenix rising up from the ashes, reborn—stronger and wiser somehow—ready for life again. She saw herself as a sort of phoenix, risen from the ashes of the Shoah, nurtured as much as her mother could nurture her, and then ready to fly away. In her own way and in her own time, her mother had prepared her for life: the time to fly comes for everyone, yet its arrival is rarely the same for any of us—and accepting that is what makes each of us ready, or not, to take flight and to endure the heartbreaking crashes that must accompany the soaring and gliding we so delight in.

The perfection of all that had come and all that was yet to be appeared to Josselyn in a single, breathtaking flash—and then it departed just as suddenly. She was growing used to these bursts of insight, but they still filled her with awe and wonder and hope, and she prayed that they always would—if they continued. She promised herself that she would never, ever take them for granted. It was as if her mother, having gained wisdom from God, now passed it on to Josselyn. The beauty and peace of it was quite beyond anything else she had ever experienced, even the magic and fire she'd felt with Cameron.

She would let herself heal from this crash landing, let the pain and grief come when they did, even though they overwhelmed her. Nothing to do but wait till she felt strong enough to fly again. Someday she would glide, even soar, but it would take time.

Verses from a modern translation of the Twenty-Third Psalm filled her mind: "The Lord is my shepherd ... he restores my soul ... though I walk through a valley of deepest darkness, I fear no evil ..." *For I will never be alone.* Resting her head on her knees, Josselyn wept, but it was with relief, not despair. In letting her mother go, she found the blessing of peace, however fleeting it might be. She accepted that life had to go on—ever moving forward—and so did the living.

Crossing off the last remaining items on her packing list, Josselyn placed them in one of her suitcases. As she zipped and locked all the bags, she felt as if she were symbolically sealing an era of her life, which she needed to do so that she could move forward to the next one.

In the months following her mother's death, she had felt adrift, vacillating between moments of intense clarity and awareness and moments of deep despair and confusion. She was glad to leave that behind. She had not heard from Cameron since his phone call while she was sitting shivah, and although she tried to tell herself that he was fine, that he had warned her this would happen, she worried about him constantly. She knew she wouldn't be able to leave that worry behind, but her upcoming adventure at least gave her something bright and exciting to focus her energies on.

Her father, invited to guest lecture on journalism in Israel, had asked whether she wanted to accompany him. She had jumped at the chance, finding to her delight that Reuters was eager to have her aboard as a foreign correspondent in their Tel Aviv office. They gave her the post on the strength of her writing, not because she was the daughter of Bartholomew Jeffrey. That's what the bureau chief there had said, and although she doubted that it was entirely true, she decided to focus on proving it true instead of dwelling on why he had really given her the job.

She couldn't wait to arrive in the Holy Land, felt confident that being there was exactly what she needed, not only so that she could throw herself into her career once more, but also so that she could feel grounded and connected to life again. For Josselyn, Israel was not just a holy place, it was also the cradle of Western civilization. The night before, she had made a list of all the fabulous places she had to visit, and the prospect of seeing them all filled her with wonder and excitement.

Nothing left to do now but wait for the cab to arrive to take them to the airport. Josselyn looked out her bedroom window, wondering when she would next see the Manhattan skyline. She had read that the plans for a world financial center off Wall Street in Lower Manhattan, begun almost a decade earlier, were all but finished. Two 110-story skyscrapers were all that still had to be completed, and the architects and construction crews were hard at work on them; she could see the buildings going up before her eyes. When she returned, they'd no doubt be finished. Those steel-and-glass-and-concrete towers would pierce the sky, completely dominating the skyline forever.

Burke had just come off his latest recon mission when the company clerk gave him a letter from Josselyn. When he saw the Reuters, Tel Aviv return address and the Israeli stamp and postmark, he felt his insides churn and then flip. He knew he had no right to tell her to stay out of danger when he courted it so aggressively himself, but that was different: he was a man. He was supposed to be the rescuer, the protector, the hero. Shaking his head, he tore open the envelope while walking to his tent. Once inside, he tossed his gear on the ground, sat down on his cot, and pulled out her letter. He took off his boots, lay back on the cot, and read.

Darling,

As you've probably guessed by the return address and postmark, I'm in Israel, a foreign correspondent with Reuters in Tel Aviv. Not long after my mother died, my father was invited to guest lecture on journalism here. When he asked me if I wanted to tag along, I jumped at the chance, and I got the Reuters posting with no trouble. I know you'll be relieved that I'm not returning to the dangers of Vietnam. Israel might not be the safest place, I realize, but it isn't a war zone either. Not technically, anyway.

I know you can't tell me where you are or what you're doing, but I pray you're safe and well, and that you'll find a way to get word to me, just to say that you're okay.

I could pour my heart out for pages and pages, telling you how much I miss you, how the day when we'll see each other again—hold each other again—shines like a beacon through my darkest hours, but I won't do more than write it just this one time. We don't need to break our hearts all over again.

Besides, we're both creatures of adventure, you and I. Neither of us could stand just waiting for the other for very long. I was going crazy at home, worrying about you all the time, even when I was writing. I had to go off in search of … I don't know … anything to fill my mind in the empty spaces where, otherwise, only fear and worry thrive. Forgive me, Cameron. I know you want me to be safe, but I also know you don't want me to go insane or be miserable, and that's exactly what was happening.

We'll be together again—someday. With so many tales to tell. My first one will be that no matter where I went and who I met, I loved and longed for only you, my darling.

Always,
Josselyn

She was right about all of it of course. Her daring was part of what he loved about her. Much as he wanted to think of her as happy keeping his house and going to PTA meetings, he knew that wasn't what Josselyn was meant to do, and he loved her as she was, not as what it would be easier for him *if* she was. She loved him the same way. That was their gift to each other. *Someday, my love, as you said.*

Burke reread the letter twice before folding it for safekeeping. As he set it back inside the envelope, he felt something else inside it. When he shook the envelope open, a snapshot slid out into his upturned palm. There she was: as beautiful as ever, though a photo could never adequately capture her radiance. He closed his eyes, letting all the aspects of her fill his senses and his memory. And his heart.

He placed the snapshot inside the folded letter, tucking it carefully into the envelope, which he stuffed into his shirt. This treasure was never leaving his side—at least not until she was there in its place.

Burke set off to find someone to take a snapshot of him, and then he returned to his tent to write back to her, letting her know she was right about all of it, and that he loved her for understanding and being honest. That he loved her for being her.

Josselyn sat down at a bistro table in a sidewalk café in Tel Aviv. She closed her eyes behind her sunglasses, relishing the brief respite. This was the first real break she'd taken in a week. At moments like this, she questioned her own sanity. What was it, exactly, that she derived from being a foreign correspondent? Journalistic acclaim, certainly—though what that meant became increasingly difficult to define. Meaning and fulfillment, yes— but it was in the realm of serving the greater good, bringing her a feeling of worthiness, not bliss. When she thought about her work as a journalist, wide, sweeping words always came to mind, never deep-down, honest feelings. It felt so odd, even to her, that she confided in no one. The only two people she could tell it to—Cameron and Natalie—both were so far away, and she would never be a long-distance burden to either of them. Confusion could so easily be mistaken for despair or depression when heard or viewed from a great distance.

The waitress set a Turkish coffee and a plate of dates and figs in front of Josselyn, who downed the coffee in three gulps and then nibbled at the fruit. She caught the waitress's eye, signaling she wanted a refill on the coffee. She was bone weary today. Sustenance, in the form of pure caffeine, was what she needed. Finishing the fruit, she pushed away the plate and waited for the second coffee to arrive.

While she waited, she opened her bag, rummaging through it. Her hand found its way instinctively to what she sought: Cameron's snapshot. He had sent it to her a few months before, together with a long, passion-filled letter. His letter echoed the sentiments in the letter she'd sent him a few months prior to that. The essence of it was that even though they were the loves of each other's lives, and each recognized the other as such, their individual callings were too important to them, had a power and a life of their own. Neither one of them could give up those dreams for anything or anyone … not even each other.

Swallowing hard, Josselyn fingered the already-wearing edges of the snapshot, pulling it out of the bag and gazing at it with a mixture of reverence and tenderness; a borderline maudlin display that she would have derided as little as a year ago, and yet could not suppress now, no matter how hard or how often she tried. Truthfully, it was more than just their callings that stood in their way: it was their demons and fears too. Josselyn sensed this at a deep, almost visceral level, without really acknowledging it consciously.

The waitress set down the second coffee and cleared the dirty dishes, as Josselyn tucked the snapshot back in her bag, withdrawing her fingers from it in an act of conscious will. This coffee she sipped slowly, feeling the blend of acridity and syrupy sweetness coat the back of her throat. She loved the intensity of it, loved intensity, period—which was the root of her problems. The calm sea always beckoned invitingly, but it was the tempest that pulled her each and every time.

Josselyn didn't need to read Cameron's letter again: she had long since memorized it. Good thing too. She doubted they would ever see one another again. Not in this life anyway. *You chose this life,* she berated herself, hearing her own harshness in her mind, though she had not spoken the words aloud. But to a great extent, the writer's life had chosen her as much as she had chosen it. She'd just never counted on falling in love with Cameron Burke. The curveball love had thrown her, not the life she had chosen long ago, was what wreaked havoc on her now.

If only loving Cameron could be enough for her, she'd gladly build a life around it. But it would never be enough for her. Words would always call her: the next great story, the great American novel, sorting out her mother's story and her father's legacy. And heroism and service would always call him. No matter how much she and Cameron loved each other, their missions would always stand between them. If they were destined to be together, it would only be once they had fulfilled the dreams they each had to pursue. They each knew this. Knowing it was the easy part. Accepting it was what was hard. Her father always said that the untrodden path held great rewards, but their price was desolation. As a girl, she had never realized how true those words would prove to be for her. Desolation was something she could only understand once she had experienced a true soul-level love and passion for another person. Desolation was meaningless unless compared to that kind of deep connection.

She wouldn't let herself think about the fear of loving him without the drama—the dread that they couldn't sustain their love without it; they both needed the all-but-unendurable peaks of their passion, even though that entailed an inescapable despair. The despair she was in the midst of now, and that she knew he was in the midst of too. She could deal with the sacrifice of losing him—or giving him up—but could never deal with the all-too-human weakness of failing in a day-to-day relationship with him. She hated the very thought of it as much as she knew he would.

Deriving a strange sort of comfort from knowing this stubbornness and vaunted pride was something the two of them shared, Josselyn drained her coffee cup. Again, she swallowed hard to steel her resolve, as well as to convince herself that she had lost Cameron to her single-minded dedication to perfecting the printed word, not to her inability to exorcise the demons that paralyzed her. It felt better to focus instead on renewing her commitment to becoming the great writer she had dreamed of being before she'd ever met Cameron Burke. She resurrected that lifelong dream as if nothing—and no one—had ever usurped its importance. Her destiny assured and her dreams crystalline, she set her money on the table and strode away, forcing herself to relegate Cameron to an incandescent memory, so she would no longer be haunted by the ache of letting him go.

Taking one last puff of his cigar, Captain Swinton put his hands behind his head and leaned back in his chair. After deliberating a moment or two, he sat up and looked Burke square in the eye. "Well done, soldier."

"Thank you, sir." Swinton's taciturn pronouncement meant more to Burke than all the flowery—and most likely empty—praise of a man of less integrity and honor.

"You realize this means you can pretty much name your posting."

Burke nodded.

"Any preferences? The Middle East, maybe?" Swinton maintained his no-nonsense tone, but he knew Josselyn Jeffrey was in Israel.

Yes! screamed the voice in Burke's head, but all he said in reply was, "Wherever I'm most needed, sir."

"Son, you've got to fight for what you want in this world. We're needed everywhere, and one battleground is essentially the same as another. But there's only one woman for each of us. If you've found the one for you, don't let her go—not for your country, not for what you see as your duty, not for anything."

"Not even glory, sir?" Burke smiled, touched by Swinton's warmer demeanor but taken aback by it too.

"No greater glory than the love of a good woman. Trust me. Don't make the same mistake I did." A flicker of pain glinted in Swinton's eyes. Not raw pain, more like the ache of an old injury that flares up now and again. "I need your answer by 0800, soldier," he finished, resuming his usual tone.

"Yes, sir."

"That's all."

Burke saluted, exiting the captain's quarters and returning to his own. Climbing into his bunk, he wondered about the insanity of it all. He had undertaken reconnaissance missions as part of his resolve to be a hero, to make his efforts in the war count. And he had succeeded. His recon work had garnered the attention and approval of big brass, and Swinton had been instructed that once Burke's official tour was up, he would be promoted into military intelligence. Clearly, he had a bright future—an innate ability for the work and an icy composure that awed all who worked with him. As a result, he had the opportunity to request a post in the Middle East—which was the place to be if you wanted to make a name for yourself—and he was resisting it. The same icy composure that made him a cloak-and-dagger savant also enabled him to put Josselyn out of his thoughts ... his waking thoughts, at least. But if she was within range, the pull of her would magnetize him—body, mind, heart, and soul—and he would lose his edge. Destroy the success he'd thrown himself into, initially to prove himself worthy of her and subsequently to justify letting her go until he *had* fully proved it. He was torturing himself, but he knew that without that success he would never feel worthy of her, never be able to ask her to be his. He was caught between a rock and a hard place.

Burke turned on his side, fishing Josselyn's snapshot out of his shirt. He balanced it between his thumb and forefinger, noticing the already-fraying edges and the way the photo curved slightly from his having held it this way so many times in the past. Tilting his wrist toward the tent flap, he let the moonlight pour over the surface of the snapshot, illuminating her face in the light he most loved to see her in. She called to his soul. He could almost hear her voice, smell the sweetness of her, feel her hair falling against his face and her lips on his, tentative at first, then urgent as her body melted into his. … Burke quickly tucked the photo away, closing his eyes in a futile attempt to push her back into his subconscious.

"No good," he whispered aloud. *The Middle East it will be.* He lay awake until reveille, waves of emotion swamping him: rapture then dread then pain, over and over and over again. It would never be any other way for the two of them, but knowing it didn't make that fact any easier to bear.

Three weeks later—Swinton had insisted that he take some time stateside to see his family before he began his intelligence career—Burke was on an air force transport headed for the Holy Land. *And destiny,* he thought with a mixture of excitement and grim apprehension. He knew in his bones that he was meant to accomplish great things as an operative in the Middle East—no less than he knew that he was meant to love Josselyn as long as there was breath in his body. Better to just accept both and let life evolve.

"Thy will be done, Lord," he whispered as the plane began its descent, carrying Cameron Burke headlong toward his fate. And hers.

Burke settled against his duffel bag, using it as a shock absorber against the rough terrain the jeep bounded over. No matter how hard he tried, he could not shake the feeling that he had made an irreparable mistake by coming to the Middle East, and yet he knew he would have made the same choice if given a second chance. He was caught up in fate's inexorable weaving, felt the threads of it pull tight around him. He didn't like that feeling. Not one bit. *So much for putting it in God's hands,* he all but laughed out loud at himself.

He had wired Josselyn before coming to Israel. A terse, single line indicating when and where he was arriving; nothing else. It could easily have been a wire sent to a secretary, even a stranger. He had worded it that way deliberately to protect her in case her messages were intercepted, but now he wondered whether she might interpret it as a change of heart on his part. Saving and serving were always his primary objectives, his way of identifying himself and relating to his environment and the world at large. Ensuring Josselyn's safety stemmed from his generic concern for her as a human being, his being in love with her only deepened his concern, making it much more complicated. Nevertheless, he would not apologize for who he was, and he would not ever be able to change his automatic behavior, even if he tried.

She would understand. She had to.

He leaned his head back, pressing his eyes shut in a vain attempt at sleep; he would settle for rest. His superior at the defense office had informed him that sundown marked the holiest time of the Jewish year: Kol Nidre, which ushered in Yom Kippur, the Day of Atonement.

None of them knew what an unforgettable one it would be.

Josselyn sat alone in the kitchen of the apartment she and her father shared in Tel Aviv. She had discarded Cameron's telegram, couldn't bear to read the terse and impersonal words. It didn't matter that she realized his perfunctory message was intended to ensure her safety. Knowing that he was so close but not necessarily within her reach was impossible to bear. She had tried—was still trying—to tell herself she was being ridiculous, acting like a schoolgirl, and being entirely selfish, to boot. How had such a cool-headed literary type as she turned into this boiling mass of insanity—this creature of pure passion? Her own inner shift terrified her. She hated feeling out of control.

Gazing into the flame of the yahrzeit candle, she breathed deep, letting the violet heart of the flame mesmerize her. The candle was in remembrance of her mother, and she had lit it before sundown, as the memorial aspect of Yom Kippur dictated. Looking ever deeper into the flame, Josselyn prayed her mother's tortured soul had at long last found peace.

Gradually, the flickering flame soothed and calmed her, and her focus returned. She grew vaguely aware of her father's presence in the doorway.

His voice floated over her softly, "You cannot be great in love and in your work. Few can be great—truly great—in either. None in both."

"I never wanted to be great at anything *except* my work. I never even sought love. I don't understand why this is happening." The words spilled out of her in a rush. She had not meant to say these things to her father.

"Love finds us. And the best kind of love is the love we *don't* seek."

Josselyn nodded. Her father's love had always surrounded her. She had never questioned it. Her mother's love she had sought daily and never felt she had attained until it was too late. Even so, the powerful connection she had felt so keenly during the moments while life was slipping away from her mother's body waxed and waned of late. No matter how powerful a moment it might have been, it couldn't make up for a lifetime of needing and hurting.

Her father stood behind her now, leaning down to kiss the top of her head the way he always did. "Don't be so hard on yourself, angel. You do the best you can. Your best doesn't have to be better than everyone else's."

Reaching up to touch his hand where it rested on her shoulder, she said, "I'm trying, Dad. I really am."

"Don't stay up too late," he said as he walked back to his bedroom.

But she knew what he meant was, "Don't make it harder than it has to be."

Why can't I just choose: writing or Cameron? Every time I think I've chosen, I waver. Why is it so hard?

The flame flickered, seemingly in response to the fierce energy of her thoughts.

You've already chosen. Make peace with it. Let go of him. Move on.

This came to her, not as her own realization but more as an external answer to her own thoughts. Weird, yet somehow comforting. The flame was absolutely still now, almost beatific. Maybe her mother, having found peace, was trying to guide her.

Josselyn rose from her chair, heading for bed herself. Casting a cursory glance at the night sky, she lowered the shade, left the kitchen, and entered her bedroom. Slipping beneath the covers, she realized she felt clear for the first time in months.

Cameron Burke had been a detour—a glorious, unforgettable detour that she would never regret having made, but a detour nonetheless. She could no more be a permanent part of his life than he could be of hers.

Best, indeed, to let go of him and move on. And pray that she never saw him again.

Within hours of having made her prayer, Josselyn would regret the words—she would regret them a thousand times over the years—the Yom Kippur War had begun. On a rational level, of course, she knew world events were outside her control. But in her heart, she couldn't help feeling that she was somehow responsible, or at least involved; that her prayer seemed to have set the events in motion—crazy as that sounded, even to her. The feeling, however misguided, that she had participated in bringing Cameron closer to danger—mortal danger, likely as not—hurt her in a way she had never conceived it was possible to hurt. Sharp, raw pain, excruciating in its fierceness and inexorable in its righteousness, cut through her heart every time she thought of him. Worst of all, she knew the agony was entirely the result of self-recrimination, and she was furious with herself for it; furious that she was victimizing herself in such a melodramatic way ... that she was so out of control. This distorted perception of justice she visited upon herself wreaked havoc on her, heart and soul. At random intervals, the thought that she was having a complete breakdown pierced through the haze of her emotional agony with alarming clarity. Each time, she would assure herself that she was too strong for a breakdown. The sardonic humor made her feel better in a bizarre sort of way.

After many hours of this brutal self-inflicted torture, she decided that the only thing to do was throw herself into the work she had come to Israel to do. As soon as she was able to secure a pass, she went to the heart of the fighting to report from the front lines. The resulting journalistic work would be acclaimed as groundbreaking and fearless; her prose as evocative, yet mordant. No one, friend or foe, would ever discover that the secret to her brilliance and fearlessness was her need to escape pain. She could not bear to face the pain she felt because of Cameron—not of losing him, or even of giving him up, but of *praying* to lose him.

It would be almost thirty years before she herself fully acknowledged what the secret was.

BOOK III
WITHOUT YOU

Cameron Burke opened first one eye, and then the other, taking shallow breaths in a vain attempt to stave off the agony that threatened to overwhelm every cell of his body. It was an odd feeling; he could feel himself held within the soft net of heavy drugs sure to be keeping the full force of the pain at bay, yet he knew the pain was there. Waiting.

Burns. He knew that was the source of the pain, even though he couldn't feel it precisely. Steeling himself for the searing excrucation that any movement was sure to bring about, drugs notwithstanding, he attempted to shift his head ever so slightly, just enough to assess the extent of his injuries. *Attempted*, being the operative word. Pain like he had never before experienced, nor ever would again by the grace of God, ripped through his body like a river current, sucking the breath right out of him and leaving him panting and helpless. All he had managed to glimpse was a sea of white: bed sheets and bandages. He could have guessed as much and saved his strength.

If it wouldn't have been so torturous, Burke would have laughed at his own folly. He, Cameron Burke, of all people, ought to have known better. A seasoned firefighter. A Vietnam vet. A military-intelligence operative. He thought of himself by name, rattling off his credentials purely to test his mental faculties. So far, so good.

It would be better if he could remember where the hell he was, of course. Not in America, that much he knew for sure. Far from home; he knew that too. *Think, man, think.* But no matter how fiercely he exhorted himself, he could not remember—not if his loved ones were threatened life and limb, not if he himself faced torture.

Easy, he told himself. *Try again later.*

Slowly, lest the pain rip through him again, he let his eyelids drift closed again. In the next instant, visions of her danced in his mind's eye. Damn! Had the fire that seared his skin and nerves burned her even more deeply into his memory? Was that even possible?

Burke prayed for the coma that had held him in blissful oblivion to overtake him again. Anything but the never-ending haunting of his every waking moment. But it was no use. He knew he would never be free of his longing for Josselyn Jeffrey. Not as long as he lived. The agony of *that* would last forever, and its scars would never heal.

"Time for your morphine," said a voice as soothing as what it promised to deliver. Burke waited for the haze to mercifully descend, providing the oblivion that alone kept her out of his consciousness.

Standing at the kitchen window, Josselyn Jeffrey stared into space. She could see the familiar view of Tel Aviv, but her mind was looking past it. The last time she stood this way, she'd prayed to never see Cam again. Her father had stood in the doorway, trying to ease her pain. He had always tried and usually succeeded. But not that time. She'd wanted the pain. As much as her mother had. In the end, no matter how hard she tried not to be like her mother, she'd become her. Perhaps she tried *too* hard.

Her mother. Her father. Cameron. One by one, she'd lost them all. They'd each slipped away, out of her grasp, out of her reach. Had she held on too tight or not tight enough? She knew she would always wonder, but would she ever know for sure?

God, how she wished Nat were there with her now. Natalie was all she had left in the wake of her father's sudden death from a massive coronary a few weeks after the Yom Kippur War broke out, followed by Cam's sudden disappearance during one of the fiercest battles. As a correspondent assigned to cover the war by Reuters, she'd been able to track what was happening to him. Even though she'd vowed never to see him again, she knew she would always love him and need to know that he was all right.

She'd promised her father that she would stay out of harm's way, but he ought to have known that she would never be able to keep such a promise and still garner the journalistic accolades that she'd become all but obsessed with attaining. Had his concern for her safety precipitated his fatal heart attack? She knew she would always wonder about that too.

The worst part was that she hadn't even gotten to say good-bye, to say one last I love you that she would have meant with all her heart and soul—both of which were now in tatters. She had gotten to say good-bye and I love you to her mother, whom she had neither understood nor realized how much she loved until those last moments. But her father, whom she had adored unabashedly and unequivocally for her entire life, had slipped out of her life without a parting word. Not even the chance to say she was sorry for reneging on her promise to stay out of danger. Perhaps there was no need. He knew she was sorry, and he knew she loved him. He would have said that where love exists, there is no need to apologize or to say good-bye.

Josselyn blinked back her tears, briskly brushing away one bold enough to seep out of the corner of her eye when she'd willed them all back. No time for tears or grief now; she was leaving Israel in less than an hour. Directing her gaze downward, she noticed a cab waiting at the curb and realized it was the one she'd called.

She breezed out of the kitchen, picked up the suitcase that held the few belongings she hadn't already shipped stateside, and exited the apartment without looking back.

"Do you know where you are?" asked the now-familiar soothing voice.

"Heaven?" Burke teased, catching a glimpse of auburn curls and a creamy complexion. He could see well enough through the eye-holes in his bandages, as long as what he looked at was directly in front of him.

"At least I know you're feeling better," she teased back, turning to face him.

He was pleased to see she was pretty. Not beautiful. Not haunting. So much the better. Pretty suited him just fine.

"Nice green eyes," he remarked.

"Thanks. Yours too."

"Mine are blue."

"I know. I can see them. I meant yours are nice too."

"Thanks."

She smiled at him. A sunny smile. Completely ingenuous and devoid of mystery. That suited him just fine too.

"I'm Patricia Callahan."

"I read your nametag. I'm Cameron Burke."

"I read your chart." She smiled again.

So she had a sense of humor. That was good. But better was the fact that she was as unlike Josselyn Jeffrey as she could possibly be. Not that he could imagine any woman being even remotely like Josselyn, but the farther from the possibility, the better. The haunting of his body, mind, heart, and soul would be more than enough—a living hell and exquisite torture. More likely than not, he would never see Josselyn again. They had gone their separate ways. More to the point, Josselyn didn't want him. She would have found him if she did—she was a reporter, after all. She didn't want him, plain and simple. That was what he had to accept so that he could move on. He was sure of that. Even if he wasn't sure of anything else.

But Patricia Callahan he'd be seeing more of. A lot more, and often, maybe even after she was no longer his nurse.

Burke observed Patricia's continually sunny efficiency as she notated his chart. "Do you know where you are?" she asked again, as if the intervening conversation had not happened.

"Not heaven?"

"No, but I am flattered."

"Does that mean you'll go out with me?"

"Aren't you getting a little ahead of yourself, Burke?"

"Cam."

"Okay. Aren't you getting a little ahead of yourself, Cam?"

"I'm an eternal optimist, Nurse Callahan."

"Patricia."

"See? It paid off."

Patricia laughed.

"Does that mean you'll go out with me, Patricia?"

"Yes, it does, Cam. I mean, when you get those bandages off and you're out of traction," she added quickly.

"Sure about that? Don't want to wait to see what's under the bandages?"

"Nope. I'm an eternal optimist too." She smiled when she said it and then resumed her nurse's tone. "Try to get some rest. I'll be back when I finish the rest of my rounds."

"Where am I, Patricia?"

"I can't tell you. You have to tell me. I'm sorry, Cam. Doctor's orders. It'll come to you when you least expect it. Don't try so hard," she soothed, placing a gentle hand on his bandaged brow.

Patricia turned, smiling at him over her shoulder as she walked away, and he felt his spirits lift a bit. Life would go on—no matter what lay beneath the bandages, no matter what bones were broken. His body would heal, sooner or later, and he would learn how to live with whatever scars remained. Even the ones that would never disappear from his heart. He kept watching Patricia until she was out of sight.

Patricia Callahan knew Cameron Burke's memory would return because, whenever the morphine took over, he always mumbled the same name over and over again: Josselyn. But once the bandages came off, and he no longer needed anything for the pain, Patricia would help him forget her. Whoever she was. She knew she would make him forget because, whoever Josselyn was, she had either driven him away or not known how to keep him.

But Patricia knew how to keep a man like Cameron Burke, and she intended to do exactly that.

⤨

"Tel Aviv. Or at least somewhere in Israel," Burke said decisively the next time Patricia checked on him.

"Good for you, Cam," she said brightly.

If it wouldn't cause him to yelp in pain, he would have grinned in triumph—and relief.

"I was beginning to wonder if I'd ever remember where I was," he admitted.

"Well, it's not where you are, Cam. But it is where you *were*, so it's the place where you would remember being."

"Then where am I?"

"VA hospital."

"Where?"

"Virginia. Not far from DC."

"How did I get here?"

"You were flown stateside once your condition was stable."

"Patricia, what happened to me? I need to know how bad it is."

"You should wait for the doctor to tell you."

"I want you to tell me."

"I can't, Cam."

"Please, Patricia," he said softly, inching his unbandaged left hand toward hers and grasping it. "Please," he said again.

Arching an eyebrow, Patricia acquiesced. "All right, but it has to be our secret that I told you."

"My word of honor."

Patricia smiled. A man like Cameron Burke wouldn't use such a phrase lightly.

"You were in an explosion. A land mine blew up. You saved three people and nearly got yourself killed," she told him. "You're a real hero," she finished, her voice holding the exact measure of adoration she knew he needed to hear.

"Thanks." He squeezed her hand.

"Cam, you really need to talk to the doctor about the details." She slipped her hand out of his.

"What is that supposed to mean, Patricia? Whatever it is, just tell me." He steeled himself for the worst.

"They won't know if you'll walk again until they take you out of traction." She said the words quickly to be sure she got them all out, adding softly, "I'm sorry, Cam. I didn't want to be the one to tell you."

"I wouldn't have wanted to hear it from anyone else."

She was astounded by his calm reaction. "You did hear what I said, didn't you, Cam?"

"I heard you: I might be paralyzed; they won't know till they take me out of traction."

"Aren't you ... scared?"

Burke looked at her for a few seconds before he answered. "I was a New York City firefighter and a soldier in Vietnam before ... what happened in Tel Aviv. Whatever happens, happens. I've knowingly put myself in harm's way too many times to worry."

"I didn't ask if you were worried, Cam. I asked if you were scared."

Again, he paused before answering. Longer this time.

"I'd be scared to death, and so would anyone else with a lick of sense," she blurted out before she could stop herself.

"I guess I don't have much sense then," he said.

"I'm sorry. I shouldn't have said that." Patricia flushed deep red.

"Why not?"

"Because I'm your nurse. I've crossed the line. … I'm supposed to take care of you, not—"

"Not what?"

"Fall in love with you," she whispered, looking him straight in the eye.

Burke knew he would never get Josselyn back, but he could do far worse than Patricia Callahan, who was pretty and kind and adored him. Even though Josselyn was the only woman he would ever really love, he would be a good husband to Patricia. That is, if she would have him … if he weren't paralyzed and disfigured … *if* …

Forcing the thoughts from his mind, he reached for her hand again with his unbandaged one. "You sure it was wise to tell me that before you see how things turn out?" She did not take her hand away this time.

"Nothing will change how I feel about you," she said. She entwined her fingers with his, and he clasped her hand tight.

"I'll see to it you never change your mind," he said.

As Patricia Callahan smiled at him, Cameron Burke vowed to keep that promise. And Patricia vowed to drive Josselyn—whoever she was—out of his heart forever.

Josselyn moved through her parents' brownstone like an automaton. Of course, it was her brownstone now. All she had left of them. *Not all,* she chided herself. She had other things … memories … love. True, she would have those wherever she went, but she still needed the house. This was home: the place where she felt safe. She wondered how much of that safety was the house itself, the four walls of solid brick, and how much was her parents. Her father, really. Her mother had never helped her feel safe.

Don't think about it now. Plenty of time for that later.

She let her gaze drift around the room and then toward the window. The Twin Towers were finished. Soaring steel sentinels, piercing the sky with insouciant defiance. Already, they were the subject of fierce criticism. Too mighty, too fearless, too sleek. "Too American," the critics might just as well have said. But she loved the towers, not in spite of those criticisms but because of them. Loved her country in the same way. Maybe because that was the best way that she could thank her parents for all they'd sacrificed so that she could be born to live in freedom.

The doorbell rang, and she hurried to answer it, knowing it would be Natalie. She was eager to see her best friend. Rachel Tevner had been diagnosed with, and then succumbed to, ovarian cancer shortly after the Jeffreys left for Israel, and the rabbi had suffered a stroke two days after he and Natalie got up from shivah. A week later, Natalie was sitting shivah again. Josselyn had offered to come home each time, but Natalie wouldn't hear of it. Josselyn wondered if she could ever be that strong. Her own parents' deaths were separated by some time, at least, and she had never shared the closeness with her mother that Natalie and Rachel had always enjoyed. Natalie insisted that was exactly what enabled her to get through it all. Death had not separated her from her parents. Love was unending. Immortal. Eternal. Josselyn sighed as she reached the front door, wishing she could believe that as unequivocally as her friend did.

She opened the door for Natalie, and the two friends threw themselves into each other's arms. They would have to be each other's family now. Closing and locking the door behind Natalie, Josselyn linked arms with her friend, and the two of them headed for the kitchen.

"Want some coffee?"

"How about tea?"

"Tea?!"

"It's more soothing," Natalie said, reaching into her pocket and pulling out two teabags, which she waved in Josselyn's face.

Josselyn rolled her eyes, plucking the teabags from Natalie's fingers.

"Do you want to be a jangle of nerves your whole life?"

"Writers drink coffee."

"Uh-huh. That's why they're all nuts."

As they walked through the dining room and into the kitchen, Josselyn released Natalie's arm and turned toward the stove. Putting the teabags on the counter, she filled a kettle with water, set it on the stove to boil, and then turned to put up the coffee for herself.

"Why not try the tea? Think of it as an adventure."

"An adventure," Josselyn echoed.

"Yeah. Aren't writers supposed to be adventurous?"

Josselyn shrugged as she scooped coffee into the filter.

"What about Hemingway?" Natalie pressed. "He was an adventurer, for sure."

Josselyn nodded, the fantasy of herself as "the next Hemingway" flashing through her mind. All that seemed like a lifetime ago. "And a big coffee drinker," she said.

"I know how he felt about alcohol," Natalie retorted. "His coffee drinking never made headlines."

"It didn't have to, Nat. It's a given. All writers are coffee drinkers."

Natalie said nothing.

"Anyway, I'm more into emulating Carson McCullers at the moment," Josselyn added.

"She was a coffee drinker?"

"I'm certain she must have been."

"I see," Natalie enunciated deliberately, exaggerating what she knew Josselyn thought of as her "shrink tone."

Josselyn looked at her over her shoulder. "Nat, don't—"

"Carson McCullers is your role model."

"What's wrong with that? She wrote her masterpiece at twenty-three."

"Bully for her, Joss. She also suffered a stroke, lived in constant pain, and attempted suicide. None of which had anything to do with her being a caffeine addict, I'm sure. Let alone whatever else she was addicted to."

"I'm impressed you know so much about her," Josselyn remarked. "You didn't mention she was quite a drinker and smoked like a fiend."

Natalie rolled her eyes.

"But a caffeine addict! Nat, whoever heard of such a thing?" Josselyn laughed, finished setting up the percolator, and turned it on. She joined Natalie where she sat at the kitchen table.

"Laugh all you want, but it's true. I'm following a study on it. Caffeine is connected to anxiety, strokes, and high blood pressure. The conclusions in this study will make medical history; you mark my words."

"If you say so, doctor."

"Does that mean you'll try the tea?"

Josselyn shook her head.

Natalie narrowed her eyes. "Have you heard a word I've said? Are you going to wait to read the study?"

"No. I have no intention of reading the study. I love coffee, and I'm not giving it up. Besides, doesn't tea have caffeine?"

"Fractional amount compared to coffee."

"I'm not going to have a stroke, Nat."

"My father didn't think he was, either. He practically had a coffee IV." Natalie locked eyes with her friend.

Josselyn relented. "Okay. Tea. And I promise to give up coffee."

Josselyn shut off the whistling kettle, took two mugs from one of the cabinets, and scooped up the two teabags from the counter. She tore off and discarded the tea packets, put one teabag in each of the mugs, and poured in the boiling water. The tags of the teabags lifted lightly with the briskness of her steps as she carried the steaming mugs back to the table. Setting one mug in front of Natalie and one at her own place, she sat down.

As Natalie sipped her tea, Josselyn sighed, missing her coffee already.

"I know it's not the same," Natalie soothed. "I missed it at first, but—"

"All right, all right. I won't have you worrying that I'll have a stroke."

"Look at it this way, Pearl S. Buck won the Nobel Prize for Literature, and I'm sure she was a tea drinker, Joss. I mean she grew up in China, so how could she not have been?"

Josselyn smiled at her friend. "Can't argue with that."

"We can have Chinese every night."

"It's growing on me," Josselyn said, sipping the tea tentatively and grimacing.

"I told you it takes getting used to, but you'll learn to love it."

"Don't push it, Nat."

"It's better with fortune cookies." Natalie grinned.

Josselyn grinned back. "It couldn't be worse." To change the subject, she told Nat her theory about why she loved the towers. Finishing with, "What do you think?"

"You've read too much Ayn Rand."

"I'm calling Imperial Dragon to deliver lo mein."

Natalie grinned again. Chinese food was her secret vice, a nonkosher treat she indulged in at the Jeffreys' without her parents' knowledge, though now she suspected her mother had known all along. It didn't matter any longer. In the place they were now, her parents would forgive her.

"Chicken," Natalie said.

"I wasn't going to give you pork or shrimp, for goodness sake."

"Some things I just can't do."

"I know."

Josselyn went to the phone, placed the order, and turned to face Natalie. "Aren't you going to ask me how I'm dealing with my father's dying, Nat? Don't you think it's weird that I haven't brought it up when it's why I asked you to come over?"

"Grieving is personal, Joss. When you're ready to talk about it, you will—and I'll be here."

"I don't even have a grave to visit." Her father had insisted on cremation, had specified it in his will.

"It doesn't matter. You carry the loss and the pain with you, and the happy memories too. The love most of all. Be glad he didn't give you the burden of a grave. It's depressing to go … and to leave. Take it from me."

"I hadn't thought of it that way," Josselyn said. She hadn't been to her mother's grave since the burial. "Losing my mother felt so … different. My father was everything to me."

Natalie walked to where Josselyn stood, putting her arms around her friend. "You don't have to change the way you feel about your father. Ever. He's with you always."

"Then why does it feel like I've lost him forever?"

"Maybe because you're trying too hard to hold on to what was."

Josselyn pulled back to look at her friend, staring at her uncomprehendingly.

"You have to let him go, Joss. Only the love you have for each other is left now, and that can only be felt, not held."

Arching an eyebrow at her friend, Josselyn said, "Philosophy *and* psychiatry now?"

Natalie shrugged. "It makes sense, doesn't it?"

"Theoretically. Easier said than done, I'm sure."

"So are most things that important," Natalie smiled.

"Then I guess I've got a lot of work cut out for me."

"Everyone does, Joss. No hurry. It'll be there when you're ready to tackle it. No one else is going to do the work for you."

Josselyn smiled, but in the back of her mind, she knew her father wasn't the only one she was trying to let go of. But she wasn't ready to tell Natalie about Cam. Not yet.

Months later, Cameron Burke waited in wild anticipation for the doctor to remove his remaining bandages. He felt as if he'd been waiting his entire life for those bandages to come off his face and head. For the first time in his life, he was afraid. It would be easier if Patricia weren't going to see what was beneath the bandages before he was, but there was nothing he could do about that. Nothing he could do about any of it. Burke had never thought of himself as good-looking—and had never really cared whether women thought he was good-looking—but he did care about being disfigured. And not just about how Patricia would feel if he were disfigured. She had said it wouldn't matter, and he knew she meant it. Her training as a nurse notwithstanding, he didn't want to be with a woman who pitied him. Nor did he want to spend the rest of his life knowing that other people were staring at him in horror, disgust, pity, or some combination thereof.

I'll deal with it … whatever it is, he told himself hastily, pushing to the back of his mind the thought that he was relieved Josselyn wouldn't have to see him this way. He chastised himself, thinking of Patricia and how much she adored him, but knowing that Josselyn would haunt him forever. There was no getting around that. She was the woman he'd never stop thinking about, never stop missing, never stop wanting. Hers was the love he would never forget. He told himself that it wasn't as if he didn't care for Patricia; he did. It was just different. And it always would be. But what could he do? He'd tried to come back into Josselyn's life when he knew he would be in Israel, but she hadn't wanted him to. For the umpteenth time, he reminded himself that he had to just accept that and move on.

And moving on was just easier with Patricia there to move on to. Besides, he had promised Josselyn that he wouldn't consign himself to a life alone. And he never could have envisioned what pain and misery his choosing to make a life with Patricia would cause in the future.

Patricia and the doctor arrived at last, cutting short Burke's reverie. Giving crisp directives to Patricia, the doctor removed the bandages swiftly. The air felt cool against Burke's skin once the last layer of gauze was unwound. He scanned Patricia's face for signs of the horrible disfigurement he had been steeling himself for, but she was inscrutable.

"You've healed far beyond what we expected," the doctor told Burke. "Nurse Callahan will take it from here."

"How bad is it?" Burke wanted to know. When they removed the bandages from the rest of his body, it hadn't been too bad. Some scarring on his inner arms, but they would heal. He hoped his face had fared as well as the rest of him, but he'd known too many burn victims to believe that hope stood much of a chance.

"I'll get you a mirror. You can see for yourself," Patricia said.

"I can make it to the mirror by myself," Burke retorted, motioning to the crutches beside his bed. He'd come out of traction a week prior, finding to his great relief that he was not paralyzed. "I'm asking you because I want to know what you think before I see it for myself."

"You look good to me, Cam," she said, applying some salve to the skin below his jaw and on and around his ears. "I wouldn't lie to you."

Burke looked into Patricia's eyes and knew she wasn't lying.

"Let's go take a look," he said, starting to get up and reach for the crutches in the same movement.

"Hold still and let me finish."

Burke did as he was told, swinging off the bed and onto the crutches Patricia held for him after she finished tending his skin.

The walk to the mirror a hundred yards away felt like miles. The only glimmer of hope was Patricia's green-eyed smile of encouragement, coupled with the adeptness he'd achieved on his crutches within so short a space of time. He wouldn't need to be on them much longer, but it felt good to have mastered them nonetheless, especially after feeling utterly useless for so long. Uselessness was a feeling Cameron Burke could not abide.

Deliberately averting his eyes from the mirror as they neared it, Burke looked at Patricia instead. She squeezed his hand where it held the crutch, placing her other hand on his shoulder.

"It's all right. Look for yourself," she encouraged.

Better to just get it over with. Burke lifted his head and looked square into the mirror at his own reflection, surprised to see not an unrecognizable version of himself, but the self he remembered—just with skin that seemed redder than it ought to be, more like a severe sunburn than an explosion's handiwork.

"It really isn't that bad," he told Patricia, as if she hadn't been telling him the same thing all along.

"I'll never lie to you, Cam."

He peered closer. Below his jaw and on and around his ears, the skin was still pretty raw. He knew he'd have some scarring, but it didn't matter. Seeing himself whole and almost the same as he had been before gave him a jolt of he wasn't sure what—hope, courage, strength, joy, gratitude, perhaps a mixture of all of them—and he felt alive, really alive, for the first time in he couldn't remember how long.

"When do I get out of here?" he asked Patricia as she led him back to bed.

"What's your hurry? Don't you like the nurses?"

"Well there's one who's really something."

"Uh-huh."

"And she promised to go out with me when I get out of here, so …"

"Well, you'll be here a while longer, so you have plenty of time to plan a pretty fantastic first date."

Burke laughed.

Patricia smiled at him, and he knew everything would turn out all right. He would begin to live again in earnest—without Josselyn.

During the months that followed Josselyn's return to the States, she went through the motions of living, but only felt half-alive. She didn't know how Natalie, who had been even closer with her parents than Josselyn had been with Bartholomew, was able to move on from a double loss with such grace and fortitude. Recognizing that it must have had something to do with Natalie's philosophy—that love did not die with the person who died—only brought Josselyn more despair. Certainly, that had not been her mother's experience. Her mother had been dead to life and the living for all of Josselyn's life, as well as for most of her own—from the moment her parents had brought her to the platform to board Wallenberg's train. Their saving her even when they knew they would be dragged off to Mauthausen was what her mother had never made peace with, because she'd always believed her parents had traded their lives for hers. Her mother had never gotten to say good-bye either. Josselyn had never specifically thought about that until she had to grapple with her own unsaid good-byes.

One morning, Josselyn awoke, got out of bed, and crossed the room to the windows to look out at the Twin Towers piercing the sky. She realized that she was becoming exactly like her mother: dead to life, just under different circumstances.

And the only way back to life was by living. She wasn't living, would never truly live again except with Cameron.

She had made the choice not to let Cameron back into her life in Tel Aviv because she feared that what they'd had in Vietnam had been magical and could never be repeated in day-to-day life, so it was better not to even try. Hadn't she sworn to herself a million times that she wouldn't waste her life the way her mother had? Her circumstances might not be anything like her mother's—certainly her mother's were indescribably worse—but she would wind up wasting her life the same way her mother had. Never living fully because she was afraid to love.

You're a journalist. You can find Cameron Burke. You can and you will.

With that, she breezed out of the bedroom and went to take a shower. From this day forward, things would be different. Josselyn Jeffrey had come back to life.

When Josselyn arrived at her desk in the New York Times newsroom later that morning, she sent a Telex to Reuters in Tel Aviv, asking about Cameron. Because of the time difference, she knew she wouldn't hear back until the following day at the earliest, but at least she'd made a start. That was enough for now.

With her mind clear, she started on her work for the day, lifting her head at the sound of a familiar voice coming from the front of the newsroom, near the editor's desk: *Luke Lanvin!*

In the next instant, she was out of her chair and hurrying to where he stood, saying his name aloud.

Luke turned and burst into a grin at the sight of her, moving forward to kiss her cheek and give her a hug. After exchanging greetings, they arranged to have lunch that day to catch up.

The morning sped by as Josselyn lost herself in the story she was writing, and before she knew it, Luke was at the corner of her desk, hat in hand. He extended his arm, and she took it. They left the Gray Lady, the term of affection for the building that housed the Times, and headed for a nearby deli.

"The work you did in Israel was first-rate, kid. You'll be on the short list for every journalism award worth winning."

Josselyn dismissed such a thought with the wave of her hand.

"Oh I get it. Only your father can win awards?"

"Luke, I've only just started. Look at all the veterans I'd be competing with."

"Wasn't your father pretty young when he won his first?"

Josselyn nodded.

"I read your stuff, kid. Start writing the acceptance speech."

Josselyn only laughed in reply, but she couldn't help feeling pleased. Acclaim as a journalist was all she'd ever wanted. Till she met Cam, and even then, loving him had not been enough to make her set aside her lifelong dreams and ambitions. She mentally shoved the thought away; she would do what she could to find Cam, but she couldn't think about all that right now.

"What about you, Luke? What have you been up to?"

"Vietnam just got to be too … intense. I had to come home. I'm glad you left when you did." *No place for a woman*, he'd been about to say, but with this whole feminism thing, you couldn't be too careful.

"You did good work over there, Luke."

"Thanks, kid."

"What happened to IQ?"

"He'll stay forever. The place suits him." A Saigon whore was the only way a guy like Carlton Quiggley could ever get laid, but Luke wasn't about to say that to Josselyn.

Josselyn nodded. "I know what you mean. What a creep." She slowed her pace. "This is it," she said, stopping in front of the deli.

Luke opened the door and steered her inside.

"So whatever happened with you and that soldier you knew in Nam?"

"We sort of lost touch," she said, sitting down on a stool at the counter.

Luke took the stool next to hers. "Sorry."

"War has all kinds of casualties, I suppose."

"He'd be crazy to leave you unless he was one of them." The instant he saw the expression on her face, Luke regretted his words. "I meant it as a compliment, kid," he added hastily.

"I know," she patted his arm. "It's just … complicated. Let's talk about something else."

They each ordered hot pastrami on rye with mustard, then turned to talking about Luke's daughter, who had left the master's program at Berkeley to study law. She was a public defender now. Their disparate views on politics and government continued to be a bone of contention. They hadn't spoken since his return from Vietnam.

Josselyn couldn't think of a thing she would not give for one last conversation with her father. She willed herself to swallow the lump in her throat, smiling at Luke so he wouldn't suspect she was falling apart.

Soon she would know where Cam was. She'd call him, tell him that she realized she'd made a terrible mistake, and they'd be together again. And this time she wouldn't ever let him go.

Focusing all his energy on recuperation, Burke made incredible strides in his recovery, amazing the entire staff of the VA hospital, Patricia most of all. Having progressed from crutches to a cane, he went for a walk around the hospital grounds one afternoon. Patricia took her break and found him pausing beneath an enormous Dutch elm.

"You're being discharged next week, Cam." He heard Patricia's voice behind him, a sudden interruption in his stream of consciousness. She had the unnerving habit of sneaking up on him this way. He hoped he'd learn to get used to it, knowing he'd never break her of it.

"That's great news." He turned to face her, leaning against the tree and extending his hand to her.

Patricia clasped his hand, and he pulled her toward him. "Don't let on that I told you, Cam. Wait till the doctor gives you the official word."

He nodded.

With tentative fingers, she stroked the scars beneath his jaw. "Any pain?"

Burke shook his head, and Patricia knew it was in earnest because he no longer winced. In the first weeks following the removal of his bandages, he had cringed at even the lightest, gentlest touch. Patricia liked to think it was her nursing skills— more so even than Cam's tenacity and iron will—that had wrought his miraculously swift recovery.

"I've decided to accept the posting at the Pentagon," he told her abruptly. A few weeks before, he'd been notified of the opportunity by a lieutenant colonel who had told him to take his time considering; the job would be his if he wanted it. The prospect of it alone had spurred his convalescence. Burke was itching to get back to work.

A look of dismay clouded Patricia's green eyes before she could stop it.

Burke didn't miss it. "This is what I do," he said quietly, squeezing her hand harder. "You knew that."

"Of course," she said quickly, her eyes bright again. "You'll never really feel completely yourself again until you're back to doing what you do." Inwardly, the prospect of Cam's returning to the arms of danger terrified Patricia. She could feel darts of fear pricking her insides, but she forced herself to ignore them. Cameron Burke was the kind of man she'd always dreamed of, and she wasn't about to scare him off.

"You sure you're okay about being with a cloak-and-dagger guy?" Burke teased, but he was sincere about wanting her to be sure. It was a tall order for a woman to be involved with an operative. Far taller than Patricia could possibly envision, even though Burke knew she really did love him—with a kind of hero worship mixed in that boosted his ego enough to make him not pay attention to the potential problems of being involved with a woman who related to him through the veil of adoration.

"As long as you're the cloak-and-dagger guy, yes."

"I'd better be." He winked at her, and she smiled.

"I've got to get back, Cam. Coming?"

"In a while."

"Don't stay out here too long, sweetheart." She dropped her voice at the last word, letting it hang in the air like a lingering caress.

"I won't, honey." There was only one woman he could ever call "baby," and he was glad Patricia hadn't called him "darling." He wouldn't have been able to bear having any woman but Josselyn call him that; inwardly, he could still hear her voice forming the word.

Patricia smiled over her shoulder at him as she walked away. He watched her until she disappeared into the hospital, and then he turned back and resumed staring off into space. He couldn't start his job at the Pentagon or his life with Patricia too soon. Not that he'd officially proposed, but he knew she would say yes. He didn't want to be discharged from the hospital before asking Patricia to marry him. Tonight. Right after she went off duty … yes, that would be perfect.

When a prestigious journalism award's short list came out and her own name was on it, Josselyn's first reaction was shock. It quickly turned to sheer delight and a deep sense of fulfillment. She thought of her father not living to witness her achievement, and her grief returned full force, as if she were losing him all over again. Sitting at her desk in the Times newsroom, she was all but overwhelmed by her sadness.

Picking up the phone, she dialed Natalie's number to share the good news and also to get a pep talk. When Natalie answered, Josselyn blurted out the news without taking a breath.

"That's fantastic!"

"I still can't believe it."

Natalie didn't miss the catch in Josselyn's voice. "Your father isn't missing this, you know. Wherever he is, he knows."

But I can't tell him, can't see his smile light up the room because he's so thrilled. All Josselyn said was, "I know."

"There's someone else you can tell who'd be just as excited, you know," Natalie put in.

Natalie meant Cam, of course. Josselyn had managed to track him down at a VA hospital in Virginia, and she'd called and left several messages, but they'd all gone unreturned. Josselyn had decided this was Cam's way of letting her know that he'd tried to come back into her life in Israel, but she had ignored him, and so that was the end of it. Natalie had argued that was too simple an answer. People's reactions in relationships were far more complex than that. When Josselyn had hedged pursuing it further, Natalie had told her point-blank that she was just afraid of finding out what there really was between her and Cam. Josselyn had feigned an argument, just to save her pride, but deep down she knew Natalie was absolutely right: She was terrified of being reunited with Cam and discovering that what had once felt so powerful and magical now felt meaningless. It was better *not* to know. She would keep her treasured memories deep in her heart—safe, where nothing could destroy them.

Her idea to win him back had been foolish, and she was done trying.

"Does your silence mean you're considering calling him, or are you still being an idiot?" Natalie pressed.

"I'm not being an idiot," Josselyn shot back. She knew Natalie had said it to make her angry. It was in keeping with Natalie's theory that anger was the most organizing emotion, the galvanizer to action.

"Hmm. You're here, he's where he is, and you're both still crazy about each other. Does that make sense to you?"

"I don't know that he's still crazy about me."

"And at this rate, you never will."

"I'll think about it."

"Great. Don't wait a month to call him, Joss. You want to have a date for my wedding, don't you?" Natalie was marrying a fellow psych resident at Bellevue. The wedding was a couple of months away.

"If you keep bugging me, I'm not coming to your wedding."

Natalie laughed on the other end. "Fine. Just pick *someone* to bring. I don't want you coming to my wedding without a date. You'll be miserable."

Josselyn couldn't bring herself to even think about being with any man but Cam. She still compared other men to Cam, finding all of them lacking, even after all this time. There was no point in dating; she would never be able to sleep with another man. ... Not out of morality, but because of the pain she knew she would feel. It was easier to live without men. Period.

"I've gotta go, Nat, I'm on deadline. Talk to you later."

"Bye."

They hung up.

Josselyn hadn't told Natalie that she'd called the VA and left a message for Cam again less than a week before and still hadn't heard back from him. She couldn't let herself consider for too long that perhaps he'd been so badly injured that he couldn't contact her, or didn't remember her, or didn't want her to see him in a horrible condition. Thoughts along those lines filtered into her consciousness, and she forced them out of it, turning back to her typewriter. As always, work settled her. A few lines down, she all but forgot about her troubles. As soon as she finished this up, she'd leave for the day. Luke Lanvin had invited her out for a drink to celebrate her making the short list.

All she had to do was focus on her achievements, and she'd be fine. This was what she'd always dreamed of, always lived for. Cameron Burke was just a sweet memory from a lifetime ago, more imagined than real. She simply would not consign herself to a lifetime of regret and resultant despair. From this moment on, she would do what she was meant to do—what she'd always intended to do—write. The more acclaim and prestige she garnered along the way, the better. She would work as hard as she had to, focus single-mindedly, and that would leave no room for thinking about—or feeling—anything else.

Rolling the paper out of her typewriter, Josselyn dropped the copy on the editor's desk on her way out of the newsroom. And she left her memories of Cameron Burke metaphorically behind her forever—or at least she prayed as much.

Patricia leaned back gently against the metal rack in the supply closet. Cameron had told her to wait for him there after she got off duty, promising he had something to tell her and needed privacy. She let the anticipation flood her as she waited for him, tilting her head back and jostling a roll of gauze off the shelf. As she knelt to retrieve it, Cameron approached the closet, stepping inside. Setting a lit candle on an empty corner of the opposite rack of shelving, he closed the door behind him.

He tossed his cane aside and took her in his arms. Patricia wrapped her arms around his neck, pressing herself against him harder than she'd meant to. But she had longed for him for so long that it was more an involuntary response than anything else. Cameron leaned her back in his arms and kissed her, sending a jolt of pleasure through her body, shocking her initially but then warming her all over. She returned his kiss and nuzzled against him when their lips parted.

"Was this what you wanted to tell me?"

Burke shifted her in his arms so he could see her face, and then he smiled at her. "No. I just couldn't help myself."

Patricia blushed. "Neither could I, I guess."

"I apologize if I came on too strong," he said, reminding himself this was a Catholic-school girl, and they weren't in a war zone.

"No, no," Patricia said quickly. "You didn't offend me, Cam. I wanted you to."

In truth, he didn't trust himself to stay with her this way for too long. Better to say what he had to say and get out of there. They'd have the rest of their lives to make love.

He wanted to be poetic, romantic, but with the moment upon him, forgot everything he'd meant to say. "Patricia, will you marry me?"

Against her better judgment, which counseled her not to marry a man who hadn't yet told her he loved her, Patricia said yes. She knew that, in time, he would tell her he loved her, and she loved him so much that she wouldn't mind waiting. Suddenly she thought about all the phone messages from Josselyn Jeffrey. Knowing that this had to be the Josselyn of Cam's morphine-induced dreams, Patricia had disposed of the messages before he could receive them. She quickly dismissed the recollection now. She was going to be Mrs. Cameron Burke, and nothing could stop her, least of all some old flame he seemed to have forgotten. When Cam kissed her again, every doubt vanished from Patricia's mind.

"I love you, Cam," she whispered.

"I love you too, honey," he lied, but he promised himself that he would make her happy. He did care for Patricia, but Josselyn was the love of his life, and he would never love any other woman the way he loved her.

Patricia was pleased that she hadn't had to wait long at all to hear him say the words she'd been waiting—longing—for him to say. Her face shone in the candlelight, and Burke could not resist kissing her once more before he blew out the candle and opened the door.

The time between the publication of the short list and her actually winning the award flew by for Josselyn. The winning itself spun her into a whirlwind of activity. Suddenly everyone at the Times office couldn't wait to get to know her better. Suddenly she was on the fast track. The grief and sorrow that had descended so fiercely when she'd learned she was on the short list did not return when she won. Now she just felt happy and proud, and she kept telling herself that this was only the beginning.

At lunch one day, Luke grinned at her above the rim of his glass of Dr. Brown's Cel-Ray Tonic. "It feels good doesn't it?"

"What?"

"The fame."

"Sure." Josselyn broke into her potato knish with her fork, waving her hand through the steam that rose from it.

"As good as you'd imagined?" Luke pressed, taking a mammoth bite of his corned-beef club.

"I guess so." She nibbled a sour pickle.

Luke sipped more Cel-Ray Tonic, and then he asked, "What is it, kid?"

"It's nothing. I'm just being silly." She dove into her knish before he could catch her eye, burning her tongue in the process and needing to take a quick slug of ginger ale.

When she looked up, Luke's eyes locked with hers, and he set down his sandwich.

"It's just that there's no one to share it with. Aside from good friends, I mean."

"I knew what you meant. Trouble is, if you work hard enough to win the awards, you usually don't have time to work on anything else—people included."

"I suppose." But she thought of her father, who'd always had all the time in the world for his work, for her mother, and for her—his love had been a constant, pervasive presence, even when he was on assignment half a world away.

"Your problem is, you have no idea how young you are. You have all the time in the world to do whatever you want. Don't give yourself such a hard time."

Josselyn smiled at her friend. She wouldn't tell Luke about how much she wanted her father to be there, afraid that it might open the wounds from his estrangement with his own daughter. Then, too, she remembered her promise to herself that she wasn't going to let anything spoil the joy of accomplishment she felt. "You're absolutely right, Luke."

"You know, kid, when I'm down about things, I just write it out." Luke waited for her to take in what he'd said, polishing off the rest of his corned-beef club and chasing it with a swig of Cel-Ray Tonic.

"You mean in a journal?"

"Yeah. Or a novel."

"You're writing a novel?!"

"No, about thirty of them. Never finished a one."

"Why not?"

"Hemingway looming too large," Luke chuckled. "Truth to tell, I'm just a newspaperman. The editor's desk is the farthest I'll go. I'll never be a novelist. I'm too hard-boiled. I have fun writing them, though, and I learn a lot about myself."

"Are you saying that I have a lot of material, or that I'm so screwed up I really need to do something about it? Or am I just soft-boiled?"

"You're more … poached. And you're the least screwed-up person I know, kid. You just expect too much of yourself." Luke finished his Cel-Ray Tonic and motioned to the waitress for another. "If you wrote your parents' story from the war, it'd be a bestseller for sure. Might even get to put another prize on the mantel." He winked at her.

Josselyn laughed, but she was hooked. Her parents' story. Why hadn't she ever thought of writing it before? A book was exactly what she needed to sink her teeth into—something that would completely consume her attention for an indeterminate amount of time. Finishing her ginger ale, she grinned at Luke, scarcely able to wait for the day to end so she could go home and start her new opus. Ever since Natalie had gotten married, Josselyn found it harder to fill her free time.

The book absorbed Josselyn utterly, proving a far more therapeutic endeavor than anything Natalie could have suggested, as Nat herself was the first to agree. Deciding that she didn't want to reveal all the personal details of her parents' lives when she hadn't asked their permission, Josselyn turned their story into a novel, which she called *From Ashes to Hope*. She wrote it in record time, finding that once she began, the story flew out of her more quickly than she could type the words. Every free night and weekend she immersed herself in the book, relishing being able to savor the words, a luxury she could never indulge in as a journalist. A few months and four hundred manuscript pages later, the book was finished. Her reputation as an award-winning journalist made it easy to find an agent, and even easier to be signed by a good publisher. It seemed that before she knew it, she had received her advance check and was checking copyedited pages. Even more quickly it seemed, the book was done, off to press, and soon to be out in stores.

She couldn't imagine feeling happier or more fulfilled, and her publisher and editor had already asked her to write a second book: this one about her experiences in Vietnam. Josselyn had eagerly agreed, hoping that the second exercise would prove as therapeutic as the first.

Marking the day of the book's official release on the calendar, she counted down the days to it in her head and began to plot out her second book. She planned to call that one *Lower than Heaven,* a reference to the Eastern conception of earth as a middle ground between heaven and hell.

Cameron Burke rolled onto his side lazily, relishing the Sunday that allowed him to stay in bed until after the sun had risen. He reached out to put his arms around Patricia, who stirred slightly before settling sleepily into his embrace. Scanning her sleeping face, he was glad to see no lines on her brow. Patricia was a good wife, loving and devoted, and her daily ministrations had all but erased his scars. He had married a woman with magic fingers. He smiled to himself at all the delightful implications of that particular talent.

Patricia opened her eyes and turned in his arms, kissing his neck below the vestigial scars. "Hungry?"

"Sure," he growled playfully, pulling her on top of him.

"I meant for breakfast."

"I didn't."

Patricia laughed. "You're such an animal. Don't you ever get enough?"

A similar line of conversation from another time and place—another lifetime—flickered across the screen of his mind, but Burke shut it out, covering his wife's mouth with kisses so he wouldn't have to answer her question.

He drew her harder against him, rolling her beneath him and feeling her body respond to his. Patricia enjoyed their lovemaking, gave herself over to the pleasure much more openly than he'd ever thought a Catholic-school girl would. She arched her back now, wrapping her legs around him as he entered her with a fierce swiftness that made her gasp.

Afterward, she reached up and put her hands on either side of his face, drawing it down to hers. "I never thought I could love anyone like this."

Burke said nothing, just kissed her.

"Am I a good wife?"

"The best," Burke assured her, meaning it.

"You weren't hoping for a baby to be on the way by now?"

"No, but I'm enjoying trying."

Patricia sighed.

Burke brushed her hair back from her face, kissing her forehead tenderly and rolling to the side. He took her in his arms. "Honey, we're young, and there's plenty of time for babies."

"I want an army of your children running through this house."

"If that's what you want, it's fine with me."

"Especially making them." She kissed his cheek.

"Especially. How serious are you?"

"Very," she said, reminding him again of just how gifted she was with her fingers.

"So I see," said Cameron Burke, as he began to make love to his wife for the second time that morning.

Natalie pulled another tissue out of the box Josselyn had set in front of her. Dabbing her eyes, Natalie rasped, "How could I have been so stupid?" She blew her nose, crumpled the tissue, and tossed it into the wastebasket.

"There's no way you could have known," Josselyn assured her, pouring tea from a silver teapot into a mug, and then handing the steaming mugful to her friend. Natalie had come home early, intending to surprise her husband, but she was the one who received the surprise: her husband in bed with the college-aged daughter of the couple who lived a few doors away.

Natalie set down her mug to blow her nose again. "I should have seen it. He was always looking at her."

"So what? Men always look at pretty girls." Not a man in the newsroom failed to turn around when a young, pretty secretary from another floor dropped something off. Even Luke Lanvin, whom she liked and admired, would turn to look at a waitress in the middle of their lunchtime conversation and think nothing of it. Josselyn found it more amusing than anything else, redirecting his attention with a dry, "I'm still over here." But then again, Luke was her friend, not her husband. She couldn't imagine how Natalie felt, but she committed to doing whatever she had to do to support her friend.

"She is pretty, and men do always look at pretty girls. You're right about that. But, obviously, he did more than just look."

Josselyn sighed. "That's what you couldn't possibly have known, Nat. Why would you have even dreamed that your husband's looking at a pretty girl—a college kid, no less—meant he was sleeping with her?"

Natalie ignored the question. "Did he ever look at you?"

"Of course not!"

"You probably just missed it, as usual. Men *always* look at you." Natalie rolled her eyes.

Josselyn shrugged. It was true that she missed it when they did. If she wasn't interested, why care if they looked? She was more than her looks, and that was what she wanted a man to notice *along with* her looks. Like Cam had. She directed her attention back to Natalie so she wouldn't have to think about that. "Would you stop beating yourself up about this? Drink your tea. Do you want something to eat?"

Natalie shook her head and then sipped obediently. "What am I going to do?"

"What do you want to do?"

"Dump him! Isn't that what you think I should do?"

"I'm hardly an expert, Nat. Besides, it doesn't matter what anyone else thinks. You have to do what feels right for you. Isn't that what you would tell me?"

"Well ... yes," Natalie admitted. "You don't think I should forgive him, do you?"

"I think you should do what feels right for you," Josselyn persisted. "And I also think that you don't have to decide what that is tonight."

"Hmm. When did you get so wise and philosophical?" Natalie teased.

"Nice role reversal, huh? I give pretty good advice when it isn't *my* crisis." She rubbed Natalie's arm affectionately.

"So do we all, Joss. You just overthink, and you're way too hard on yourself, that's all. Trust me; you do a lot better than most people," Natalie said. "If a patient came to me with this, I would say pretty much what you just told me."

Josselyn nodded. "It's easier to give advice than take it—or advise yourself."

"I know life isn't perfect, Joss. I know it would be a lot worse if he had physically or emotionally abused me."

"But?"

"But deep down I also know that I don't see myself ever being able to forgive him. And part of me recognizes that if we really belonged together—if we were like my parents were—I'd be able to forgive him. But I know I'll never be able to." Natalie blew her nose hard, as if to punctuate what she'd just said. "I don't want to stay married to a man I can't forgive. I'm just postponing trouble."

Josselyn thought Natalie was psychologizing the entire situation—and doing it way too soon—but if it was what she needed to do to get through it, Josselyn wasn't about to judge her for it. Her own coping mechanisms certainly wouldn't work for most people. "If you say so, doctor," was all she said.

"But you're right; I don't have to decide anything tonight."

"Right!"

Natalie laughed in spite of herself. "And on second thought, let's order Chinese."

Josselyn went to get the takeout menu, and Natalie settled back into the sofa cushions, knowing she would have a lot of inner exploration to do, but she didn't have to let the roller coaster of her emotions control her.

As her emotions leveled off, Natalie's usual clear thinking returned. Unconditional love carried acceptance and forgiveness within it, and if she couldn't muster it, what she had thought was love was really something else. Better to correct the problem before it was too late, lest she ruin or waste the rest of her life. She'd seen far too many people do that, patients and otherwise. A lifelong marriage wasn't everyone's destiny, and Natalie could accept that; but a sham marriage was something she couldn't, and wouldn't, accept. Now or ever. She would wait to voice her decision, but she'd already made up her mind.

Patricia Burke pushed her sleeves above her elbows, out of the way of the tops of the rubber gloves she wore, and resumed her vigorous scrubbing of the bathtub. From her perch at the end of the tub, she bent over and leaned in to scrub one of the far corners. When she straightened up, she felt a bit dizzy and chided herself for not listening to what the doctor had told her that morning: bed rest all day.

Slowly bringing her head down again, she rested it between her knees. Whipping off the gloves, she ran the cold water over her left hand, and then pressed her cool, wet hand up against the back of her neck. She repeated the process a couple of times before shutting off the water. After a few minutes, she began to feel better, and she slowly brought herself up straight again.

Leaning back against the tile wall, Patricia closed her eyes against the winter sun creeping in through the bathroom window. The cold tile felt good against her neck. The bathtub's scouring could wait for tomorrow. Why had she been so anxious to do it today? Especially after what the doctor had said. Especially when she was a nurse.

Except that today she hadn't been a nurse, just a woman. A wife. Up until early this morning, she'd been thinking of herself as a mother too. Tentatively, of course; she knew the highest risk of miscarriage was during the first trimester ... but she'd felt fine.

Patricia bit her lip to stave off a fresh spate of tears. Maybe she should just let herself cry, but tears did not come easily to Patricia. Never had. Besides, if she started to cry, she'd have to think about all that she was crying for: losing the baby, having a husband who was away more often than not—and doing life-threatening work, no less. She had thought that Cam's being stationed at the Pentagon would guarantee a normal home life, or at least as normal as could be expected for a military-intelligence operative. But it hadn't turned out that way, and Patricia had learned that an absent husband might just as well be halfway around the world as around the corner if he was going to spend all his time at work. She should just accept it, as her mother had advised. Deep down, though, Patricia knew that the mysterious Josselyn Jeffrey, whoever she was, would have kept Cameron Burke home—but Patricia would never be able to. She knew that now.

No tears, Patricia commanded herself inwardly. God, how she wished Cam would come home. She pressed her neck harder against the tile, hoping the coldness would somehow ease the hot knot of unshed tears constricting her throat.

The familiar sights along the way barely registered in Burke's consciousness as he drove home from the Pentagon. Ice crystals around the moon gave it an otherworldly halo; he noticed that much as he stopped at a red light. He had stayed far longer at the office than necessary. No crisis, national or international, but he'd have to invent something to tell Patricia. A false-alarm type thing, nothing that would make her lose sleep. Some incident averted by the wiles of her husband. And hero. He loved that she still thought of him that way. Something with Red China, he decided. That would work; he never gave her details. Couldn't, of course, so she wouldn't suspect anything.

Turning the wheel to hug the curve of the cul-de-sac, Burke wondered what he was so bent out of shape over. Nothing had really happened. While reading the newspaper—the *New York Times,* not the *Washington Post,* which was the paper he usually read—he'd caught sight of her name. Josselyn Jeffrey. *New York Times* byline. She'd won a major journalism award too; he remembered seeing that. Somehow the award hadn't struck him the way seeing her byline had. Winning an award was a one-time thing; having a byline in a major newspaper was a daily event. To be reminded of her every day was more than he could even bear to think about; he would have to stick with the *Post.*

He told himself he was glad that she had achieved what she'd set out to, and he knew she would be glad to know that he'd done the same. Except that the ache he felt in his heart told him he hadn't achieved anything that meant anything. Not really. Not when seeing her name sent him into a tailspin. Not when he still woke up in the middle of the night unable to rid his mind of the thought of her. It was as if she inhabited the very cells of his body—the scent and taste of her filled him as strongly now as they had years before when he held her in his arms at night. He could almost feel the texture of her skin against his sometimes … intoxicating and intense. And heartbreaking.

There was nothing he could do at moments like that. Nothing could shake the specter of her from his soul. Not even the wife he cared for; the wife who adored him. He just would never be able to love Patricia the way he loved Josselyn—the way he would always love Josselyn. And the worst part of it all was that there wasn't a damn thing he could do about it.

Patricia was fast asleep on the living-room sofa when Burke came into the house. She lay on her side, snuggled beneath an afghan. The upside-down book resting across her hip told him that she must have been waiting up for him. Burke knit his brow. It was better than it would have been if he'd come home unable to stop thinking about Josselyn, and he prided himself on the fact that his wife had no idea of his secret. He had never, and would never, let on.

He hung his overcoat on the coat tree, rested his fedora on top, and then noiselessly set his attaché case on the floor beside it. Stepping gingerly toward the sofa, Burke bent at the knees and gathered Patricia into his arms, wrapping the afghan around her and leaving the book on the sofa. She stirred slightly and then settled against him, her head instinctively finding his shoulder.

"Cam?" she murmured.

"Mm-hmm," he answered, heading toward the stairs.

"Are you all right? I tried to wait up. …" Her voice trailed off into a yawn as she burrowed contentedly against his shoulder.

"It's late, honey. Go to sleep. We'll talk in the morning."

"Mmm …" Patricia managed before sleep overtook her completely.

Burke carried his sleeping wife upstairs, tucked her in beneath the covers, undressed, and slipped into bed beside her, wrapping his arms around her and willing the memories of Josselyn Jeffrey from his mind.

Butter sizzled in the pan as Patricia cracked eggs into it. Cam had just mentioned something about an averted incident with Red China, telling her as casually as if it had been a weather report, and then taking the glass of orange juice she'd handed to him, swallowing its contents, and putting the glass in the sink. Now he sat at the kitchen table, drinking coffee while he waited for his breakfast. Scrambling the eggs and putting two slices of bread in the toaster, Patricia wondered how she could have envisioned herself as suited for this kind of life. She eyed Cam surreptitiously as he read the morning paper between sips of coffee. God, how she loved him. Her heart felt like it would burst with love for him more often than not. But was that enough? She'd thought it was when she married him; she'd thought it always would be. Now she wasn't so sure. Aftereffects of the miscarriage, she told herself. But she wasn't convinced.

Turning off the flame but leaving the eggs in the pan, Patricia opened the cupboard and took out a plate, walking toward the toaster just as the toast popped up. She pulled each piece out with tongs, set them on the side of the plate, and then scooped Cam's eggs out of the pan, leaving them in a steaming mound beside the toast. She brought the plate to him at the table, and he set aside the paper and started to eat.

Crossing back to the counter, Patricia poured herself coffee, joined her husband at the table, and sipped while he ate.

"Now that you know all about Red China, tell me about your day yesterday," Cam said lightly.

Patricia had rehearsed a thousand times what she was going to say. *Just get it over with,* she told herself.

"Cam, I miscarried yesterday. I didn't want to tell you I was pregnant until I was sure." She snapped the words out quickly, expecting to feel better when she finished, but finding that she actually felt worse.

Cam set down the toast he'd been about to butter. He reached across the table and took Patricia's hand in his. "Are you all right?" He looked at her as tenderly as she'd hoped he would.

"I'm fine. The doctor said we can start trying again as soon as I feel ready."

"Then as soon as you're ready, we will." Cam stroked the back of her hand with his thumb. "I should have been with you. Why didn't you call me?"

"What about China?"

"You're more important than China," he told her, still reeling from the shock. While he had been mooning like a fifteen-year-old over Josselyn Jeffrey's byline—and his reminiscences of her charms—his wife had been miscarrying. Alone. *Never again*, he swore to himself, watching Patricia's eyes fill with tears. With the hand that still held hers, he drew her toward him around the table, gathered her into his lap, and held her.

"I'm so sorry, Cam," she whispered, fighting her tears.

He had never known a woman more averse to crying than his wife was. "It's all right, honey. Go ahead and cry." He stroked the back of her head with one hand, his other arm circling her even tighter.

"Crying won't solve anything. I want to have another baby right away." She sat up as she said it, looking down at him slightly from where she sat in his lap.

"If that's what you want, okay." He kissed her.

"Don't you want it too?"

"Of course I do. I just want to make sure you're all right."

"I'm fine. I was only a few weeks along. I am a nurse, you know."

"And a very good one."

189

She fingered the edge of his almost-faded scar. "Finish your eggs and get going." She kissed him and then stood up.

"Yes, ma'am!" Burke was amused. Patricia rarely gave him orders.

"I don't want you to be late tonight. That's all I meant," she added hastily, turning back toward the counter.

He caught her hand and pulled her back, standing up and taking her into his arms. "Patricia, I won't be late." He kissed her again, a deep, full kiss this time. The kind that made her knees go weak. She settled into his arms as he gripped her even tighter, wondering if she'd still melt this way when they were married ten years or twenty or fifty—and praying silently that she would.

Burke tried to convince himself that someday he would no longer be haunted by the deepest passion—and the truest love—he had ever felt with any woman. He knew he would never feel any of that with his wife, but he vowed to be a better husband.

"Go finish your eggs," she said.

Burke kissed the side of her neck just below her ear, and then he did as he was told.

Patricia studied the eggs she was cracking into the pan to scramble for herself, but it was her own eggs she was thinking about. Nothing mattered to her but giving Cam children, because then no one would mean more to him than she did. Not even Josselyn Jeffrey.

"So he's married," Natalie said, spooning shrimp with lobster sauce onto her rice-filled plate. As more time elapsed since her parents' deaths, she'd begun to indulge in all sorts of nonkosher food, including shellfish, surprising herself when she discovered how much she liked it.

"What's that supposed to mean?" Josselyn shot back.

"Nothing. He's married." Natalie passed a takeout container to her friend.

"I'm sorry, Nat. I'm not angry with you."

"I know."

"I drove him to do this."

"Right. You were the love of his life, but he's spending his life with another woman."

Josselyn knew Natalie was only trying to keep her from getting hurt. "We just knew that we were meant for each other. I can't explain it."

"Must have been lust," Natalie quipped after chewing and swallowing.

"Ha, ha, ha. It was the real thing; you just have to believe me."

"*You* just have to believe you. It doesn't matter what anyone else thinks, me included."

Silence.

"Who are you trying to convince?" Natalie persisted.

"I'm not trying to convince anyone."

"Well, sweetie, just remember: *he's* married … and not thinking about you."

Without answering, Josselyn speared a shrimp, wondering how much of it she'd driven him to and how much he'd have done on his own, regardless. Her tireless search of the Life and Times of Cameron Burke had yielded information, albeit sporadically. He'd been wounded in an explosion in Israel during the Yom Kippur War, endured a fairly long convalescence from the burns and fractures he'd sustained, and then been assigned to the Pentagon at around the same time that he married his nurse from the VA hospital—the same one Josselyn had called so many times.

Luke Lanvin, who knew everyone everywhere, had gotten the information for her, although he'd done so with misgivings when none of the messages she left at the VA were returned. "Leave the past in the past, kid," was what he had said, but then he'd done what she asked, waving away her promises to return the favor someday. Now that she knew, she wished she didn't. She should have paid more attention to Luke's concerns.

"Keep moving forward and don't look back," Natalie said, without prompting.

"Is that your best advice as a psychiatrist?"

"It's just my best advice, period," Natalie said pointedly.

"I would never have an affair with a married man, Nat." The implication hurt Josselyn more than it angered her.

"You think you wouldn't, Joss. But what if you ran into him somewhere? You don't know what you would do."

"Well, I know what I *wouldn't* do."

"Do you? Before you left for Vietnam, would you have guessed that you'd sleep with a man the same night that you met him?"

Josselyn's eyes widened as she opened her mouth to answer, but then snapped it shut, realizing that she didn't know what she would do if she met him now. And she didn't know what she would have done all those years ago if he had been married then. After a minute or two, she said, "I suppose love does strange things to people."

"No, it doesn't. Lust does strange things to people. You live in your head, Joss. Maybe you confused love with lust. There's nothing wrong with that, you know. Lots of people—"

"It wasn't just lust, Nat, whatever you might think."

Picking up on Josselyn's tone, Natalie dropped it. No point trying to help anyone see what she wasn't ready to.

Josselyn was relieved that Natalie didn't persist; her whole relationship with Cam had become a mystery to her. If it had been love, how had she let him just slip out of her life? How had she let the one person who had awakened such powerful feelings in her just … go? And more important, *why* had she? The girl she had been before she met Cam would have concurred with Natalie. The woman she was now could not. That weak-in-the-knees feeling Cam brought about in her, that intoxicating blend of euphoria and excitement, was as irrational as it was delicious. Maybe that was more lust than anything else. But what she experienced with Cam had been so much more than *just* that. And she knew it had been for him too. It was the soul-to-soul connection that made her know he was the love of her life; the man who made her feel intensely alive and incredibly happy, more so than anyone else ever had or ever would. If Nat had never felt any of that with a man, she couldn't possibly understand.

All Josselyn knew for sure was that she was going to spend the rest of her life regretting that she'd let Cam go. The two of them were made for each other and meant for each other, and nothing could ever change that—even if he had married someone else.

On the day that his daughter was born, Burke received word that the president had brokered the peace accord between Israel and Egypt at Camp David. Several miscarriages and a stillborn son behind them, Patricia and Cameron Burke were at last the parents of a healthy, beautiful baby: Margaret Anne. Burke had never believed it would be possible for a human being to feel as much pure love and tenderness as he now felt for his baby girl. It was as if God had somehow attached a cord from her heart to his, and he was now bound to her for as long as they both lived. Longer even, he guessed. Gazing at the tiny baby in his arms, he understood eternity for the first time—more deeply than he'd ever understood it in flames or in battle ... or at the height of passion. Nothing would ever mean more to him than his daughter.

Perching on the edge of her bed, Burke smiled down at an exhausted Patricia.

"Happy, Cam?" she asked, stroking his arm.

"How I feel redefines happy, honey."

"Me too." She beamed at him, glowing even in her weariness.

Mission accomplished. At last. Patricia had hoped to give Cam a living son, but he couldn't have loved one more than he loved this baby girl. She realized, almost wistfully, that she had never seen him more adoring. But she was determined that if anyone would supersede her in Cam's affections, it would be their daughter. That was far better than some stranger she'd never see and never know, but who had been the silent third in their bed from the very beginning.

It had been a hard, painful delivery, and Patricia burrowed gratefully into the pillows. The obstetrician had already told them there could be no more children. The multiple miscarriages, the stillborn, and this one were all that she could take. It didn't matter. All that mattered was that she'd given Cam a child, and he was more attentive toward her than she'd ever seen him.

"Will you be all right if I just close my eyes?" Patricia asked him.

"We'll be fine," Cam assured her, squeezing her shoulder and kissing her forehead quickly before returning his rapt attention to his daughter. *We don't need anyone or anything but each other, do we, my little muffin?*

He didn't need to say it aloud; Patricia already knew. But she reminded herself that as long as the one he adored was their daughter, it didn't matter. She couldn't have known that she was about to spend years convincing herself of that fact, that his never having loved her as much as she loved him was something she would never get over.

But in the moment, Patricia Callahan Burke was too bone weary to care about anything but drifting off into oblivion.

Josselyn walked along the Promenade, vainly trying to clear her mind. After their conversation about lust, Natalie had called to apologize, saying she shouldn't have passed judgment on how Josselyn and Cam felt about each other, or what each meant to the other. Josselyn had accepted Nat's apology, admitting that she herself wondered what she and Cam had really meant to each other. She hadn't told Nat the rest of it—the part she knew Nat would never understand. Instead, she'd ended the phone call with an abrupt excuse about an imaginary deadline.

Feeling as if the four walls would close in on her, Josselyn had gone outside, heading for the Promenade. A walk there usually brought her clarity, or at least some semblance thereof, but not this time.

What *had* she and Cam really meant to each other? Had it really been the once-in-a-lifetime magical experience she remembered, or had she just tried to convince herself of that? Why couldn't she just relegate it to the past—whatever it had been—and live in the present? Her self-recriminations told her she was still doing all the things she'd always sworn she would never do. She was wasting her life, accomplishments and awards notwithstanding. If he were still in love with her would it even matter? He'd married someone else, as Nat continually pointed out. But that didn't necessarily mean that he wasn't still in love with her; she'd told him to find another woman if they didn't find each other again. How she wished she'd never said those words! If only she'd known. ... Now there was no way of knowing whether he'd merely done what she'd asked, continuing to think of her as much as she thought of him, or if he'd just met someone else and relegated her to the past. As he never returned any of the calls she'd made to the VA hospital, she couldn't help but wonder if he'd kept his promise to never forget her, but she didn't really want to know for sure.

The sky above the Promenade closed in on her now as much as the four walls had before. *No escaping myself, is there? Never will be.* The peace she'd always longed for seemed farther away than ever before.

Shortly after the signing of the historic Camp David Peace Accords, Josselyn Jeffrey won a literary fiction award for *From Ashes to Hope*. She considered the thinly veiled fictionalization of her parents' lives to be her best writing so far. She was prouder of the book than of anything she'd ever done, feeling that all the pain her family endured had produced something worthwhile—at last.

She recalled turning in the manuscript to her editor, how she had gone home and cried—not heaving sobs, but a steady trail of tears that had seemed to flow in response to everything she'd ever grieved, both long ago and recently. When her tears finally stopped, she'd felt stronger and more serene than she had since her parents' deaths. And since Cameron.

Natalie had sobbed through the entire manuscript. So had Luke Lanvin.

Josselyn's publisher and his staff had been over the moon from the beginning, certain they had a bestseller on their hands. The popular success of the book had been thrilling, and still was; but garnering the critical acclaim of an illustrious award for literary fiction was a dream come true. Every time she browsed in a bookstore and saw the book, the emblazoned medallion on the cover proclaiming the award, she felt a flush of excitement and pride. Not that she had any intention of resting on her laurels—constant activity and immersion in her work were what she thrived on—but she did enjoy the validation of her artistry.

Now she was hard at work on *Lower than Heaven*, the novel about her experiences in Vietnam, including her love affair with Cameron Burke. It was a different kind of story entirely, of course, but her publisher was still expecting big things from her second book. Josselyn Jeffrey was a "name" now, a bestselling author. It all still felt a little unreal.

Unrolling page 212 from her typewriter, Josselyn's gaze fell upon the name of Kyle Hanrahan, her fictitious moniker for Cam. She found herself unable to release her eyes from where they focused, chided herself for being ridiculous, and frowned. Flipping the page over and resting it atop the stack of manuscript pages set upside down on her desk, she turned off the typewriter and checked her watch. In less than an hour, she had a date with Ron Levenson, an author she'd met the last time she was in her editor's office. Ron, who called himself a "cultural critic," taught at The New School. He had given the pretense of needing a contact at the Times office when he asked for her number. She had offhandedly told him to just call the main number, not realizing he was coming on to her. Natalie was right: she was absolutely clueless about things like that. In any case, Ron had found what he thought was her playing hard to get to be an irresistible turn-on. He'd pursued her pretty relentlessly, and finally she'd just given in, not sure which she had grown wearier of: making excuses for why she couldn't see him or just feeling lonely.

Slipping into a black dress and heels, Josselyn brushed her hair and picked up her purse, less sure of what she was doing, and why, than she had ever been. But nothing—not even writing—had taken her mind off Cameron Burke. Maybe *nothing* ever would, but *someone* might.

Patricia peeked into the nursery. Cam sat in the rocking chair, holding Margaret in his arms and smiling with infinite tenderness. The baby's hair was growing in red and curly, and Patricia hoped it would darken to auburn as she got older so she wouldn't be a carrottop for her entire life. Patricia had jumped for joy when her own red hair had burnished. Cam couldn't have cared less. As far as he was concerned, Margaret Anne Burke was the most exquisite creature God had ever breathed life into.

Patricia tiptoed away, turning down the hall and going downstairs to the kitchen to put on the coffee and cut the coconut-custard pie. When he wasn't on assignment, she and Cam always waited to have dessert until after she'd bathed Margaret and Cam had rocked her to sleep with a good-night story or a lullaby. Patricia had never seen a more devoted father. Cam's bedtime ritual with Margaret was the most cherished moment of his day. And for her part, Patricia couldn't have been happier. Being Margaret's mother gave her a standing in Cam's eyes that nothing else could, and it also ensured Cam's spending as much time at home as possible.

Since Margaret's birth, Patricia had scarcely thought about Josselyn Jeffrey, the faceless rival for her husband's affection. In truth, she had all but convinced herself that she'd exaggerated the elusive Josselyn's importance to Cam from the very beginning. Morphine-induced dreams produced strange reactions indeed. She might have been nothing more than a high-school crush he'd never gotten up the nerve to ask to the senior prom, for all Patricia knew. She would not let herself think about all the messages Josselyn had left at the VA, which she, Patricia, had intercepted and disposed of before Cam could see them. She did what she had to do, then and now.

And then she'd seen the book. *From Ashes to Hope.* Josselyn Jeffrey. The title and name were etched in her mind. She could still see the book nestled between shirts and ties in Cam's suitcase as she'd unpacked it. The gold-embossed letters of the title had practically jumped off the dust jacket and into Patricia's face. Of course, he would have had no reason to try to hide the book, as he had no inkling that Patricia would make a connection to the name. At first, she told herself it was just a coincidence, but then she tried to remember the last time Cam had bought a book and read it, bestseller status and awards galore notwithstanding. No, it was the same Josselyn Jeffrey, and Patricia had been a fool to think she didn't mean as much to him as she obviously did. As she obviously always had.

Another woman might have casually remarked, "What's that book you're reading, sweetheart?" But not Patricia. She kept telling herself that she wouldn't put him in that kind of position, that all that mattered was their life together, Margaret especially. Which was true up to a point, but beyond that truth lay a deeper truth, the truth that Patricia didn't really want to know why Cam was reading the book or what feelings it brought up in him. She could endure watching him read the book—and others, if she had to—but she couldn't bear even the thought of losing him. After all, this woman was still only a name, not a voice, not a face.

And then, bitterly, she reminded herself that Josselyn did have a face; Patricia had seen it on the book-jacket photo. She would never again be a faceless rival. In fact, Patricia wished she hadn't ever seen Josselyn's face, wished she hadn't been compelled to open the book's back cover to look at the photo. A beautiful face, far more so than Patricia had expected. She'd actually felt herself involuntarily draw in her breath at the perfection of its exquisiteness, the dark hair and eyes against alabaster skin. Patricia had not expected her to look like that, realized she hadn't known *what* she'd expected. Josselyn was alluring and mysterious in a way Patricia could never hope to be. To put it bluntly, Patricia was everything Josselyn Jeffrey was not. Patricia knew that. And because she knew it, she also had to face the fact that Cam had only married her because she was nothing like Josselyn. He had determined to marry a woman bearing no resemblance to the woman he still carried a torch for, wanting his only reminders to be his own memories. His own fantasies. Nothing could ever convince her otherwise, not even Cam himself. Not that he'd ever have the chance, because Patricia had no intention of telling him she knew about Josselyn. Ever.

She drove the knife into the pie, hunks of coconut slathered in custard sticking to the blade as she drew it up to slice the other side. Patricia conceded she might be overreacting, but she didn't care. She had married a man who was supposed to be a hero, a shining exemplar of what men were supposed to be, and she felt somehow cheated—even though she didn't think Cam ever had, or ever would, actually cheat on her. The knowledge that he had never considered himself to be a hero, let alone a shining exemplar of masculine virtue, she dismissed. When she told him what she thought of him before they were married, Cameron Burke had told Patricia Callahan to wait for the guy who would truly be those things. But Patricia was so infatuated with him that she could not possibly have believed that anyone but Cam could ever be her hero. He might no longer be her hero, but he still was her husband. He might not be perfect, but he was still as driven, tough, honest, and decent as she always described him as being. Beyond all that, she was still every bit as much in love with him as she'd ever been. And that love was what she intended to cling to. If he didn't love her as much as she loved him, she would make her love be enough for both of them.

As she heard his footfalls at the base of the stairs, she lifted each piece of pie out of the pie pan and onto a plate, carrying the plates to the table and setting them there. When Cam came into the kitchen, she was bringing the coffeepot to the table, her right hand gripping the handle and her left supporting the base, with a trivet between it and her palm.

"Sleeping like an angel," Burke told his wife, his deep-blue eyes twinkling in the same way that any mention of Margaret always engendered.

"That child just adores her daddy," Patricia said, beaming at him while she poured his coffee, as if she hadn't a care in the world and were the happiest wife in it.

Burke chuckled. "I suppose every father thinks it, but she *is* the most beautiful baby in the world." As Patricia set down the coffeepot, he reached for her hand, drawing it to his lips. "Of course, given she looks like her mother, this father happens to be correct."

Patricia swallowed hard, managing to force a too-bright smile, but Cam was so absorbed by his joy in Margaret that he didn't notice. "You can hardly think I'm the most beautiful woman in the world, Cam."

"I can and I do," he assured her, pressing her hand against his cheek and kissing her palm and then the inside of her wrist.

Patricia lowered her eyes. He so seemed to mean it. She willed herself to believe him, to banish thoughts of Josselyn Jeffrey from her mind, to reclaim her husband.

"Don't be so modest," he went on.

"The woman who wrote that book you're reading—she's beautiful." The words rushed out of Patricia's mouth, unbidden, before she could stop them. But once they were spoken, she couldn't help but want to see what her husband would say.

Cam's face stiffened almost imperceptibly. Patricia knew no one but she would have picked up on it.

"Don't tell me you didn't notice her photo, Cam," she teased.

Relaxing a bit as he realized she was just ribbing him, didn't know—couldn't possibly know—who Josselyn was or what she meant to him, Cam said, "Well, yes, she is beautiful, but not the way you are."

"Right, because she looks like a movie star."

"No man in his right mind would want a movie star. A woman like that is nothing but trouble and heartache for any man."

Watching despair flicker across his face for a split second, Patricia felt vindicated. So Josselyn had jilted him; she wasn't really a threat, after all.

"Come here." Cam tugged on the hand he still held, pulling Patricia into his lap. "You're the only woman I want."

As he slipped his arms around her and parted her lips with his, Patricia reminded herself that he hadn't said, "You're the only woman I ever wanted or ever will." But she told herself that it didn't matter. She hadn't expected a man like Cam not to have had other women before he met her. And as she kissed him back, she prayed that he meant what he *had* said. That was the best she could hope for. What did the past matter? The present was all anyone could really count on. Pressing herself harder against her husband, Patricia was determined to show him just why he would have no reason to think about any woman but his wife in the future.

Pressing her hands against the counter, Josselyn said softly, "Just go, Ron."

"It's the sex, isn't it? Why can't you just tell me what you want?"

Because what I want is another man, and every time I'm with you, every cell of my body is crying out for him … and always will. Turning to face him, she said, "It isn't the sex, Ron. And it isn't you. I'm just not cut out to be in a relationship."

"If you convince yourself you're not, then you're not," Ron retorted.

"You pushed me to go out with you, Ron. How many times did I say no?"

Ron just glared at her.

Again, she said, "Just go," but this time her tone was leaden.

Ron swung on his heel and left.

Even though he'd been wrong for her from the beginning, he was a nice-enough guy. If he turned into a jerk near the end, it was largely her fault. She didn't *want* to be with any man but Cam, plain and simple.

Sex with Ron had been … nothing. Just a series of groping motions with no connection. She had felt the sensations, of course, the physical release of pent-up frustration. But afterward she always felt empty. She should have ended it after the first time, but each time she kept hoping she would feel something the next time. She should have known better. A connection like she and Cam had came once in a lifetime—or not at all. At least she had proved to herself that she hadn't just been convincing herself it had been magical. But the proof didn't bring her any measure of comfort or peace. It only made her feel worse than ever. Nevertheless, it made her keenly aware of what she had to do—and what she couldn't keep doing. She wasn't going to hurt any other men in the course of trying to prove to herself that she could make Cam not matter.

She'd made her bed, and now she had to lie in it … alone.

Almost four years had passed since she'd won the award for *From Ashes to Hope*. Josselyn had achieved everything she'd ever dreamed of … more even. The only thing she'd ever really wanted that she didn't have was Cameron Burke. But seeing Natalie's misery through a bitter breakup and divorce, Josselyn knew she'd done the right thing. The passion she and Cam had been able to sustain in a war zone would never have survived the monotony of day-to-day life. Even if part of it was her fear that she wouldn't have been able to make him happy long-term, that he'd loved the part of her he'd seen, not all of her—he couldn't have loved all of her, hadn't gotten to know all of her any more than she had gotten to know all of him. What they'd shared had been real and magical, but that didn't mean it would have lasted. She had made peace with that, mostly because of what had happened with Ron, which still made her wince inwardly. It also showed her that she knew who she was—had always known—and she could never be anything else. *Just keep it in the past. …*

With a sigh, Josselyn closed her suitcase. She was heading to DC to cover the return of the hostages freed in Tehran, and she'd been thinking about Cam ever since she'd received the assignment. Just the prospect that she might see him filled her with a mixture of excitement and dread, a feeling she was rapidly growing to detest and eager to be rid of.

"What are you, fifteen years old?" she demanded aloud of her reflection in the mirror. "You didn't even do this when you were fifteen. Pull yourself together. You're a journalist, a professional. If you meet him, you meet him. If you don't, you don't. That's not why you're going. You're on an *assignment.*" She enunciated the last word with emphasis and precision, as if saying it to a non-English speaker.

She wondered whether years of pining away for someone could truly drive a person insane. Or maybe it was just that her longing for him had become habitual; she was so used to it that she just couldn't let it go. If she wouldn't get a psychobabble-laden lecture in return, she'd ask Natalie. Better to just convince herself that she was not insane and not heartbroken, just acting like a fool.

Acting, being the operative word, because she wasn't a fool. Cameron Burke was a high-level operative in military intelligence. He could have gotten word to her a million times if he'd wanted to. He was also married and a father—she still followed his life and career sporadically—and she was many things, but not a home wrecker. No, things had worked out the way they were supposed to. Her life was what it was meant to be: she had her writing, her fulfilled dreams—just like she'd told him, minus the coffee. She'd never expected to be with any other man, but then she had given in to Ron's relentless pursuit. She considered that a mistake because it was the best description she could come up with. And it was a mistake she would never repeat for the unsuspecting man's sake, as well as her own.

If she and Cam were meant to be together again, it was in God's hands, not hers. That brought her some measure of relief, but no peace. She couldn't decide whether to pray that she would meet him—or that she wouldn't. Luke was going to DC also, and she was glad she wouldn't be alone at night in the hotel with nothing but the four walls and memories that ripped her heart to shreds.

A cab honked in the street below. Looking out the window and seeing that it was hers, she grabbed her suitcase, went out the door, and hurried down the front stoop to the curb. The cabbie stowed her bag in the trunk, and they sped off to La Guardia, Josselyn catching a glimpse of the Twin Towers as she looked out the window after settling in. She liked seeing the image of something she could always count on when she felt so unsettled, so caught up in despair. She watched the towers through the cab window until she couldn't see them anymore.

Once in DC, Josselyn found herself caught up in the journalistic whirlwind to which she surrendered herself gratefully. Not that she was driven to garner kudos for her stories about the freed hostages; she wasn't. All she wanted was something to throw herself into body and soul so she wouldn't think about Cam. But in spite of her own intention, she found herself wrapping her mind around the events, sinking her teeth into them, and turning out stories she felt proud to write.

She passed a copy of her latest story to Luke, who sat across from her at a small hotel-bar table where they sat sipping brandy into the wee hours. She'd taken to doing that when she worked late on deadline; otherwise, she was too pumped up to fall asleep, and if she didn't get a good night's sleep, she was worthless the following day.

Luke swirled the snifter in his left hand as he read her story, taking a sip when he turned over the last page. "You turn it in yet?"

"Before I came to meet you. Why? Is something wrong?"

Luke grinned at her. "Only that another year has come and gone when I won't stand a chance to win an award. Or even make any short list."

"Oh come on, Luke," she demurred, but she smiled at the praise.

"You don't care about the awards, do you?"

"Of course I do."

"Not really. Not the way other people would. Putting the words down, the process of it more so than the product, is all that matters to you."

"I suppose so," she said softly, realizing it fully as she answered him, even though she recognized it was something she'd always known, just never articulated.

"What a gift it is to love it that much and expect nothing."

Josselyn nodded, understanding that she did love it enough not to need any additional acknowledgment. Writing was the meat of her soul; she didn't need any gravy. She enjoyed gravy, but enjoyment and need were not one and the same. "I wish I could say that of myself about other things."

"You're wrong, Joss. Writing is your great love, your singular passion, not Cameron. He was just a step on your path. Leave him in the past."

Luke didn't ordinarily say things like that to her. Having long since voiced his misgivings, he largely kept silent on that score, so she knew that the brandy had loosened his inhibitions. All she said was, "Maybe so."

"Life is just life, not necessarily what we expect it will be, and certainly not fair. Don't beat yourself up, kid." Luke had certainly had more than his fair share of disappointment and heartache. After his wife's diagnosis with inoperable uterine cancer a year or so before, he and his daughter had forged an uneasy truce for her sake, but then she died soon afterward. He and his daughter remained in touch now, but it was always strained.

"I won't if you won't," Josselyn told him, setting down her snifter with a trace of brandy still at the bottom. Standing up and leaning across the small table, she gave him a good-night kiss on the cheek.

"Sleep tight," he said, smiling because she never minded his treating her like a daughter. If his own daughter had to be the way she was, at least he had a sweet kid like Josselyn for a good friend.

The following night, there was a press party. Josselyn went with Luke, planning to beg off early and head back to the hotel. She was still exhausted from the night before. But she knew at least showing her face at these things was a must; she was a senior journalist now, responsible for all the expectations that entailed.

She walked into the party on Luke's arm, scanning the room more out of journalistic reflex than in search of anyone in particular, least of all Cameron Burke, but there he was, framed in a doorway at the back of the room. Josselyn's breath caught in her throat, and she involuntarily gripped Luke's arm tighter.

"See a ghost?" he teased, patting her gloved fingers.

Without a word, Josselyn released Luke's arm and walked across the room toward the doorway in back. And Luke realized that was exactly what she'd seen: a ghost from her past. He headed for the bar and ordered a scotch, neat. She would find him when she was ready to leave.

Something—he'd never be sure what, precisely—prompted Cameron Burke to look up. The shock of seeing her made him all but fall against the door jamb he was standing beside. She was even more beautiful than he remembered, if that were possible. A black strapless gown hugged her body in a way that was elegant more than revealing; and her creamy skin, exposed above the gown and black evening gloves, all but gleamed in the glow of the ballroom chandeliers. She was still radiant; always would be. Before he knew it, she was standing in front of him. The scent of her skin catapulted him back into the past and almost out of his mind.

"Hello, Cam," she said, her voice still low and musical, her smile still sweet with just a tinge of mystery. Not the kind that seemed a forced allure; he knew it was real, had known it the second he laid eyes on her. Josselyn's mystery was simple: She knew who she was and had nothing to prove to any man. Hers was still an I'll-take-you-where-you-only-dream-of-going smile. Many men would be all too glad to embark on the journey, but very few were brave enough to stay the course, himself included.

"How are you, Joss?"

"Good. You?"

"Good."

"I saw you across the room and had to come say hello."

"I'm glad you did. I didn't see you; I would have come over."

"I know you would have."

"Let me get you a drink."

"No, really, I just wanted to say hello. It was good seeing you," she said, turning back toward the party. She didn't trust herself to stay, considered it a victory that she hadn't collapsed into tears or thrown herself at him, hollow a victory though it might be.

Burke caught her gloved hand, imagining the pleasure of peeling it off her long, slender arm, pressing his lips against the sweet, tender flesh inside her wrist and elbow.

"Cam, I'm begging you. Just let me walk away."

"Didn't I do that once already? Or didn't you?"

"Cam, don't."

"Come away with me," he said, shocking himself with the words. He hadn't ever expected to say anything of the sort, but he hadn't ever really expected to see her again either.

"Don't be ridiculous." Her voice was sharp, her eyes even sharper, as she wrenched her hand free of his grasp. "You're a husband and a father. This isn't Vietnam." She softened at the last part, putting her hand on his arm in the same way she had the first time they met.

You're a husband and a father. Her words reverberated through his brain. He couldn't hurt Margaret, didn't want to hurt Patricia either. But he had not realized until now, when she was actually within reach, that his feelings for Josselyn were still this powerful. He had to use every ounce of his will to restrain himself from reaching out and pulling her into his arms.

He stepped almost imperceptibly closer to her.

"Cam, don't," she said again, the sharpness gone from her voice and replaced with weariness. "Please." She hadn't moved her hand from his arm.

"Have you been happy?"

"Yes. I've done all I set out to."

"That doesn't mean you're happy." He looked into her eyes.

"I suppose it doesn't, but I am. I've never wanted what other people want. You know that."

"Aren't you going to ask if I'm happy?"

"You're doing what you've always wanted. You've made a life for yourself."

"But I'm not happy. And neither are you. Neither of us could possibly be."

"Stop it, Cam. We each chose the life we wanted. Neither of us could have made the other happy for long. You know that as well as I do."

Maybe we should have tried. But all he said was, "All I know is, the most alive I ever felt was the time I spent with you. That's no small thing to just toss aside, Joss."

"We tossed it aside years ago. You married someone else and had a child together. We both made a choice a long time ago, never realizing how much heartache and longing it would bring us. We can't visit that kind of pain upon your wife and daughter, Cam. I just won't do it." Josselyn moved her hand away abruptly, as if she didn't realize she'd kept it on his arm all that time. Dropping her voice, she continued, "And don't mistake me for someone who's going to just overlook the fact that you're married with a family, or pretend it doesn't matter because I'm still in love with you."

"Are you?"

"It doesn't matter." She turned on her heel, casting a final glance at him over her shoulder, her dark eyes blazing. "I'm sorry I came over to talk to you at all. I should have just left things the way they were. At least my memories are ... never mind." She rushed off before he could reach out to stop her.

Burke stood all but paralyzed, watching the journalists and politicos close around her. He stared at the white curve of her neck and shoulders, the graceful line of her hair swept up from her neck and piled high on top of her head. Watching her make her way through the crowd, he saw her go up to a man at the bar, say something to him, and then walk briskly out of the room. In that instant, he decided he was not letting Josselyn Jeffrey walk out of his life a second time. He was not considering the implications of what that meant, only that he couldn't bear the thought of letting her go. It didn't occur to him that she was no longer his to hold on to.

He'd been assigned to attend this party, to mingle with the press because he'd been instrumental in the ultimate liberation of the hostages. He'd come alone because Patricia had taken Margaret to visit her parents before he'd learned of the party. Not being much of a mingler, he knew he wouldn't be missed if he disappeared for a while. Just long enough to convince Josselyn that he was serious, that he hadn't meant for her to sneak off to a hotel room with him for a night of endless passion, but to start over. To be together … for good, this time.

As he hurried through the side corridor that led to the main lobby, he made up his mind that he'd leave Patricia—he would find a way to remain as much a part of Margaret's life as he possibly could, but he was not going to let Josselyn get away … not again. He'd tell her so straight out and wait to see what she said. Spotting her in the lobby, he dashed toward her, calling her name, and then catching her by the shoulders from behind before she could rush off.

"Why are you doing this?"

He could hear the tears she was holding back catch in her voice as he turned her around to face him. "I love you, Josselyn. I've never stopped loving you. I'll leave Patricia. Marry me."

"You're not giving up your life for me, Cam. It's not that simple. I could never be the kind of wife you need. I'm too self-absorbed, too driven by my own work and my own dreams. It would never work. We'd make each other miserable."

"We made each other happier than anyone else ever made either of us."

"That was different. It wasn't real," she lied.

"It felt pretty real to me."

"That's not what I meant. I'm not talking about the sex."

"It wasn't just sex. Is that all you think it was to me?"

"I don't know what it was to you. I don't know what I was to you." She let ice creep into her voice and lowered her eyes.

"You don't mean that, and you were always a rotten liar. You know I loved you with my whole soul and still do. Damn it, Josselyn! Look at me."

She lifted her eyes, the tears seeping out of them and hanging briefly on the edges of her long lashes before dropping to course down her cheeks. "Of course I didn't mean it. I know how much you've always loved me."

"Good. And I know how much you've always loved me. So why are we still debating? I'll tell my wife I want a divorce as soon as she gets back from visiting her folks, and I'll leave the house right after."

Thoughts of Natalie, of all that pain, flashed through Josselyn's feverish mind. No matter how much she loved Cam, she couldn't be the source of another woman's heartbreak and upheaval, let alone a child's. And Cam didn't need to tell her that his daughter adored him, or that his wife did. She knew the kind of husband and father he must be.

"No, darling," she said softly.

"No, what?"

"No to all of it. I'm not going to be a home wrecker."

"You aren't a home wrecker. I never should have married Patricia. I've been in love with you from the minute I laid eyes on you."

"That's not Patricia's fault. Do you expect your confessing all that is going to make her feel better? That she'd rather lose you to the woman you've been carrying a torch for than to one you met since you've been married to her? And what about your daughter?" Stepping closer to him, she put her hands flat against his chest. "Don't you see that there's no way for us to be

211

together without innocent people who you love getting hurt? You do love your wife, don't you?"

"I care for her, but not the way I love you."

"You don't want to break her heart and ruin her life, Cam."

"She'll be better off. She's a terrific girl; she'll find someone who'll love her more than I do—who'll be a better husband."

"Will she think so?"

Burke didn't answer. Patricia would never think so. Josselyn was right, of course: his leaving Patricia would destroy her; she'd rather die than lose him. "So you and I are the ones who'll have to suffer," he said at last.

"We're the ones who made the mistake. Isn't that as it should be?"

No, this is as it should be: you lying in my arms every night; us losing ourselves in each other every time.

Josselyn continued, "We got what we asked for, Cam, we just didn't realize *what* we were asking for when we asked for it. 'Be careful what you wish for, you might get it.' You've heard that before, haven't you?"

He nodded. "I didn't ask to lose you or to never hold you again," he rasped.

"You'll never lose me, darling. Every word on every page has you running through it."

Her eyes locked with his, and they held each other's gaze for a long time. What she most loved about him was exactly what would keep him from ever leaving his wife to be with her. And what he most loved about her was exactly what wouldn't let her demand that he do so.

Finally, Burke said, "I need some air. Take a walk around the block with me."

"All right." She walked through the door he held open, taking his arm as they stepped out into the street.

"That hotel's crawling with reporters."

"Watch it, mister," she quipped, squeezing his arm where she held it.

"You know what I mean."

"I know exactly what you mean, so tell me what you're up to."

He saw a large niche at the side of the building as they neared the corner. A large tree shielded the recessed space from the streetlamp. He steered her toward the niche.

"I didn't ask to never hold you again."

"You said that already."

"I meant it both times." He put his hands on her hips, drawing her close to him.

"Cam, this is hard enough on both of us as it is. Don't make it worse."

He covered her mouth with his, pressing her against him until her body melted into his. Over time, he had almost forgotten just how intense it was with her. It wasn't just her body that melted into his so perfectly, it was their hearts and souls joining too. He held her tight in his arms until he felt his heart would burst. The rest of him was certainly about to. Josselyn eased away first, the look in her eyes a mix of unaffected tenderness and mild reproach.

"Did I really make it worse?" he asked, knowing he had—for both of them.

"Yes and no."

"Sorry, baby, but the last time we said good-bye I didn't think it would have to last me the rest of my life."

"Will it this time?"

"No," he whispered.

"Well, it really is good-bye this time, Cam. Anything more will make it worse, so let me just go."

He stepped back.

"We both hate long good-byes," she reminded him.

He nodded.

"Have a good life," she said softly, reaching up to stroke the side of his face with her gloved hand and kissing his cheek on the other side.

"I'll always love you," he told her, clasping her wrist before she could move away and kissing her palm. The heat of his breath through her silk glove sent a frisson of pleasure up her arm, running like a shock wave through her body.

"And I'll always love you. Every word is you. Remember that."

She broke away before he could pull her close again—before her steely resolve crumbled—and she strode back to the hotel without looking back, knowing that if their eyes met, she'd run back into his arms and never again muster the will to leave them.

Back in New York, Josselyn worked feverishly to finish *Lower than Heaven,* turning it in well ahead of deadline, complete with the cryptic dedication, To C., WITH LOVE IN EVERY WORD, NOW AND FOREVERMORE. Whatever happened, Cam would always have that. She knew he would buy the book, knew he would know he was Kyle Hanrahan and she was Giselle Garreau.

More than that, she knew she would always regret having turned him away that night in DC. Perhaps she had done the right thing, but her heart was broken. And every book award in the world couldn't make up for it or take away the pain. Nor could moralizing about it. If love was everything, how could turning away from it be right? She wondered if she would ever really find the answer.

When Burke first saw the display of *Lower than Heaven* in the bookstore that he was walking past, he went inside and bought a copy, flipping to the dedication page automatically. He smiled to himself in spite of the vise of pain gripping his heart. This was a book he was going to read over and over again. Patricia's remark about how beautiful Josselyn looked in her last book-jacket photo flashed through his mind suddenly, but he brushed it aside just as quickly, certain it was not connected to anything.

Couldn't possibly be. There was no way Patricia could know. A guilty conscience could reveal more than hard evidence, Burke knew all too well. But this book was all he would ever have of Josselyn for the rest of his life.

Paying for the book and tucking it in his attaché case, he crossed the street to the bakery that had been his original destination. He was going to Margaret's school later that day to talk to her class, and he'd promised to bring her favorite cinnamon-crumb muffins for their drive home. Margaret was his little muffin, had been from the minute she was born. He'd actually taken to calling her "Muffin" because she so loved their version of sharing a muffin: his giving her the entire top and eating the bottom. That was the smallest sacrifice he could make for his daughter, for whom he would gladly lie down in the road at the height of rush-hour traffic to spare a moment's pain.

Josselyn had been right about their parting, right about pushing him away after the embrace he contrived. But knowing she was right didn't make it easier. There was the kind of right you knew in your head and the kind of right you felt in your heart, and his heart would always feel empty without her. Margaret was the only joy in his life now, the only thing that made life without Josselyn worth living. But even so, he knew he would never really get over losing the love of his life. Secretly, he hoped Patricia would confront him; if she did, he would tell her the truth, hoping it would force her to throw him out. But he knew his wife, and she would never confront him, no matter her suspicions … if she really had any. Probably he was just imagining it all.

Stepping inside the bakery, he got the two muffins and went back to the car, heading off to Margaret's school.

Patricia Burke was in the bookstore, looking for a gift for her father, when she caught sight of Josselyn Jeffrey's latest book.

Skimming the jacket copy and seeing that the book was about Vietnam, Patricia's breath caught in her throat. Part of her wanted to read the dedication, to confirm her own deepest fears, but part of her didn't want that confirmation. Everything would change if her fear was confirmed; there would be no going back. Ever.

Her fingers actually itching to flip the pages, Patricia carefully set the book back down on the display and continued toward the military-history section to find the biography of General Patton that her father had mentioned wanting to read. She knew all too well what she would find on that dedication page, and she didn't really want to see the words that would surely confirm all her nagging suspicions.

Quite simply, she just loved Cam too much to lose him, and if he knew that she knew, he'd insist that they part, that she find someone who would be the husband she deserved. But she didn't want that husband. Cam was the only husband she had ever wanted, and she would do whatever she had to do to keep him. Even if it meant living with the painful truth that he'd been in love with another woman for as long as he'd known Patricia. That woman didn't have him; Patricia did. With a smile of secret triumph, she slipped the Patton biography off the shelf, carrying it to the cash register to pay for it and then leaving the store with her purchase.

As she stepped out into the street, Patricia let the bookstore door close behind her. Close, too, on Josselyn Jeffrey, whom Patricia Burke vowed never to think of again.

When Margaret Burke was twelve, she discovered a book in her father's closet. Intrigued because her father rarely read books, she read the jacket copy: "*Lower than Heaven,* the gripping story of the love of a lifetime, ignited by the jungle heat of Vietnam, but doomed to fail. ...." Margaret's eyes widened to green saucers as she devoured the rest of the copy, sinking to the floor of the closet and then beginning to read the book itself, holding it open across her bent knees. As she turned page after page, Margaret lost herself in the story, and the purpose of her original mission to her father's closet vanished from her mind.

After a while, her father came in search of her. She heard his voice on the periphery of her awareness. "Muffin?" But Margaret was so engrossed, she didn't even respond.

"Muffin? You okay?"

Jolted, Margaret fumbled to collect herself and hide the book in the same instant that her father came to the door of the closet. "Um, fine, Daddy!" she chirped, scrambling to her feet.

"Did you find the shirt?"

The shirt? Margaret forced her brain, still feverish from her reading, to focus. Right. That was what she'd come in search of, an old shirt to use as a painting smock. Her current smock had so much paint on it, her mother had told her that if she didn't replace it, she was locking up her painting supplies. Margaret, in a panic, had appealed to her father, who had told her not to worry; he had plenty of old shirts that she could use just as easily. "Um ..."

"Right here, honey." He pulled out a once-white sleeve, mere inches from her face, and looked at her inquisitively.

Knowing she could never lie to her father—her mother, yes; her father, never—Margaret came clean. "Daddy, I never got that far. I found this. It practically jumped out at me!" She said it all quickly, her face serious, her eyes darkened to emerald and still wide as saucers, the "guilty" book clasped in her hand.

Burke suppressed a chuckle. Margaret's flair for drama drove Patricia to the end of her tether, but he found it adorable. "I see," he said in an equally serious tone, taking the book from her.

"You never read, Daddy. And a novel?"

"I saw the book display in the window of the bookstore across the street from the bakery one day ... and it just ... I don't know ..."

"Called out to you?" Margaret had that happen often enough with books. Next to painting, reading was what she most loved to do.

Chuckling aloud now, Burke said, "Sort of. Take it to read if you want to." He handed the book back to her, pulling the shirt off the hanger.

"Really?"

"Sure. Careful your eyes don't pop out of your head when they get that big."

Margaret laughed as her father dropped the shirt over her shoulders. "But Daddy, it says it's about a passion ignited by jungle heat." She opened the book cover to quote directly from the jacket.

Burke put his hands on her shoulders. "If I say you can read it, you can." He didn't want Margaret to think he was keeping a secret by having the book tucked away. He'd read it multiple times in the several years he'd had it. How long had it been? Five years? Six? He couldn't even remember. It felt like a hundred, that much he knew for sure. The point was, he and Margaret had no secrets from each other—except his work, of course, but she understood why he couldn't share that with anyone. He didn't want her to think his having a secret from her would justify her keeping secrets from him, especially since she would be starting to think about boys soon. Burke knew his daughter would come to him with her questions, not her mother. Margaret and Patricia never seemed to have bonded at all. Either they ignored each other or they fought, and all they did agree on was that he was the center of the universe, and the greatest man who had ever lived.

"Do I have to tell Mom?" Margaret was saying now.

"Of course. Why wouldn't you?"

"Well … the passion thing, Daddy. You know how churchy she is."

"Muffin, it's not that kind of book. I hope you won't be disappointed." He winked at her. "You didn't think I'd started reading romance novels, did you?"

"Daddy!!!" Margaret's cheeks flushed as she shook her head in indignation, her red curls flouncing around her shoulders.

"It's a war story, honey." The romance part was overlaid on an incisive portrayal of the war from both the soldier's perspective and the journalist's. Burke guessed that his imagination ran far wilder at the love scenes than any other reader's would. Understandably so; he'd lived them. Reading—and rereading—was like giving in to a bad habit that he just couldn't kick. In any case, if Margaret was going to read a love story, he'd just as soon have it be a tasteful one like this, with some real history she could learn from too.

"But there is *some* romance?" Margaret asked hopefully.

"Just the right amount for you."

She folded her arms across her chest and narrowed her eyes at him.

"Take it or leave it, Muffin. I'll square it with Mom."

"I love you, Daddy!" Margaret exclaimed, setting the book on the floor as she bounced out of the closet and into his arms for a squeeze.

Burke squeezed her back and then released her, putting the book back in her hands and ushering her through the bedroom, into the hallway, and toward the stairs. "Come on. Mom's going to wonder what happened to us."

"Not likely. She's reading one of those new books."

"Oh." Burke gave his daughter another wink. Patricia had recently begun taking adult-ed classes. She was currently enrolled in "The Empowered Woman," and reading books with titles like *Awakening Your Inner Aphrodite*. Patricia had hastily assured him that it wasn't *that* kind of book. It was the powerful-woman side of Aphrodite, not the sexpot. He hadn't dared to hope. A few years after Margaret was born, Patricia's approach to lovemaking began to change. It became more of a wifely duty and less of an erotic pleasure. She was still willing, just no longer eager. Because this change occurred at the same time that she became more of a churchgoer, Burke linked the two together in his mind. He wasn't happy about the changes in Patricia—more for Margaret's sake than his own, as he didn't want her to be force-fed religion—but he accepted it all. Margaret, for her part, was content as long as her father was the center of her world and she of his, so things seemed to go along well enough.

"There you two are," Patricia said, looking up from her book as they walked into the kitchen. "Much better," she said to her daughter, referring to the clean shirt now serving as a smock.

Margaret nudged her father.

"Honey, while Margaret was smock-hunting she found this old book in my closet, and I told her she could read it."

"You read a book?" Patricia quipped.

"*Lower than Heaven*," Margaret told her mother. "It's sort of a history book, but with a teeny-weeny love story."

Setting down her own book and looking up at them, Patricia said, "That's a familiar title." She rose from her chair and crossed to the counter island where Margaret had set down the book. Taking it in her hands, Patricia mused over the cover, "Hmm. Number-one bestseller. Multiple awards. No wonder it's familiar."

"Then it's okay if I read it?"

"Sure, if your father says so."

Burke detected something odd in Patricia's voice, something she was perturbed about, but guarding. No, hiding. Her expression was as inscrutable as ever.

"It's a great book for understanding Vietnam."

"Well, your father served our country bravely in Vietnam. You ought to know about it. Besides, you know the rule: one book a week over and above what you have to read for school, or no painting."

"I know," Margaret said dutifully. It was the one rule of her mother's that she didn't mind. It seemed to her that reading and adoring her father were the only things she and her mother did agree upon, their only common ground. She was her father's daughter, through and through.

"Might as well start now. You've painted enough for one day."

"But Mom ..."

"Don't 'but Mom' me, missy. Clean up your stuff and go read." Patricia inclined her head toward the enclosed studio Cam had built for Margaret on half of the patio that stood behind the kitchen.

"You heard your mother, Muffin."

Margaret did as she was told.

"I don't ever remember your buying that book," Patricia said lightly.

"Why would you? It's just a book."

"It's the only one you've ever bought." Patricia let him think she had forgotten about the other book from years before; about their conversation regarding Josselyn Jeffrey's book-jacket photo too.

"A slight exaggeration." Burke smiled at her. "I read the reviews and wanted to read it. It's set in some of the places where I was when I was in-country."

"I know you don't like to talk about Nam. If the book helps, I'm glad." She reached over and squeezed his forearm. Although her passion had ebbed over the years, her affection hadn't. The inscrutable expression he'd long since grown accustomed to remained, but as Patricia's eyes warmed and the odd tone of voice vanished, Burke wondered if she'd ever looked at or spoken to him oddly at all. Just his guilty conscience playing tricks on him again, no doubt.

"Thanks," he said, drawing his wife closer and kissing her cheek.

As he turned to look out the window to watch Margaret rinsing her brushes under the outside faucet, he missed his wife's turning to look at the book. When he turned back, she was all sweet wifely smiles again.

Patricia was biding her time, just as she had been for years and could for years longer still. Being Mrs. Cameron Burke remained the most important thing in the world to her, but the books she was reading were beginning to impact her thinking in a way her husband would eventually find most unpleasant.

Margaret read far into the wee hours, burrowing beneath the covers with a flashlight long after her mother had come in to tell her it was time for bed; even if it was Saturday night with no school the next morning, she still had to be up in time for church. Margaret didn't care. She knew how to nap with her eyes open during the sermon. It was worth it to read this book. Quite simply, Margaret found it impossible to stop turning page after page, until there were no pages left to turn. Then she wanted to just read it all over again. To cry when Kyle Hanrahan went off on a desperate mission and his lover, Giselle Garreau, didn't know what had happened to him, thinking him dead and so deciding to take a dangerous assignment herself. It seemed to Margaret that everything each of them did doomed them to be apart. She didn't understand how or why love that was so deep and so strong couldn't work out in the end. It was awful and heartbreaking, but glamorous at the same time. She hoped someone would love her that way someday.

Yawning contentedly, Margaret snapped off the flashlight, set the book on her nightstand, and instantly fell asleep.

Because she didn't want her mother to figure out that she'd stayed up half the night reading, Margaret didn't mention finishing the book for a few days. "Mom, you really ought to read the book Dad lent me," she said at the dinner table.

"Oh?" her mother said casually, doling out peas on each of their plates.

"Uh-huh. I learned a lot about Vietnam."

"Tell your mother what the title means." Burke poured some gravy on his mashed potatoes and then passed the gravy boat to Margaret.

"The Vietnamese believe that there's heaven and hell, and earth is in the middle. But not like we think of it. Heaven isn't just where good people go, and hell isn't just where bad people suffer. The suffering happens here on earth. That's why the book is called *Lower than Heaven*; it's like saying, 'War is hell.' And love is too, I guess."

"I think 'hell' three times in the same explanation is quite enough, Margaret Anne."

"War *is* hell. Besides, I told her to tell you what the title meant." Burke cut into his pork chop vigorously, casting a sharp look at his wife. He reserved sharpness only for when he felt Patricia was being unfair to Margaret, and if Margaret was there, he never let it creep into his voice, only glint in his eyes, so Patricia would see it but not be demeaned in front of their daughter. Burke thought Patricia was a good mother, even though she and Margaret had never been close. But he also felt that the emphasis on the church stuff was too high-handed. He didn't want Margaret to hate religion because it had been forced down her throat. Bad enough that he'd had to go through that. But this was just something that he and Patricia would never see eye to eye on.

Patricia raised her eyes to meet her husband's. "All right, but I still don't like the word used. I want to be sure you understand that, Margaret."

"I understand, Mom." Margaret wondered how her mother could think that she might not understand something that had been drummed into her head daily for as long as she could remember.

"Good girl. Now eat your dinner."

Margaret had never seen her mother not want to talk about books, and she wondered why something as silly as her saying "hell" three times would have had such a powerful effect. Deciding that she'd rather talk to her father about love and why it was hell, she dug into her pork chop and didn't say another word.

Once she finished helping her mother clean up after dinner, Margaret went off in search of her father. She found him in the den, drinking coffee and reading the *New York Times*. Sitting on the floor at his feet, she leaned her head against his knee. Burke reached down to stroke his daughter's hair. Catching a red curl between thumb and forefinger, he said, "What's up, Muffin?"

"Do you think anyone will ever love me the way Kyle loves Giselle?"

"Sure." He let go of the curl.

"As much as Kyle loves Giselle?"

"Yes." Burke set down the paper.

"Daddy ..." Margaret lifted her head abruptly.

"Muffin, right now there's a boy asking the same question. Someday you'll find each other. You'll see."

Margaret sighed. "But look at how much Kyle and Giselle love each other, and it never works out. Is that why love is hell?" She lowered her voice at the last word, in case her mother could hear.

"Love is only hell in a war zone because war is hell ... and the worst place to fall in love."

"I don't know, Daddy. It seems so romantic and glamorous."

"That's because it's a story. It's heartbreaking when it happens, nothing romantic or glamorous about it." Burke moved into the far corner of his club chair, patting the small patch of leather beside him. Margaret sprang to her feet and pounced into the chair, settling herself half on it and half in his lap. He closed his arms tight around her.

"I hope I fall in love like that someday."

"Not like that."

"You don't want someone to love me like Kyle loves Giselle?"

"Muffin, any guy who treats you the way Kyle treated Giselle will have to answer to me."

"But, Daddy, he only left because she told him to. Wasn't that right?"

"No. A man has to be a man, Margaret. When he loves a woman, that's all that matters in the world. Taking care of her, protecting her, being a good husband and a good father, eventually. That's it." Captain Swinton's long-ago advice and Josselyn's more-recent entreaty flashed through his mind.

"Like you and Mom," Margaret said, snuggling contentedly, even though she really didn't understand why her father, a sweeping and heroic figure, loved her mother, who was pretty but dull.

"That's right." Burke kissed the top of her head, willing his mind to stillness.

"Do you love Mom more than anyone else in the world?"

"Only until you were born. Now I love you the most, but that's different. You'll understand when you have kids of your own."

Burke pressed his eyes shut. Only part of it had been a lie, and he didn't believe that the truth should be told when it was something that couldn't be changed and would only hurt the person you told it to.

Outside the den, Patricia stood with her back pressed against the wall, wondering whether what Cam had told

Margaret was true. The following day, when Cam was at work and Margaret was at school, Patricia was going to read that dedication. Then she would know the truth. One way or the other ...

As soon as she got home from dropping off Margaret at school, Patricia went upstairs in search of the book. Nothing in Margaret's room, so she must have given it back to Cam. It wasn't lying about; Patricia would have seen it. At dinner, she should have just told Margaret that she wanted to read it. Of course, she could casually mention that to Cam tonight, but she didn't want him to see her reaction to what she read in the dedication. She would ask him, but she needed to make her discovery first so that she could be prepared to reveal nothing if she had to read in his presence.

Opening his closet door, she stepped inside and looked near his shirts; Margaret had been looking for a shirt to use as a smock, so that must have been where she'd first seen the book. Sure enough, there it was—the gold embossed letters of the title and the author's name gleaming in the morning sunlight that streamed through the bedroom's east-facing windows. Seizing it, Patricia balanced the book on her open left palm, lifting the cover and then flipping the first few pages until she reached the dedication: To C., WITH LOVE IN EVERY WORD, NOW AND FOREVERMORE.

Patricia forced herself to breathe slowly, but already the blood was rushing to her head, her mind racing. How could it be a coincidence? Knowing she would never be able to wait to read the book—not even until that night ... she would never get through the day—Patricia clutched it to her chest like a schoolgirl and hurried downstairs. A mixture of dread and wild anticipation flooded her as she sat down at the kitchen table, setting the book on it and then putting up a pot of coffee. Before the day was over, she would know the story of her husband and Josselyn Jeffrey, once and for all.

Patricia spent the day drinking coffee and reading *Lower than Heaven,* or more precisely, losing herself in it. Much as she hated to admit it, the book was among the best she'd ever read, deserved every award it had garnered, as well as its bestseller status. She found herself crying at the heartbreaking love story, despite the fact that the protagonist, Giselle Garreau, was the fictitious incarnation of the woman Patricia's own husband had been in love with all these years. The worst part of it was that Patricia knew she would like Josselyn Jeffrey if she met her. Blowing her nose as she turned the last page of the book and shut it, she filled her mug one last time, setting it to cool while she went back upstairs to replace the book in its spot in Cam's closet.

Patricia's mind raced now: What to do? Her latest reading and course work told her she should confront Cam. If he didn't come clean, she should demand a divorce. No woman should stay married to a man who didn't love her. Definitely not. Patricia's feet punctuated her thoughts as she planted each one firmly in front of the other, descending the carpeted stairs, the beige pile tufting around the edges of her shoes. The flat heels of her penny loafers clicked on the ceramic tile when she moved from the living room to the kitchen. In the silent house, the sound jarred her. Usually she kept the radio on for company while she went about her housework. Patricia picked up her mug and drained it. Glancing at the kitchen clock, she put her mug in the dishwasher and picked up her purse and keys. The day had run away from her; it was already time to pick up Margaret at school.

While she drove the familiar route, Patricia pondered her dilemma. She didn't really want to hear Cam defend himself or deny the truth—or worse yet, refuse to apologize and admit that if he had it to do over again, he would marry Josselyn, not Patricia. The realization shocked her. She hadn't ever wanted to hear his side of it, only to know the story. Deriving no pride from unearthing her true feelings, Patricia breathed uneasily as she stopped at a red light. Nothing to do but bury the truth in her mind in much the same way as she had buried her suspicions all these years. She still loved Cam and still wanted to be married to him. Confronting him would be to no purpose.

Patricia wondered if any of the feminists who taught the classes she took and wrote the requisite reading materials had ever been in love with a man—really in love. When she looked at Cam, her heart no longer skipped a beat, but she was reminded of how it once had. Those memories were not to be easily or lightly tossed aside. And even if they ought to be, Patricia didn't want to toss them. There was also the church, but more than that, she felt bonded to Cam, felt in her heart that the vows they had taken were sacred ... felt it clearly and deeply, beyond what the church decreed. Couldn't imagine life without him; couldn't imagine who she would be if she were no longer Cam's wife. She still loved him; that was what it boiled down to and always would.

Arriving at the school and moving around the traffic circle behind where the buses were lined up and pulling out, she caught sight of Margaret and pulled up to the curb, unlocking the door.

Margaret hurried over, her red curls bouncing against her shoulders. She hopped into the car, dropping her books on the floor at her feet with a groan of, "I hate school!"

"How about going into town for some ice cream, sweetie?"

Margaret gaped, wide-eyed. Her mother hadn't called her "sweetie" since kindergarten, hadn't offered to go for ice cream just like this since about that time either.

"Are you okay, Mom?"

"Sure. Just want to have a fun afternoon with my girl. Is that so strange?"

Her mother was smiling so happily, Margaret didn't have the heart to say that strange was exactly what it was. "Sounds great, Mom."

Patricia pulled around the circle and off the school grounds, heading for town. "Your father's not the only one who enjoys doing fun things with you, you know. Now that you're getting older, there's shopping and all sorts of things we can do together."

Margaret nodded, smiling brightly to mask her utter lack of enthusiasm and, beyond that, her consternation. "Mom, is this about that mother/daughter bonding thing I saw you reading the other day?" she blurted out in spite of herself.

Her mother laughed, although Margaret was sure she would have been in trouble had she said the same thing the day before. She would have to be on her guard. No way of knowing when her real mother would return. "Sweetie, you don't miss a thing. I have been doing a lot of thinking since I read that, but about my own mother and me. I've never questioned my bond with you. I love you more than anyone in the world."

"So does Daddy," Margaret whispered.

"I know. You're a lucky girl," her mother told her, pulling into an empty spot on the street a few stores away from the ice-cream parlor.

As her mother shut off the car and pulled the key out of the ignition, Margaret could have sworn she saw tears in her eyes. But she must have been mistaken. Maybe it was just the sun in her eyes. Her mother seemed happier than she had in a long time. Who knew when she would next get to go for ice cream in the afternoon, just like this and for no occasion? Margaret wasn't going to spoil the day. She hurried around the car to the curb.

"Come on," Patricia said, putting her arm around her daughter's shoulders and giving her a sideways squeeze. "What do you want to have?"

"Just a cone, I guess."

"Not a sundae?"

"Mom, are you sure you're okay?"

"Why? Because I'm not telling you that you'll spoil your dinner?"

"Yeah ..." Margaret answered hesitantly, as they stepped inside the ice-cream parlor and each sat on a stool at the counter.

"Well, it's Dad's late night, so we can eat when he gets home or ... whatever."

"Okay." Margaret spun on her stool. Her mother usually reprimanded her for that, but today she didn't seem to mind. "I guess I'll have a hot-fudge sundae with wet nuts, marshmallows, and coffee-fudge-ripple ice cream."

"Me too," Patricia said to the woman behind the counter. The place was empty, so Patricia knew the woman had heard them.

"Coming right up," the woman replied.

"I've never seen you eat a sundae, Mom. Even when Dad and I get sundaes, you always get nonfat frozen yogurt. And never chocolate."

"Life is short, Margaret. You don't have to indulge every day, but you shouldn't let joy pass you by either. If you feel like having a sundae one fine Thursday afternoon, I say, go for it!"

"Me too!" Margaret said, sincerely gleeful this time.

"Don't waste your life expecting other people to make you happy. Make your own happiness, sweetie."

"Does that mean I can be a painter?"

"If it's what you really want to do—"

"You never said that before."

"If it's what you really want to do when you're old enough to decide, yes, you can be a painter. In the meantime, keep learning and working at it like you've been doing. I know how serious you are about your painting." Patricia meant it. Margaret was talented; every art teacher confirmed that fact. Patricia just didn't want her to close off her options. But after today, she realized that being happy was all that mattered. More than anything, she didn't want her daughter to tie up her happiness in a man who would break her heart. Much better that she find happiness within. That way, no one could take it away from her. "You make your own happiness, sweetie," she said again. "If painting is what does that for you, paint."

"Okay, Mom."

"And when you fall in love, make sure he loves you more than you love him." Patricia couldn't explain the need for inserting such a non sequitur, something so completely beyond Margaret's comprehension at her age, but she had Margaret's rapt attention now and wasn't sure she would ever again have the opportunity to tell it to her. It was something Patricia wanted her daughter to know—the most important thing she could ever tell her, it seemed in that moment—and Margaret would understand it someday, even if she didn't now. Patricia knew Margaret would remember this afternoon, and everything Patricia had told her during it, for the rest of her life.

"Okay, Mom," an uncomprehending Margaret said for the second time, relieved when the sundaes came and her mother stopped talking. She hoped this was a passing mood. Fun as it was to go for ice cream in the middle of the week and spin on the stool without getting into trouble, she didn't want her mother to stay weird like this forever. It was unnerving. At first, she thought about asking her father why her mother was behaving so oddly, but then she remembered the mother/daughter thing and decided she shouldn't tell him. Getting closer to her mother might be nice, but she would never be closer to her than she was to her father, that was for sure. She would keep her mother's secret, however, even though she had no idea what it was.

After she won two awards for *Lower than Heaven*, Josselyn backed off her schedule at the Times office. No longer a full-time reporter, she wrote special features, book reviews, that sort of thing. With his recent promotion to editor, Luke Lanvin let her do whatever she wanted. She had also become a featured contributor to the *New Yorker.* The flexible schedule suited her. She had started another book, a memoir of her experiences in Israel. Luke teased her that the next overseas event that piqued her interest would turn her into a foreign correspondent again, and Josselyn agreed, but right now she was perfectly content to be as she was, where she was, doing what she was doing. In her mind, that contentment was a greater accomplishment—and far harder won—than the writing or awards had ever been. They came easily to her; writing had always been like breathing. Serenity, on the other hand, was as arduous to attain as it had ever been.

In the years since their encounter in DC, Josselyn thought about Cam, hoping against hope that he would read the dedication she'd written to him and reappear, despite her insistence that he stay away. If Giselle's heartbreak and confusion read like the real thing, as all the reviewers praised it for doing, it was only because Josselyn had put her own heartbreak and confusion on the page as candidly as she knew how.

Of course, he hadn't reappeared and never would. She loved him even more for not coming; his loyalty to his wife was much the same as his honoring Josselyn's request that he stay away. He was just decent. That was what she'd loved about him from the beginning.

Some people were destined for a lifetime of happiness. She just didn't happen to be one of them. But she had the blessing of a short time of sheer joy, a few exquisite moments of rapture beyond describing; so sublime, in fact, that she couldn't put them into words, and so she had made the love scenes ethereal and symbolic, hoping that the only other person on earth who could conjure up the same images from them as she did would someday read those passages in the same bittersweet mixture of joy and pain that she felt writing them.

Josselyn had come to accept that it was what it was. Any attempt at happiness with another man was doomed to fail. She knew that in her heart. Trying to prove that she could just go out with other men and not care was something she'd decided she would never do again. One Ron was more than enough. She was done with seeking love in this lifetime. She was no longer disappointed or even sad; merely resigned to the fact. The past was the past. She'd gotten what she wished for. In her next lifetime, she would be more careful with her wishes.

There was an almost imperceptible change in Patricia shortly after Margaret finished reading *Lower than Heaven,* but Burke couldn't put his finger on it. For the most part, he attributed it to his own feelings of guilt. At least a thousand times, he thought about asking Patricia straight out, but if he were wrong, he would be opening up a can of worms for nothing, hurting Patricia irreparably when she didn't suspect a thing. He would not clear his conscience at her expense. If she knew and confronted him, they'd have it out, once and for all. Otherwise, he would take it to his grave.

Only when he knew Patricia and Margaret were out of the house would he take the book out of his closet, sit on the edge of the bed, and run his fingers reverently over the surface of Josselyn's photo. Closing his eyes after a while, so his other senses would kick in and he'd be surrounded by the scent of her, by the memory of the texture of her skin against his, by the sweetness of everything about her. Usually, at about the time he had made himself absolutely crazy with desire for her and miserable because he'd never be with her again, he would hear the garage door open and Patricia's car pull in, and he would stash the book, go into the bathroom to take a cold shower, and emerge reasonably composed by the time she came upstairs to the bedroom.

He never stopped wondering if Josselyn regretted telling him to stay away as much as he regretted obeying. But he knew he wasn't capable of doing anything else, and he wouldn't want her to turn into the kind of woman who accepted less, no matter how much they both might want to give in to their desires and pay no heed to what they knew was right. He loved her even more than he wanted her, and he knew she felt the same way. Some people never even had a glimmer of the kind of moments they had shared. Better to just be grateful and leave it in the past where it belonged.

Years passed. Busy ones for both of them. The Gulf War. Somalia. Kosovo. Each hearing snippets of what the other was doing. But for Josselyn, confirming that Cam was still married was all that mattered. As long as he was, nothing had changed. Whatever tied him to his wife—whether it was only his daughter or something more—she didn't want to know. And Burke knew that was exactly how she would feel.

Margaret moved to New York at the height of the war in Bosnia. She'd been accepted to Pratt on a full scholarship. Burke knew his mother would look after Margaret—with plenty of help from the rest of the family, including his cousin, Dylan, and Dylan's wife, Erin—so she went with his blessing. Patricia was less than enthusiastic, but she didn't put up a fight either.

It seemed to Margaret that her mother had pretty much forgotten the day at the ice-cream parlor, a day that Margaret thought of all the time, particularly when she was out of patience with her mother's perpetual self-help odyssey, which was even worse than her churchgoing, though in a different way. To Margaret, the two seemed diametrically opposed, and so she couldn't believe that her mother was sincere about either one. More than anything else, Margaret detested hypocrisy.

In 2000, Margaret graduated from Pratt and moved into a loft in SoHo, her graduation present from her parents. They used the money they'd put away for her education but hadn't used because of the scholarship. Margaret was surprised and thrilled. She bridled when Dylan reminded her that accepting the gift was a tacit approval of the capitalist system she abhorred because it perpetuated underprivileged societies, but, otherwise, she was singularly joyful. Burke knew his daughter just needed to grow up a little, and then she'd see that what he called her "Berkeley ideas" were naive and misguided. He respected her commitment to her convictions, though, and hoped her lessons wouldn't have to be learned the hard way, even though he knew the best-learned ones always had to be.

A few months after Margaret's graduation, Patricia asked him for a divorce, saying they were no longer compatible when he asked her for a reason why. She said she was tired of being married to an inflexible workaholic, which he hadn't known she thought he was; tired, too, of being a housewife, even though he'd never stood in her way of going back to work or doing anything else she might have liked once Margaret was old enough to fend for herself.

Of course, incompatibility had not been the reason, but it was the only one Patricia ever intended to give. She'd simply come to find it increasingly unbearable to live with a man she knew was in love with another woman. When Margaret was in the house, it had been bearable, but without her, Patricia felt confronted by the truth at every turn. The specter of Cameron's long-lost love was everywhere. She couldn't stand it anymore. She'd given incompatibility as the reason, called Cam things she didn't really mean, all because she didn't want Margaret to ever learn the truth, didn't want her opinion of her father to be shattered, or to have her think of her mother as the kind of woman who didn't think enough of herself to leave the husband who would always love another woman. Patricia wanted more for her daughter than she'd ever demanded for herself, but she couldn't prevail upon Margaret to demand more for herself than what she saw her mother settle for. *Do as I say, not as I do,* echoed hollowly, and Patricia hated it. So she went against the church, loving her daughter more.

Telling Cam that she didn't want to be married to him anymore was the hardest thing she'd ever had to do, the one thing she'd never envisioned herself having to do. But she was glad to see he'd never guessed her suspicions. If he didn't know her real reasons, he couldn't ever suggest them to Margaret, and Margaret would believe whatever her father told her. Patricia wished she could have continued to be the person she'd been in the ice-cream parlor that long-ago afternoon, but she didn't have enough happiness inside her to muster that kind of joy for more than a few short hours, so she'd reverted back to her normal self, pretending to forget all about it. She knew her semblance of forgetting hurt Margaret, but it was nothing compared to the hurt Margaret would feel if she knew the truth. Patricia loved Margaret enough to accept that she loved Cam more than she loved her. And she hoped that Margaret still remembered that long-ago afternoon and all that Patricia had told her, especially about making sure that the man in her life loved her more than she loved him. She hoped her daughter would always remember that, no matter what else she might have already forgotten.

Patricia knew all too well that Margaret could not control why and how she loved the people she loved any more than Patricia herself, or anyone else, could. Love was an eternal mystery that way. The irony of it was that the only person Patricia thought would understand that in the same way she did was Josselyn Jeffrey.

BOOK IV
FOREVER CHANGED

$\mathcal{M}$argaret Burke strode down Montague Street, entering the church that now doubled as a trauma/crisis-intervention center. The sheer number of people filling the space overwhelmed her. How ridiculous it had been to think that she could just show up, not even knowing the psychiatrist in charge, and do anything.

"You look lost," a woman's soothing voice interrupted Margaret's self-chastisement. She turned in the direction of the voice. "Maybe I can help," the woman continued.

"I … I came to help … to … I don't know …" Margaret stammered.

"Neither do any of us. Do you have any specific skills?" The woman took Margaret's arm and led her away from the crowd, toward a table where a group of efficient-looking people were working—one putting papers on clipboards, another talking on a cell phone, still another rocking a sobbing child.

"I'm an artist. I thought maybe I could help some of the children express their feelings," Margaret replied, surprising herself with the statement. When she entered the church, she'd had no idea how to help. The despair of the child—the raw, unbridled pain of the cries—focused Margaret instantly, and she knew what she had been brought to the center to do.

"Excellent idea," said the woman, in the same soothing voice, at once comforting and authoritative. "I'm Natalie, and I'm usually much better about introductions."

She extended her hand.

Margaret shook her hand with a warm firmness that Natalie immediately felt good about. "I'm Margaret."

"Ever done grief work?"

"No. But for as long as I can remember, I've used painting and drawing to express feelings I couldn't put into words."

"Well, experience can be the best training ground. Let's start with this little one." Natalie nudged Margaret ahead of her, and they both knelt beside the dark-haired woman rocking the still-sobbing child. The woman looked familiar to Margaret, but she couldn't place from where.

"All right, sweetheart, it's all right to cry. You're safe here. You don't have to talk to us if you don't want to." Natalie stroked the child's hair, and the head lifted suddenly, loosing a crop of long red curls. Seeing Margaret's own auburn mane, she hurled herself from the lap she was occupying into Margaret's surprised arms, nearly toppling her and clinging to her for dear life.

Margaret gathered up her charge, moving toward the desk where the clipboards were being assembled. Securing a few scraps of paper and a pencil, she spotted an empty space by a window and walked toward it, carrying the child who clung to her. As Margaret sat on the floor in a pool of sunlight, the little girl allowed herself to be settled into Margaret's lap, but she did not loosen the grip of her small arms around Margaret's neck.

Shifting the little one to her left side, Margaret took the pencil in hand and began to sketch what she saw through the window: the sun's rays glinting off a brownstone roof and illuminating the sycamore tree a few feet from the front stoop. At the sound of the pencil against the paper, the child lifted her head ever so slightly, gradually turning to peek. Intrigued, she turned to fully examine what Margaret was doing.

"You're making a picture!" she announced.

"Mm-hmm," Margaret smiled. "Would you like to help me?"

"But you're *big!*" exclaimed the child, ignoring the question.

"I know," Margaret answered seriously. "When I'm sad, it's easier to draw than to talk."

The little girl nodded, sniffling and lowering her lashes over eyes that Margaret noticed were startlingly blue once she could see the child's face. "Is your daddy a fireman too? Was he *there?*"

"No. My daddy's far away. In Washington."

"Is he okay?"

Margaret nodded.

"I'm Bernadette."

"I'm Margaret."

"Can I draw a picture for my daddy? We can give it to him when we see him."

"Of course." Margaret squeezed her. "My cousin is a fireman too."

Bernadette picked up the pencil and began to scribble on a blank sheet of paper.

Margaret held the child tight, silent tears streaming down her own face as she prayed for little Bernadette's father, adding a prayer each for Dylan and her own father, God knew where. All the brave—and impossible—men and women who sacrificed everything for the rest of America to be safe. *God, bring this child's father home safe and sound. Don't let her grow up without her daddy. Please, God. Your infinite mercy upon this child. Amen.*

Burke had put key operatives in position, and he was in remote contact with each of them. For the first time he could recall, he was glad that he was out of the field. Now all he wanted was to be home—even though he hadn't thought of New York as home in years.

He laughed out loud at his own sentimentality—a short, gruff chuckle. Connecting to the Internet from his laptop, he pulled up the *New York Times* online. Scanning the headlines, he caught an op-ed byline by Josselyn Jeffrey. He clicked on it, snatches of memories flooding his mind, rapid-fire, as the article loaded onscreen and the text came into focus.

Burke let Josselyn's words pull him into her mind, her torment. Her writing was clean and sharp, her legendary journalistic style, crisper than the lyrical grandeur of her fiction, but every bit as evocative. He still marveled at her prodigious talent, still stood in awe of all she had accomplished. All she had become … without him.

The name of his cousin—Dylan Burke—popped out at him. Dylan had saved her. *There, but for the grace of God, go I. It should have been me. It should have been me. It should have been me.* …

"It should have been me," he growled aloud, all but choking on the words. And in that instant, Cameron Burke decided that he was not going to live the rest of his life without the only woman he had ever really loved … the only woman who had ever understood him … the only woman who loved him exactly as he was, which was all that he knew how to be.

Natalie peered through the throng, trying to catch sight of the artist who had come to help with the children. Young; flashing green eyes; long curly auburn hair. Name with an *m* … Meghan? Mallory? Margaret? Yes, Margaret. Natalie shook her head. On September 10, she would never have forgotten the name of someone she'd spoken to at some length, especially not within hours of the conversation. Definitely an occupational hazard. How would people trust her—open up to her—if she couldn't remember their names?

Get a grip, Nat, she told herself fiercely. *It's only September 12. You have to pull yourself together. You have to hold it together for these people. You owe it to them. It's why God put you on this earth: to help people, to illuminate what they can't see by themselves alone. Now do it.*

A tap on her shoulder interrupted Natalie's internal pep talk.

"You holding up?" Josselyn's familiar voice.

"You're asking me?"

"So it would appear." Josselyn smiled at her over the rim of a Styrofoam cup, tilting it back and draining its contents.

"I'm fine. You?"

"Fine." Josselyn tossed her empty cup in a nearby wastebasket.

"We'll get through this, you know."

"I know. One foot in front of the other. Right?"

Natalie nodded. "Just keep walking." She paused and then asked, "Joss, have you seen the artist who came to work with the kids?"

"Not since that little carrottop attached herself to her." Josselyn smiled. "She'll find you if she needs you, Nat. You said we each came here to find a way to help and connect with one another."

"But I'm responsible for what happens here."

"So are we all. This is a collective wound. And don't look at me like that. I've read Carl Jung." With a quick wink, Josselyn patted her friend's shoulder and made her way back into the fray.

Margaret hurried back toward the church, toting a bag filled with the construction paper and crayons that she'd purchased at a drugstore a couple of blocks away. She was so lost in her own thoughts that she all but collided with a woman in front of the church.

"Sorry! I don't know where my head is today."

"Who does? Don't worry about it." The woman extended her hand with a smile. She was the same woman who had been holding little Bernadette when Margaret arrived at the center. Why did she look so familiar? "I'm Josselyn Jeffrey," the woman said. "I admire how you handled that little girl earlier. You're a natural. That's what Natalie would say."

"I'm not. But thanks," Margaret smiled back, shaking hands. "Josselyn Jeffrey? As in THE Josselyn Jeffrey?" *That* was why she looked so familiar. Margaret could have kicked herself for not realizing it.

"I guess so," Josselyn laughed. "And you are?" She had been observing Nat's "artist" all day but had no idea what her name was.

"Margaret Burke." *And I'm not a total idiot.*

"Pleased to know you, Margaret. You *are* a natural. I'm nowhere near as good with people as you were with that little girl."

They headed back into the church together.

"Well, I'm not a world-famous, award-winning author and reporter."

"That doesn't matter much today, does it?" Josselyn forced herself to stay focused on the conversation, but she couldn't help dwelling on the name Burke. Feeling her heart skip a beat, she stopped short. She had to find out if Margaret was connected to the other two Burkes whose brief but indelible appearances in her life had been so significant. So unforgettable.

Gripping Margaret's arm, Josselyn said, "Margaret, did you say your last name was Burke?"

Margaret nodded.

Josselyn released her grip. "I'm sorry. I ... I was there yesterday. ... When the South Tower ... collapsed, a firefighter named Dylan Burke saved my life. I just thought—"

"He's my cousin!" Margaret exclaimed. "This is *too* bizarre."

"Oh my God. Have you heard from him? Is he all right?"

"He is. He's still down there, of course. Rescue and recovery."

"Thank God." Josselyn clapped her open hand over her mouth, suddenly swamped by a mixture of relief and worry— knowing full well that in the midst of this newfound prevailing chaos, any relief she might feel would be tenuous at best. The roller coaster of emotions would either kill her or drive her insane. All she said was, "I'm amazed he got word to you so quickly."

"Well, my father is a big wheel at the Pentagon, so ..."

Josselyn's face went white. Feeling all the blood in her body drain toward her feet, she forced herself to breathe deeply—rhythmically—so that the shock would not completely overwhelm her. Josselyn struggled to remain on an even keel while Margaret looked at her quizzically, asking if she was all right.

"Margaret, is your father Cameron Burke?" she managed at last, her voice strained.

Margaret nodded. How could her father have missed telling her that he knew Josselyn Jeffrey, when they both so loved her books? Margaret had read *Lower than Heaven* six times since she was twelve, and *From Ashes to Hope* almost as many. "I know he knows *you,* because he and I always read your books. Everything you write, actually. But how do you know *him?*"

"I don't. I mean, I did. We knew each other a long time ago; that's what I meant," Josselyn sputtered, wishing now that she'd never brought up Cameron to his daughter, who stood before her now, confusion and dismay clouding her lovely young face.

Dylan Burke struggled to straighten his aching back as he emerged from the rubble. Masses of steel and concrete, so recently seeming invulnerable and permanent, lay in twisted, grotesque heaps, smoldering and reeking. As oxygen trickled into the wreckage of the disaster, new fires would break out at will. He and his team—like all the rescue-and-relief workers—were beyond exhausted. Drained of all their strength, sheer hope of finding their comrades, as well as other victims, was all that kept them going throughout the days following the attack.

Standing straight now—as straight as he was going to get with how his back was feeling—Dylan squinted, surprised. Day. He knew it was day from the sun in his eyes, on his face and back, but he had no idea what day it was. Day to night,

night to day—how many times had it turned since the towers were felled by jet-fueled assassins?

A few feet away from him, a portion of steel protruded from the rubble, a contorted ziggurat of metal, glowing with an infernal heat that brought the taste of bitter bile to the back of his throat. He wanted to find his friends, he wanted to protect his men from the still-real danger at the site, he wanted to go home and take his wife in his arms and never let her go.

Suddenly his own impotence in the face of this catastrophe struck him full force, rendering him incapable, in that instant, of proceeding with what he had to do. Dropping down to a squat, he rocked back on his haunches and wept, bawled like a baby as he had not let himself do since the night of the fire that claimed his father's life. Only this time, Dylan Burke knew he would not be done weeping for a long, long time.

Day after day, Josselyn and Margaret worked side by side, helping Natalie minister to the endless stream of people—some grieving, some filled with hope against all reason, others numb, still others not even knowing what they were feeling.

In whatever few spare moments they had, Josselyn and Margaret shared with each other what they knew about Cameron—Josselyn, from the distant past; Margaret, from the present—discovering together that neither one of them knew him as well as she thought she did.

Through Margaret's descriptions, Josselyn realized that Cameron had wasted the years just as she had, each of them pursuing dreams and goals that, in the end, had fallen short of their illusions. The only real, true thing that had never disappointed her was his love—or the way his love made her feel about herself and about living. She didn't know how to separate the two from each other, didn't want to, and was coming to see that she wasn't supposed to. What was love if not the lens through which to see ourselves and embrace life? She suspected that, wherever Cameron was, he was reaching a similar—if not identical—conclusion. *Come back to me, my love. I promise I'll never leave you—never let you go. Never.* She intoned the words in her mind, at once a solemn promise and a desperate prayer.

Margaret ricocheted between feelings of elation and guilt. In the midst of the greatest tragedy of the nation—and of her own life—she was filled with joy that, at last, happiness was within her father's reach. Relieved, too, of the enormous lifelong burden that she'd fallen short somehow, not been the kind of daughter he'd really hoped she would be, his protestations notwithstanding. Now she felt completely secure that he'd been absolutely honest and unequivocally devoted. Any doubt she'd ever felt evaporated. The faraway sadness in her father's eyes had never been about her at all, but about the lost love of his life.

Margaret vowed that she would bring her father and Josselyn Jeffrey together if it was the last thing she did, and she would find Bernadette's father too. Yes, she would do both; hope and joy and love arose within her—in spite of everything, or perhaps *because* of everything; she wasn't really sure which. She felt as if she could accomplish anything, but even more so, she felt that something good had to come of this tragedy. Steeling her resolve and casting her eyes heavenward, she crossed her heart and inwardly repeated her vow. An abiding sense of peace, as she had not felt since childhood, filled her.

For the first time, Margaret understood why her grandmother had bent over the rosary with such devotion. Before she left the church that night, she would light two candles: one in memory of the souls departed, the other with hope for the living.

That evening, Margaret sat with Erin, whose courage and faith seemed endless. To say that Erin inspired her almost demeaned what Margaret felt. *Awe* was the only word that came close to providing an adequate description. But Erin was only glad that they had bonded, that Margaret would be more a part of her and Dylan's life now—that Dylan was safe and coming home when his work was done was a given; neither of them even entertained an alternative thought. Erin also promised that if Dylan or anyone else in the department called, she'd ask about Bernadette's father.

Sometime after midnight, Erin went to bed, but Margaret lingered. After a while, she went to the small spare room Erin had fixed up for her to stay in, but she couldn't sleep.

In the middle of the night, Margaret fired off an e-mail to her father, telling him briefly about Josselyn in a code that only he would understand:

Dad,

Met Kyle's muse. As terrific as I'd expect. *You* already know that, though. She still loves you. So do I.

Kyle Hanrahan was their all-time favorite Josselyn Jeffrey character. Only her father would know exactly which Kyle she meant. Margaret now realized that Kyle was really her father—or Josselyn's reflection of him—that Josselyn was Giselle Garreau, and that the entire book was a recounting of his and Josselyn's time together in Vietnam. She also wondered whether her mother had never read Josselyn Jeffrey because she had started *Lower than Heaven* and been shocked to see Cameron Burke jumping off every page. But then she quickly decided that her mother never would have even noticed. Not if Margaret herself had missed it. Besides, her mother would never read what she called "war stories." To Margaret, Josselyn never wrote about war specifically, but about life cast against the backdrop of war, just as other writers cast other backdrops.

As Margaret became more involved with the artist set, she began to scorn her younger days and so much of what she loved—like those books, though she'd forgotten how much she loved them until she met Josselyn. No wonder she'd felt so lost and disconnected. She had all along, knew it, but just couldn't admit it to anyone … herself least of all. That would have been tantamount to saying she was human. To her, "human" was synonymous with "ordinary," and that was something Margaret could never abide being. She had confessed all this to Josselyn, who remarked that the two of them were a lot alike and she hoped they would remain friends.

Margaret reflected after that conversation that all artists didn't feel compelled to create a persona and then become it, and she didn't have to either. Just the thought of how easily she and Josselyn had connected was enough to make Margaret smile. The fact that connecting with others had been a lifelong challenge for both of them made their instantaneous connection even more special. Quite simply, Margaret felt like herself again for the first time in a long time. Everything would be okay. Somehow. It had to be. …

Snuggled beneath the covers again, more in an attempt to feel safe than because she was really cold, Margaret watched the lights of the city and the stars through the window's parted curtains. To her, the lights were even more beautiful than the stars. The city had always been an enchanted place for her at night, the artist in her spellbound by the myriad wonders of its incandescent glow, the singular stubborn resistance to her scorn of the "bourgeois." Margaret laughed inwardly at her own folly. As if Manhattan could ever be anything but incomparably cosmopolitan, the shining exemplar of humankind's potential, made visible in the skyscrapers that soared to heaven itself, their silvery spears unequivocally surmounting every challenge. God's promise that life was a gift had never seemed truer to her than it did now, and the only way to honor that promise was by living to the fullest.

The night sky was more magical than ever. Myriad points of light rose above the Brooklyn Bridge, struggling to be visible in the midst of the smoke that still partially shrouded New York City. Margaret's hope was fortified by that light, brighter in its determination to shine through the smoke than it could ever be on a midnight clear. She had to make sure that her hope stayed alive and strong so that she could keep her promise.

Having just drifted off, the phone's chirp seemed an annoying insect on the periphery of Margaret's awareness. At the third ring, she awoke fully with the recognition of "phone," groped for the cordless, and pressed the TALK button.

"Hi, Dad," she said, knowing it wouldn't be anyone else. Dylan called Erin whenever he could, but always after six in the morning or before eleven at night. During the ensuing pause, she mused that Erin must be dead to the world. Margaret was glad the phone hadn't woken her. "Daddy?" she said to the phone's persistent line crackling. "Is that you?"

"Muffin, are you all right?" Her father's voice came through as the static cleared.

"I'm fine, Daddy. Are you?"

"Fine. A little surprised."

Margaret laughed. "Imagine how I felt."

"Is she … how is she?"

"She's her, Dad. I expect she's pretty much the same as she was when you knew her, just sad for all the years in between."

Like I've been. Like I still am.

"Dad, are you okay?"

"Yes, Muffin, I'm okay."

"Oh, before I forget, Dad … I told her you and Mom are divorced. You're not mad that I sort of blurted it out, are you?"

"Of course not. If I send a message, will you print it and give it to her?"

"Sure. I won't even peek."

"I love you, Muffin. You could have just ..."

"Just what? All I ever wanted was for you to be happy. Feeling like I couldn't make you happy was all that my artsy-fartsy futzing around was ever about. I never even realized it till now. It's going to be fantastic, Dad. We're all going to be so happy. Finally."

"What about your mother?"

"Come on, Dad. Mom is Mom. You just never really saw her for who she is. She has things exactly the way she wants them. She wouldn't stand for it any other way."

"I'm sorry, honey."

"Don't be. I'm not." Margaret paused and then added, "I won't abandon Mom, Dad. She's my mother, but she is what she is. I accept her, and I accept you. I want both of you to be happy, but she doesn't know how to be happy. You do. Don't let your happiness slip away again. Send the message. I'll give it to Josselyn."

Patricia, for her part, would have been glad to know that her subterfuge had succeeded so utterly; her daughter never even guessed the reason for her mother's unhappiness. That was a secret Patricia would take to her grave.

"Thanks. Take care of yourself, Muffin. I'll call you soon. The line's going out."

"I love you. Be careful."

"I promise. Love you."

They both hung up, and Margaret logged back on so she could print the message, knowing her father was already typing away.

Don't let your happiness slip away again. Margaret's words kept echoing in Burke's mind. *You got that right, Muffin. I did let it slip away, and with my eyes wide open.* He couldn't bring himself to say that to Margaret. No, it was more that he couldn't bring himself to *hear* the words because they were true. If he was going to be honest, he might as well be completely honest.

Cracking his knuckles, Burke stared at the laptop's blank new-message screen, the blinking cursor mocking him, daring him to do what he knew he ought to have done years before.

"Just do it," he rasped aloud. *If we still love each other—if she's loved me as much as I've loved her all these years—the time apart won't matter.* He thought of the last time he'd seen her, watching her walk away without looking back. If she had, they both would have lost their resolve. ... *No more regrets. That was then, this is now. Type.*

Joss,

I know at the time doing what we did seemed our only choice, but now ... what I mean is, I don't want to dwell on the time that's past. I want to start over, if that's what you want. Margaret will tell you how to reach me.

As ever,
Cam

He clicked on Margaret's e-mail address and hit SEND, taking a deep breath as the message wended its way through cyberspace. Now all he had to do was wait for Josselyn's reply.

The following morning, Margaret practically flew to the church, the printout of her father's message for Josselyn folded neatly inside her bag. Once inside, she sought Josselyn immediately, lest the glee she could barely contain seem offensive to the grieving.

Catching Josselyn's eye, Margaret gestured toward an empty corner, and Josselyn met her there.

"What? You're practically grinning."

"Pretty tacky at a trauma center, huh? Can't help it, though," Margaret said, opening her bag and pulling out the message. "Read this." She handed the folded paper to Josselyn, adding hastily, "I didn't read it. When the message came through, I printed it and folded it with my eyes closed."

Josselyn smiled, opening the folded piece of paper. Margaret continued to chatter away happily, but Josselyn barely heard a word, just the faintest tinge of a voice on the outer edge of her awareness. She scanned the message three times, knowing she would analyze it countless times throughout the day, and then take it home and read it all over again. At home, she would allow herself to read it slowly, punishing and delighting herself at the same time. Loving Cameron had always been an exquisite blend of agony and rapture. She was equally addicted to both.

"You're not mad, are you?"

Josselyn let Margaret's voice guide her back to the present, focusing on it with all her might as memories of Cameron began to flood her consciousness against her will. She would drown in them and never rise to the surface if she didn't focus on Margaret's voice now.

"What? Mad at you? No! No, of course I'm not mad at you."

"Oh good." Margaret exhaled audibly, her green eyes shining and high color suffusing her cheeks. She looked for all the world like a child, not much older than the little girl she'd ministered to on her first day at the trauma center.

Margaret's eyes sought hers. In that instant, Josselyn realized that this didn't have to be excruciating any longer. Cameron's e-mail could mark the end of their mutual despair and longing, but only she had the power to make it be so ... for him and for herself. In the midst of so much suffering beyond anyone's control, why would she continue to choose to be miserable? To prove what, exactly?

"How do I reach your father?" she asked Margaret, laying her hands on the younger woman's shoulders, as if she were afraid she'd soar to the ceiling upon hearing her answer.

Margaret remained still, but couldn't resist a fervent, albeit softly spoken, "Yay!"

With her answer to Margaret just past her lips, Josselyn felt as if the pain of a thousand years had been healed and the weight of the world lifted from her shoulders. A bitter, burning pain that had lived inside her for so long it had become part of her seemed to dissolve, and she marveled at how easy it was to just let go of all the despair and longing she'd held on to for so long.

Perhaps what she'd witnessed at the feet of the towers changed her view of love and loss. It made her realize how blessed she was to have a second chance with Cameron. She would love and be loved, and in the end, that was all that really mattered.

The day dragged for Josselyn, but passed quickly for Margaret and Natalie, who learned, through Erin's tireless search, that little Bernadette's father was alive and working at the Pile. Bernadette's mother wept with gratitude, and Margaret solemnly promised the little girl that they would remain friends, no matter what. It wasn't easy to have a father who saved lives for a living, who always had to look out for other people—strangers—first. Margaret knew that all too well. Bernadette would be in her life for as long as she wanted to be.

Toward evening, the next shift came on, and Josselyn, Margaret, and Natalie prepared to leave. Josselyn had given Margaret her home and cell phone numbers, along with her e-mail address, and they exchanged a meaningful but wordless look as they parted. Natalie didn't miss it.

Margaret headed for Dylan and Erin's, and Josselyn and Natalie headed the opposite way.

"Want to have a bite?" Natalie asked when they reached her place first.

"No, you come to my place."

"You've cooked every night so far."

"You work harder at the center."

"I saw that look. What's going on with you and Margaret?"

"Margaret's last name is Burke."

"You told me. The firefighter's her cousin. Big reunion as soon as he takes a break. You already sent the story to the paper and—"

"Nat, I said, 'Margaret's last name is Burke.' *Burke.*"

Natalie started to speak, and then she covered her mouth with her hand.

"Don't tell me you've got nothing to say."

Natalie threw her arms around Josselyn, and they stood in the street hugging and laughing until they cried.

"In the midst of all this, to feel happier than I have in decades seems sacrilegious," Josselyn said, wiping her tears with the back of one hand.

"When you have a chance to be happy, take it. When you feel happy, feel it. Doing the opposite is the sacrilege." Natalie had not been unhappy in the years following her failed marriage. She'd met some fun guys and had some fun times, but it was nothing more than that. She liked it that way. Her work was her life, by choice.

Josselyn smiled at her friend, knowing they were reading each other's thoughts.

"Come on. Let's go in and eat."

"You sure?"

"Uh-huh. I'll kick you out if he calls."

Laughing again, they went inside.

Josselyn stayed up late, moving from the kitchen to her bedroom at around one in the morning. No sense in trying to fall asleep when she knew she would only toss and turn in a combination of anticipation and euphoria.

At one thirty, she sat on the edge of the bed with a book in her lap. A hardcover anniversary edition of an old favorite, something she could lose herself in until her eyes closed from sheer exhaustion. Or until the phone rang. She would settle for whichever came first.

She'd read about thirty pages when the phone rang. Her fingers curled around the receiver before the ring pealed to completion, and she picked up the phone. "Hello, Cam," she said.

"I only have a secure line for about two minutes, so if it goes dead—"

"I won't worry."

They both laughed.

"I'm coming to New York—as soon as I can ... I don't know when for sure yet. This job has some benefits, you know."

"If you say so," she said.

"Can we wait to say all the things we've been waiting to say until then?"

"No."

"No, I guess not. Forgive me—I shouldn't even have asked."

"Time has a way of running out, Cam. That's why I said no. There's nothing to forgive."

"Forgive me anyway."

"Of course I forgive you ... if you need me to."

He exhaled audibly. "I've loved you all this time."

"I've loved you all this time too."

"Joss, I ... in DC, I should have—"

"*Shhh.* The rest can wait until you get here. That's all we needed to say tonight. Stay safe."

"I will. You do the same. I'll get word to Margaret when I'll be there."

"All right, darling."

He heard her voice caress that last word, and then the line crackled sharply, a sure sign that it was about to go dead. "Hang up, baby. I love you."

"I love you." He could barely hear her voice above the static now, but he knew exactly what she had said before the line went out.

The days between their phone conversation and Cam's arrival in New York passed in dream time. Josselyn would catch herself doing things—day-to-day things that she'd done all her life, as well as the post-tragedy things that, in a single day, had gone from horribly extraordinary to even more horribly ordinary—and feel like she was observing another person doing them. She lived and breathed for the instant when she would see him again, be in his arms again. Now that his return to her life was imminent, she could only wonder how she had endured all these years without him, both before and after their chance encounter in DC.

She had always thought that nothing would ever match the elation of learning that she had received a lifetime achievement award for literary excellence. To be in the company of her many literary heroes who had been so recognized was an honor that took Josselyn's breath away, filling her with a unique mixture of glee and gratitude that made her feel strong and helpless at the same time. She reveled in it, telling Luke that he was absolutely right when he quipped that it was the only occasion for which a middle-of-the-night phone call from the awarding board's headquarters in Europe would be a welcome delight. *Delight* could never capture all the intense emotions that had flooded her. No single word could. But even that award—the crowning achievement of her lifetime—paled in comparison to what she felt at the prospect of seeing Cam again. Winning, like most of the intense experiences in her life, was something she needed a string of words to use to describe all her feelings. Reunion with the love of her life couldn't be expressed in words. It emptied her heart—not in the painful, exhausting away that the decimation of the Twin Towers had, but in a mystically cathartic way that she knew would forever change her life, no matter what happened as a result. She was being emptied so that she could again be filled ... by the only man who had ever known how to completely fulfill her in every way a lover—a soul companion—could.

Her feelings were so powerful that Josselyn felt as if she could soar off into space on the sheer energy of them. In a strange way, the counseling at the center was the one thing that grounded her and kept her in the present. Being so needed was at once humbling and inspiring, fulfilling at the deepest level. This fulfillment was qualitatively different from what writing brought her, even from what loving Cameron brought her—those experiences were personal, a fulfillment she felt as Josselyn Jeffrey, writer or lover—the fulfillment she derived from working at the center was something she felt as Josselyn Jeffrey, human being and child of God. It was a radiant, exquisite feeling; one that she had never expected to feel at all, and she was all the more grateful for it because of that.

She felt completely transformed, filled with grace and serenity in a way that she had never dreamed she could feel, having always considered that such a state would make her feel inconsequential, that deep humility would make her feel invisible. On the contrary, she discovered that she felt neither small nor large, neither substantial nor unimportant. Rather, she simply felt alive. Unequivocally vital and vibrant and strong. Blessed. Grateful. Loved.

I was born to be here now and to serve now. Cam and I were meant to be together all along, but if we had been together through the interim, who knows how it would have turned out? We each needed to do what we did ... in some strange way, we needed to live through this tragedy apart.

For the first time, such a realization entailed no despair and no rancor, only peace and understanding, serenity and grace. And she smiled at the folly of all those years of longing and regret and struggle and grief. If only she'd let go, hadn't fought so hard, she might have spared herself so much pain. Yet she knew pain was the only thing—other than love—that she'd ever learned anything from, so she accepted that all was as it was supposed to be, and everything had played out the way she needed it to. Everything would be all right, after all. Somehow she just knew it would be. She couldn't, and wouldn't, lose faith or hope now.

I've finally learned how to just be. I'm not afraid anymore. I didn't pray to lose him, just to learn to live without him. She gasped aloud at the last thought, never having realized that she'd been carrying around that guilt all those years, along with the rest of her emotional baggage. And everything she'd done to prove that it was otherwise had been futile in the same way that all that wasn't true was always futile, but she knew there was no sense in dwelling on any of that. All that mattered was that she and Cam loved each other; they would never again let their fears or ambitions be more important to them than their love for each other.

As soon as he had ensured that everything on his watch was in order, Cameron Burke wended his way through the bowels of the Pentagon, exiting to the outside world. Final destination: New York—Ground Zero. All through the journey, he rode an emotional roller coaster: still-raw grief and barely contained rage over the attacks and the tragedy left in their wake; emergent, long-buried resentment and regret over the time he and Josselyn had lost and could never recoup; regret over the pain he'd unwittingly caused Margaret; unbridled joy and excitement at his and Josselyn's imminent—and lasting—reunion; relief at the prospect of seeing Margaret safe and happy, and of helping Dylan and Erin in whatever ways he could.

He had let Margaret know that he would be arriving later in the day, and that he had the cell phone she'd promised to use and leave turned on at all times. Margaret had assured him she would let Josselyn know he was on his way. He preferred to keep his contact points to a minimum, but he couldn't resist calling Josselyn to tell her he still loved her and to hear her tell him the same.

Closing his eyes, he recalled a long-ago vow he'd made to himself: that he would not leave this life without coming back to his love. It seemed, at long last, that he would be able to keep that promise.

Nothing could have prepared Cameron Burke for what he saw at the Pile. Worse than the sheer enormity of the destruction— horrific though that was—was the unavoidable knowledge that the majority of those who had lost their lives in it would never be recovered. He willed himself to believe that their souls had risen up like the phoenix, soaring above the chaos, agony, and horror, to a better place than this physical plane could ever be. God most assuredly had heaven in store for those heroes and innocent victims. Burke would not—could not—believe anything else.

Picking his way through the rubble—a sickening, twisted, horrid mess—Burke, decked out in full turnout gear, made his way toward where a firefighter had told him he'd find Dylan working with his men. A firefighter looked up, his face smeared with soot, and his bloodshot eyes an incongruously bright blue: *Burke eyes.*

"Dylan!" he called, waving his arm high above his head as he climbed toward his cousin.

"Cam? Cam!" Dylan returned his greeting, incredulity giving way to joy. He hurried to move toward his cousin.

When they were close enough, they clasped each other in a bear hug, holding on tight for a few moments before letting go. Each kept an arm around the other's shoulders as they stood together.

"My men," Dylan said, raising his free hand to point out his crew. "All good guys. Great guys." He didn't trust himself to say any more.

Cameron Burke nodded. "Tell me where you need me."

"We need you where your work is, so this doesn't ever happen again."

"That's ongoing. I took it as far as I could for right now. Besides, I needed to be here, Dylan."

Dylan squeezed his cousin's shoulders in wordless understanding, and the two of them embarked on their work together at the Pile.

Margaret had explained to Josselyn that her father was working with Dylan at the Pile, and with the same understanding and grace that Erin displayed, the two of them accepted that he was doing what he needed to do. Josselyn had met Erin a few days before, instantly liking her and admiring her besides. She reminded Josselyn of Rachel Tevner, had the same grounded wisdom and serenity.

The three women sat in Erin's kitchen now, waiting for Dylan and Cam to return. Dylan had already called Erin to say that they expected to arrive before too long. Josselyn and Margaret had raced over to Erin's as soon as she called them at the center, not wanting to miss a nanosecond of the momentous reunion.

Josselyn felt herself on the verge of what she called "autoscripting"—where she played out in her mind the entire scenario of her deepest longings—but, catching herself, she stopped. *Not this time; not anymore. Cam and I will do just fine with whatever is in store for us. I'm not afraid anymore: I can love him without the drama, and he can love me without it too. We'll be exactly what we're meant to be to each other. It doesn't have to be perfect, it just has to be love—honest, open, abiding. All we have to do is just be … just love each other and trust in each other's love.*

Dylan Burke turned the key in the lock. He could feel Erin's joy at his return pull him inside even before he pushed the door open. In the next instant, she was in his arms, no gush of words, just her sustaining devotion. Just Erin. If ever a person was truly made of love, it was his wife. He wrapped his arms around her, holding her as tightly as he had dreamed of holding her when he'd stood at the Pile, wanting more than anything to be exactly where he was right now.

Stroking his face, Erin tilted her head back so she could look up at him. "Thank God you're safe," she whispered.

Dylan held her even closer, lifting her straight up in his arms so her eyes were even with his. "God hears your prayers, babe. That's for sure."

Erin smiled into her husband's adoring eyes, and then she lowered her head and began to cry.

Dylan set her back on her feet, took her face in his hands, and kissed her forehead tenderly. He couldn't say all he wanted to say to Erin right now—not with other people around. It would have to wait until later when they were alone. Erin wiped her eyes and touched his shoulder in tacit understanding.

Turning, but keeping one arm around Erin, Dylan said, "There's my hero!" He beamed at Josselyn. "Turns out, you saved my life."

Smiling again at Dylan, Erin stepped away, and he moved toward Josselyn, extending his arms. Josselyn hugged him. "Don't be ridiculous. You know it was the other way around."

Dylan shook his head good-naturedly. "I'm *supposed* to do the saving, but I guess we could say we saved each other. Let's just leave it at that, okay?"

"Whatever you say." Josselyn kissed Dylan's cheek, taking the opportunity to peek over his shoulder in search of Cam.

"Looking for someone?" Dylan teased.

Josselyn couldn't believe how lighthearted he was, but Erin didn't seem a bit surprised, so she figured it was just a coping mechanism that worked for him. For both of them perhaps.

Straining his smoke-scorched throat, Dylan called, "Hey, Mags! Where are you? You're missing it all."

At the sound of his voice, Margaret rushed from the kitchen to greet her heroes, clasping Dylan in a hug that took his breath away as she scanned the room for her father. "Where is he?" she demanded, still hanging on to Dylan.

"He's still at the fire station. He's taking a little longer cleaning up than I did."

"I don't care what he looks like!"

Dylan disentangled himself from Margaret and rolled his eyes in Josselyn's direction. "You're not the only one he's being reunited with, Mags. He'll be here soon." His voice was raspy but had a playful tone. Taking the mug of hot tea with honey that Erin handed to him, he said, "Thanks, babe," and then sipped gratefully.

"She doesn't care either," Margaret shot back in an equally lighthearted tone decibels above Dylan's. She wasn't sure whether Dylan had said it softly in deference to her father and Josselyn's privacy, or because his throat and larynx were raw from all the smoke.

"Well, *he* does," Dylan said evenly, noticing Josselyn smile at Margaret's retort. "What kind of romantic artist are you anyway? After all these days of being in the midst of that nightmare, I find out that my cousin who hasn't been happy in years has a chance to be happier than he ever dreamed of being. I want to enjoy how great it is. I don't know about you," Dylan finished teasingly, ruffling Margaret's curls affectionately, the same way he used to do when she was a little kid.

Margaret grinned, giving him a sideways squeeze while he sipped more tea.

Smiling directly at Dylan, Josselyn mouthed, "Thank you."

He winked at her, and then he turned his full attention back to the mug. Hot tea with honey was the only thing that could ease his smoke-sore throat. *God bless my wife. ...*

"Dylan ..." Margaret began tentatively, "I'm so proud of you. I'm so sorry for every stupid thing I ever—"

"Don't, Mags. We're family." He drained the mug's contents as Margaret watched him attentively. "We love each other and accept each other, no matter what. By Christmas, we'll be at it all over again."

"Not on your life, buster."

Dylan laughed, setting down the empty mug. He clasped Margaret in another bear hug and swung her around.

Josselyn moved to the window, smiling to herself at Cam's nervousness. As if they were kids going on a date. How bittersweet it was to be frozen in time to each other. Oddly enough, she wasn't worried at all—not about the silver threading her dark hair or the lines she'd acquired as much from reporting in the desert as from a lifetime of mundane concerns and the unhappiness she had never been able to move beyond. She hoped he wouldn't be disappointed, but deep down she knew he wouldn't be. Certainly she knew *she* wouldn't be—Cam would be more attractive to her now than ever.

Hurry back, darling. A little soot wouldn't have bothered me. I've never wanted any man but you.

Lost in her thoughts, Josselyn heard the Burkes' conversation going on around her, but she could not focus on the words. Ordinarily, she would have had a million questions for Dylan Burke, would have expressed her gratitude much more profusely, his protestations notwithstanding. It was better this way, though, she realized. Accepting another's kindness gratefully was as important as reciprocating, perhaps even more so. It seemed the Burkes had an endless supply of wisdom to impart to her.

Casting a backward glance over her shoulder, Josselyn caught Dylan's eye, and he winked at her again. She winked back this time.

Day-to-day life in this clan was something she could definitely get used to. Now all she had to do was wait for Cam to arrive—wait to feel the magic explode all over again, even with all the time and distance that they had put between themselves ... maybe because of it.

Burke walked along President Street, heading toward Dylan and Erin's brownstone apartment at the end of the block. With each footfall on the pavement, he felt wild anticipation course through his veins. "What am I, sixteen?" he chuckled out loud to himself. Still, he could not contain the excitement he felt at the mere thought of Josselyn—imagining her in his arms, kissing her, touching her, making love to her. ... After all this time, it filled him with a rapture that he almost could not endure. Almost.

From the window, Josselyn made out the figure of a man walking. Straining to get a better look, she waited for him to come closer. As his long strides brought him nearer to her, she knew it couldn't be anyone but Cam.

Whirling around, she dashed out of the apartment without a word—not that anyone wouldn't be able to figure out why—and raced down the long staircase to the ground floor. She stopped at the front stoop, breathing deep to settle her nerves, not because she was winded ... she lived in the same type of brownstone, had raced up and down two sets of those stairs countless times throughout her life.

Shading her eyes with her hand, she peered toward Cam's approaching figure. The late-afternoon sun gave him an even more masculine aura, she noticed. And then she marveled that, in the moment of her most sublime happiness, the sun was shining! Even through the lingering veil of smoke. True, it was not that incongruously bright yellow that had maddened her all her life—that shining light that seemed to ever mock the depths of her despair—it was more a peaceful glow today, incandescent but for a special warmth that held just the right amount of comfort. It was, simply put, the light of love: exactly the right measure of passion and tenderness, wonder and familiarity. Tears of joy and relief sprang into her eyes. She wiped them away only so that she would be able to see him. The tears in and of themselves felt good.

Dylan and Erin's was in sight now, and Burke could make out the figure of a woman on the front stoop—slender, dark-haired, graceful in a way that only one woman he'd ever known could be. He quickened his step, glad that his years of running had kept him in shape so he wouldn't be winded when he got to her.

When he was only a few hundred feet from the stoop, he broke into a run. She sprinted down the stoop's steps in the same instant. With a few short steps left between them, they all but hurled themselves into each other's arms, laughing and crying as he lifted her up in his arms.

They just held each other close for a few moments, their silence communicating what mere words could not. He leaned her back, drinking her in with his eyes the way he always had, and then he kissed her. As sweet and soft a kiss as their first one had been all those years ago and miles away.

"The first time you kissed me was just like this."

"I remember. Every time is like the first time with you, though. Always was."

He drew her close again, their kisses deepening, igniting the fire that had never gone out for either of them, that had lived all that time not in embers, but stoked and waiting to burst into flame again. And it had taken other fires—of the most horrific kind, born of incomprehensible evil and hatred—to make them realize that nothing else mattered.

Josselyn pulled away slightly, resting one hand against his heart and caressing his cheek with the other, "Have you gotten any better at waiting?"

"With you? Probably not." He grinned.

"Time to start," she teased.

"I'd like to say we have all the time in the world now, but …" He let his voice trail off as they climbed to the top of the stoop, hand in hand.

"None of us can ever say that again. Not with conviction anyway. We have the time we have, Cam. That's all we ever had, really. The only difference is that we've all been forced to see it."

He nodded.

"Go in and see Margaret. I'm as good at waiting for you now as I ever was."

"The years in between and that night in DC—"

She brushed her fingertip across his lips. "*Shhh.* None of it matters anymore. We each did what we had to do, what seemed right at the time. I'm not losing you or pushing you away ever again—not out of fear or for my own ambition … not for any reason."

"All right. Not that I'd let you."

She smiled. "We have what we have. Remember that."

"We have each other. Remember *that.*" He squeezed the hand holding his.

"That's everything, darling," she whispered, squeezing back.

He led her inside, kissing her again at the base of the ground-floor staircase. "That it is, my love."

They climbed the stairs together slowly, relishing the sheer joy of being together in the midst of an action so simple and ordinary, rendered wonderful only by their mutual love and contentment. Neither one of them knew what lay ahead. They never would—not really. But they both understood that it was better that way. Better to not know, but instead, to have faith. Faith in life, faith in the time they had, faith in each other, faith in love.

"Remember when I told you about the phoenix?" he asked.

"Mm-hmm."

"After being at the Pile, I know that we've all become the phoenix."

"Yes," she said. "Everyone who survived, and especially the souls that have gone on. ..."

They each had come to recognize that they had to endure what they had to—it couldn't have been any other way for them, together or individually. They could only understand and appreciate love in relation to pain and suffering.

Clarity gleamed fully now, helping them both see the phoenix for what it truly represented: hope, faith, trust, love, soaring high above the flames, above the desperate pain and struggle of the tragedy of September 11, not to reach a better place, but to inspire—to remind us all that love is the only thing that really matters, the only thing that lasts, through this lifetime and into whatever existence waits for us beyond it.

About the Author

Lisa Drucker is a native New Yorker currently transplanted in South Florida.

A cum laude graduate of Vassar College with a bachelor's degree in classics, she also holds a master's degree in communications/media studies, which she earned from The New School in Manhattan. Her course of study at The New School entailed several courses in writing for film and television.

Currently she is a full-time freelance writer and editor (*http://lisadrucker.com*). She works with new clients ongoing, as well as with her established client base (since 2004), and she is also the content team leader for Synergy Publishing, LLC. Previously she was managing editor for an educational publisher; prior to that she was senior editor at a prominent lifestyles publishing house (where she was an editor for the *Chicken Soup for the Soul* series, *A Child Called "It"*, and other bestselling series and titles). Although professionally she specializes in titles within the self-help and pop-psych genres, her first love is fiction. While being a literary novelist has been her lifelong dream, she did not begin to write full-length fiction until relocating to Florida, where the tropical heat seemed to percolate her creative nature. Under the pen name Jacqueline de Soignée, she authored the *Princess-in-Training Manual*, a humorous novel published by Red Dress Ink/Harlequin. She also authored *ASVAB Flashcards*, a test-prep guide published by REA.

In addition to her editing career and writing passion, she is an avid film enthusiast and museum-goer, and is a member of the Editorial Freelancers Association (EFA) and the American Association of University Women (AAUW).

16235251R00163

Made in the USA
Lexington, KY
12 July 2012